Presented by

THE FRIENDS OF

THE URBANA FREE *and Wonderful* LIBRARY

*The Friends of
The Urbana Free Library
Book Sale*

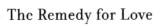

The Remedy for Love

Also by BILL ROORBACH

The
REMEDY
for LOVE

———— ❄ ————

A NOVEL BY

BILL ROORBACH

ALGONQUIN BOOKS OF CHAPEL HILL   2014

Published by
ALGONQUIN BOOKS OF CHAPEL HILL
Post Office Box 2225
Chapel Hill, North Carolina 27515-2225

a division of
WORKMAN PUBLISHING
225 Varick Street
New York, New York 10014

Printed in the United States of America.
Published simultaneously in Canada by Thomas Allen & Son Limited.
Design by Zoe Symon.

This is a work of fiction. While, as in all fiction, the literary perceptions and insights are based on experience, all names, characters, places, and incidents either are products of the author's imagination or are used fictitiously.

Library of Congress Cataloging-in-Publication Data
Roorbach, Bill.
The remedy for love : a novel / Bill Roorbach.—First edition.
pages cm
ISBN 978-1-61620-331-3 (alk. paper)
1. Young women—Fiction. 2. Men—Fiction.
3. Maine—Fiction. I. Title.
PS3568.O6345R46 2014
813'.54—dc23   2014023605

10 9 8 7 6 5 4 3 2 1
First Edition

For Poppy–
Sixty Years of Unwavering
Support

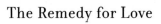The Remedy for Love

Part One

One

THE YOUNG WOMAN ahead of him in line at the Hannaford Superstore was unusually fragrant, smelled like wood smoke and dirty clothes and cough drops or maybe Ben-Gay, eucalyptus anyway. She was all but mummified in an enormous coat leaking feathers, some kind of army-issue garment from another era, huge hood pulled over her head. Homeless, obviously, or as homeless as people were in this frosty part of the world—maybe living in an aunt's garage or on her old roommate's couch, common around Woodchuck (actually Woodchurch, though the nickname was used more often), population six thousand, more when the college was in session, just your average Maine town, rural and self-sufficient.

Idly, Eric watched her unload her cart: he knew her situation too well. Sooner or later she'd be in trouble, either victim or perpetrator, and sooner or later he or one of seven other local lawyers would be called upon to defend her, or whomever had hurt her, a distasteful task in a world in which no social problem was addressed till it was a disaster, no compensation.

Ten years before, new at the game, he might have had some

sympathy, but he'd been burned repeatedly. Always the taste of that Corky Beaulieu kid he'd spoken for and sheltered and finally gotten off light and who'd emptied Eric's bank account using a stolen check and considerable charm at the friendly local bank, and who'd then proceeded to drive Eric's first and only brand-new car all the way to Florida before killing that college kid in a bar fight and immolating himself (and the car, of course, total destruction) in a high-speed chase with Orlando's finest.

Her shopping, pathetic: two large bags tortilla chips, a bag of carrots, a bag of oranges, four big cans baked beans—a good run—but then three boxes of Pop-Tarts and innumerable packets of ramen noodles, six boxes generic mac and cheese, two boxes of wine. The one agreeable thing after the produce was coffee, freshly ground, also a sheaf of unbleached coffee filters. Finally, a big bottle of Advil.

Eric turned his attention to Jennifer Aniston on the cover of five different tabloids. Was she aging well? Had she gained a lot of weight? Was a minidress appropriate? Some people in this world got all the attention. Eric noted with odd pleasure that Ms. Aniston was older than he, if not by much.

In a subdued voice, the young woman chose plastic over paper, and the kindly old bagger in his apron and bowtie packed her purchases carefully, well behind the checkout lady's pace. But good for Hannaford, Eric thought, hiring the guy at no-doubt minimum wage with his savings all eaten up by his wife's final illness—the sadness of late-life loss was in the old bird's eyes and posture, even in his hands.

The checkout lady was gruff and impatient, already turning to Eric's stuff, which probably looked perverse compared with the girl's, and had come from the new "gourmet" section of the market: organic jalapenos, organic Asian eggplants, organic red bell peppers, a bunch of organic kale for braising, two huge organic onions, a tiny bottle of fine Tuscan olive oil, five pounds good flour, French yeast in cakes, a huge chunk of very, very expensive raw-milk Parmesan (Reggiano, of course), two bottles Côtes du Rhône—and not just any old Côtes du Rhône but Alison's favorite, thirty-four bucks a pop. Also a packet of Bic razors, the new, good ones with five blades and a silicone-lubricating strip, thick green handles. He was planning to cook for Alison—they'd always had fun making pizzas—and she liked her wine, also his chin, closely shaven, had once bitten him there in passion, but only once, and a long time ago. And fruit: he'd picked out the one ripe mango in the whole display in the event of an Alison morning, unlikely, also a dozen eggs.

The druid girl ahead of him in line wasn't saying it, but she didn't have enough money. The old gent had packed everything and placed her six or seven bags of stuff into her cart. She counted out her fives and ones and piles of quarters again. "I thought I had it all added up," she said humbly.

"People are waiting," the checkout lady said.

"I'm fine," Eric said brightly.

The lady behind him made it plural, pleasant voice: "We're fine." Back after that, the line was nothing but patience.

"I'll have to put the coffee back," the young woman said.

The old gent knew right where the coffee was and dug it out along with the filters, and the checkout lady subtracted them from the register total, apparently a vexing task. Now the young woman's bill was down to fifty-five dollars and change. She should have gone generic with the Advil, Eric thought. That would have saved her five bucks or more.

"I'll return 'em to stock," the bagger said, meaning the coffee and the filters. He seemed sadder than ever, and Eric pictured the sweet old fellow using half his break to transport the items back to the correct shelf in some distant corner of the vast store.

"It's been ground," the checkout lady said. "You'll have to keep it."

"Then the oranges," the young woman said. "And the carrots."

She didn't know but Eric and everyone watching the little drama knew that the oranges and the carrots weren't going to be enough. He found himself rooting against the Advil: keep the fruit, keep the carrots! That big bottle was probably eleven dollars.

The checkout lady puffed a long breath. But the old gent in the apron said, "No, no, you need your nutrition. I'll chip in here, honey."

"I couldn't," said the young woman.

"Let's just take the oranges out, *Frank*," said the checkout lady, already tapping the buttons on her register.

But Frank dug in his pockets. "Ach," he said. He showed the girl, he showed the checkout lady, he showed everyone in line: he only had a dollar and some odd change. Time stood still. Even the motes of dust stopped floating in the fluorescent box-store light. Eric felt something rumbling inside him, rumbling up all the way from his toes, something that gained momentum, some-thing urging him to act, something physical, not articulate at all, something you would have to capitalize if you wrote it down on a yellow legal pad, something you could name a statue atop a fountain in the Vatican, not quite Grace. Charity, perhaps. His hands twitched, his mouth shaped words that wouldn't come.

Finally, just as the girl was going to say something about the Advil, he got it out:

"I'll get this. Frank, ma'am, young lady, let me get this."

But Frank had already put his buck fifty down.

"No," said the young woman. "No, please."

Eric added a crisp cash-machine twenty to her pile of wrinkled bills and simple as that, the checkout lady re-added the ticket, gave Eric the change for his twenty, gave Frank back his dollar fifty.

The young woman regarded Eric briefly, coldly, more or less curtsied in that sleeping bag of a coat, flushed further. That was it for thanks. She ducked her head back into the depths of her hood and just pushed her cart out of there, noticeably limping, her very posture humiliated.

"If these people would just learn to add," the checkout lady said. One was supposed to know what "these people" meant.

Eric's purchases were already piled in front of old Frank. Eric paid the cashier, more than double the girl's total, and for nothing but a single evening's desperate hospitality. Frank, he noted, liked him, cheerfully putting Eric's stuff in paper bags, two guys who cared about not only indigent young women but about the whole wide world. The checkout lady had no use for them at all, none of them.

Two

A HUGE SNOWSTORM was predicted, first big snow of the season, the inaugural flakes desultorily falling, some kind of unusual confluence of low-pressure and high-pressure and rogue systems, lots of blather on the radio as if a little snow were nuclear warfare or an asteroid bearing down. Eric liked his old Ford Explorer at times like this, even though (as Alison always said) it was a gas pig. He put his groceries in the back, if you could call them groceries, and swung out and across the glazed lot—last week's ice storm—and there was the young woman, staggering and limping under that mountain of a coat but making determined progress, her seven plastic bags hanging from her arms like dead animals. Eric pulled up beside her but she didn't stop walking, didn't look.

"I can give you a lift," he called.

"Okay," she said to his surprise, still without looking. He'd expected her to demur in some proud way. He helped her load her stuff next to his in the back and then the two of them got all of his legal folders and books and naked cassette tapes and envelopes and other junk out of her way on the passenger seat, and she climbed in.

"Seatbelt," Eric said.

She buckled up reluctantly.

"Where are you?" Eric said as he pulled into traffic.

She looked puzzled, peered around the edges of her hood, really caught his eye for the first time.

"I mean, where to?"

"Oh. Like, Route 138. Out toward Houk's Corners. Just out of town the other way. Before the bridge. Maybe a mile before the bridge."

"That's six miles easily. Maybe seven."

"I didn't mean to buy so much. I'd already put a bunch of stuff back. I had another box of wine. I had oatmeal. Too heavy."

"You thought you were going to walk the whole way?"

"I can't believe you still have cassettes. I love cassettes. The way the tape is right there? You can touch the fucking music." She looked at him quickly, then straight ahead, like someone driving, in fact watched the road minutely, sinking back into her coat. Her stench had begun to permeate the car. In profile, cut by the hood, her chin and nose and forehead lined up in a certain sculptural way. She wasn't just anybody, Eric realized, and began to string together a tale of mental illness in a good family, runaway patient, perhaps, or just a college kid off her meds. He'd dealt with more than a few of those, too, on both sides of the family equation. He also knew how easy it was to be wrong about these things: best not to have theories.

Gently he said, "I forgot my wallet once. I mean, it happens to everyone."

"I don't even have a wallet," she said quickly, and he realized his mistake: whatever had happened to her certainly did not happen to everyone.

After that, they rode in silence. At the traffic light by the Park 'n' Ride, Joan Killen was in the next lane, silent Prius. She didn't look, but might have been interested if she had, her proper small-town attorney accompanied by some scruffy young woman in a darkly quilted hood.

"Now where on 138 again?" Eric said.

"Across from the veterinary?"

"Oh, okay. Right. My dog goes there. Used to go there."

"You make it sound like a *girl's* school." Brief glance. Her voice was throaty, melodic despite her.

He didn't want her to stop talking. He said, "You go to the college?"

"I go wherever I want."

"And where have you wanted to go?"

"Nowhere."

"And yet you're here."

"Actually I'm not."

"Okay."

"I'm a ghost, if you want to know." She slipped the hood back to see him better, tugged it off, whiff of mildew, faint trace of amusement leaving her face. Her hair looked like it had been chopped with a machete on one side, thinned with animal bites on the other, anyway it bunched heavily, with bald spots. Hair like that, you might *want* to wear a hood.

Eric said, "What did you study?"

"Study?"

"At the college."

"Elementary ed and mathematics," she said. There was an old cut on the top of her ear, might have been pretty bad, dried blood. "I'm good at mathematics. Also archeology, which was great, and English composition, which was okay." A yellowing bruise on her neck. She said, "I got my teaching certificate, um, last spring. And then in the fall I had an actual, real job. Watch the fucking road."

The road was damp, nothing worse than that, and well paved, and empty, not that 138 was ever crowded, or even busy. Eric kept his eyes ahead, said, "You were graduated last spring?"

"Last May."

"Nontraditional student?"

"What's that supposed to mean?"

"Well. You're a little older than the usual, that's all."

"They don't get many ghosts."

"And you earned your teaching certificate."

"They gave it to me, anyway."

"Who gave it to you?"

"The college. Who do you think?"

At the sound of her tone, defensive, Eric said, "Of course. The college." But he knew from a recent and painful false-credentials case that the state conferred certification, not the college. You had to apply for certification. It cost money. You had to provide fingerprints, full set, and that cost you, too: fifty-five bucks. He also knew when someone was lying. And English composition was a first-year course. Why would you mention that when you'd just been graduated?

"I didn't love teaching," she said.

He couldn't help but return her sudden stare, unnerving, the remains of her bangs standing up as if in surprise. Still, face-on there was even more to her than he'd begun to think, intelligence, for one thing. And some kind of basic honesty. Her mouth was full with a dent in the top lip, off-center. Her nose was like a tired dog that had found a warm place to lie down and sleep. And she'd relaxed maybe a notch, kept his eye. She needed to wash her face, that's all—she was sooty, plain dirty.

"What grade?" Eric said at last. He'd done hundreds of these interviews. You look at the police report, meet with the client, keep it friendly, try to put two and two together, draw inferences, become a master of observation, figure out what's true and what's not, try, when there's a choice, to take cases you can actually win. Not much choice lately.

She let the tiniest smile arrive, cut it off short when she saw he noticed. "Maybe third," she said. "Or maybe all of them."

"All of the grades, you mean?"

She sought protection from his gaze, tweaked her own soft nose, clearly designed by the ghost shop to add some femininity to a rather hard face. "The principal adored me."

"What was his name?"

"He hated me."

"Both?"

"People are complicated."

He said, "Two sides to every coin."

So quick: "And two to most clichés."

"I'll have to think about that."

"Watch the road."

They were getting close to the veterinarian's. Eric found himself driving more slowly. He said, "What was the school called?"

"Captain Arnold Elementary, named for Benedict Arnold,

who not everyone knows made a heroic trek through Maine to attack the French at Montreal. We were happy at first."

"Who's we?"

"Jimmy and me. He taught phys ed. I loved teaching third grade—third and fourth together, actually. Nine kids with two sets of twins. I miss them slightly."

"Slightly."

"One of the twin-parents complained. About, like, nothing. I didn't explain the homework supposedly, which was like a math sheet with instructions, which I copied right off the curriculum they make you use. And Mr. Guest calls me in and there's no support of any kind coming from him. So I call my advisor back at the college here and she just says, 'Keep your head down, honey.' And then the really nice parents . . ."

"The ones you slightly miss."

"I don't miss them at all. They come in for parents' night and the other twins' dad stands up—he's like this rotund, bank-president, logger-swagger, king-of-the-garbage-men kind of guy with his wife pushing him—and he says the *meek* kids are bullying *his* kids. But, come on! The meek kids? They're like these little fragile brainy wisps five years ahead of everyone else. And what Mr. Guest didn't tell me is that these kids' very nice parents had complained the year before about how *their* kids were being bullied. And so anyway the very nice dad bravely says, Nonsense. And the bank-president, logger-swagger dad says, And you, the teacher, just letting it happen? And I'm like, I wouldn't ever! And Mr. Guest is like, Anyone else? And yes, like two other parents get up and repeat the whole thing, say that these meek little twins have been bullying their kids and as the teacher I'm letting it happen."

Eric slowed his car, stopped on the inadequate shoulder, pulled a little further ahead. He said, "There's the veterinary clinic."

"But it's just not true, outlandishly not true. So I'm like, Well, let's think about how to communicate about this as adults and role models. And one of the moms gets up and says if I don't get control of my classroom."

There was nothing across from the vet's. Eric said, "Where did you say your house was?"

She pointed vaguely to the dense forest. "I'm down there."

"Down where?"

"Oh, it's nice. Don't worry. It's down on the river."

And there was, if you looked, a bit of a path. She climbed out of the car. Eric helped her recover her groceries, and between them, Eric felt, was this overwhelming feeling of loss (or maybe it was just Eric, his lonely mood), anyway the feeling that she wasn't ever going to get to tell him the rest of her story, that he wasn't ever going to get to hear it, get to the bottom of it, clear the discrepancies, something he was very, very good at and enjoyed, the best part of his work. He couldn't help it, said, "So you're not there anymore. At Captain Arnold Elementary."

Her head jerked faintly at his remembering the name. "Not there, no. Last April I just got in my car and left. Left them in the lurch, as they say."

"So you quit?"

"Well, not really."

A cold wind was picking up, flecks of wet snow.

"Well then, you were fired. You were unfairly fired." Eric in the back of his lawyerly mind was already winning a breach-of-contract suit, with damages.

"I was fired for quitting, I guess."

Then again, it might all be rubbish. He said, "Well, maybe sometime I'll hear the whole story." The river was pretty far down, by Eric's estimation. Maybe half a mile or more, and steep terrain. Or maybe the young woman just didn't want him to know where she actually lived, laudable caution.

She said, "'It sifts from leaden sleeves, it powders all the wood.'"

"Okay," Eric said.

She said, "We had to memorize a poem. In English class. That one was short, at least."

Eric let his face brighten: "Oh, I get it. The snow. Nice."

"'Sieves,' I mean. 'It sifts from leaden sieves.'"

And here it came: one flake, two, a third one over here, and then suddenly the millions, dropping fast and hard, the wind suddenly whipping.

He said, "We're supposed to get a lot, I guess. Storm of the century, that's what I heard. Of course that's what they always say."

"And then there's something about ruffling the wrists of fence posts."

Eric's car was mostly parked on the road, and the two of them just stood behind it, as if that were where people always chatted. He said, "High winds later and over two feet of snow, three feet or even more in some areas."

"Some areas. That's us, isn't it? We're always 'some areas.' It snowed I think twenty-five feet up there last winter, in Presque Isle. The roads were like driving down canyons."

"I like your poem," Eric said. "And just the idea of fence posts with wrists, nice."

"I didn't write it." She let a long moment pass, finally began to gather her bags, picking them up by their many handles one by one till she and her coat were weighted down like a circus tent against the wind. "Well, thanks," she said.

"My pleasure," Eric said slowly. Again, that charitable rumbling up from his toes, a kind of twitching in his hands, his jaw, the words coming to his lips: "I could help you down."

"No," she said.

The snow was falling in earnest now, large, wet flakes. There had better damn well be a house down there. "Please," Eric said.

"No," she said again and put the enormous hood back over her head. She hefted those bags—easily fifty pounds dangling off her bare hands—and hunched off down the path a step at a time, definite hitch in her gait, painful to see. Eric watched her a moment, watched a little more, then climbed in his car, honked a couple of times to say good luck. She turned slightly, shrugged heavily by way of a wave, the weight of all that crap she'd bought. No ghost had ever been so tied to the earth as she.

Eric tore his eyes from her plight, drove off.

The snow had already begun to accumulate on the road—a kind of slush that would turn to ice when evening came, temperatures to plummet midway through the afternoon as the storm "re-intensified," or so the serious taller guy on the Weather Channel had warned, possibly several days of snow, likely record-breaking, if the various systems lined up.

Eric decided to go the long way, enjoy the snowfall, so no U-turn but straight ahead on 138, driving slowly, the sweeping curve down the hill and over the new bridge. Beneath which the Woodchurch River was flowing deep and swift after an autumn of rains, iced now only at the banks and fringes, boulders like mounds of glass. Long glimpse, then up and up to Houk's

Corners, the gas station there, also the defunct video club where he and Alison used to rent art movies. He felt his own temperature had plummeted, something unnamed re-intensifying inside him, that charity again, or maybe plain kindness, the stuff he was really made of and had lately kept too close. That young woman, practically dragging her bags of groceries.

He turned around in the Mobil station at the Corners and headed back, parked at the veterinarian's, which was the only building in sight, Dr. Mia Arnold, from Switzerland. He'd won a case against her just the spring before, some ultra-fancy show dog she'd euthanized in a mix-up. The snow was thick, wet, very heavy. But life continued as usual—a bearded man chunking down Dr. Arnold's wheelchair ramp with an enormous black dog in tow, a put-together college girl climbing the stairs the other way with a kitten cupped in her hands, the dogs back in the boarding kennels oddly silent. It was still only early afternoon, plenty of time, but the sky was dark and getting darker, a notch colder, too, the wind picking up, snow in Eric's face as he crossed the street to the young woman's path.

Three

HE SNIFFED THAT smell of wood smoke and dirty clothes and mildew as he caught up to her a short way into the forest—it was that old pile of a coat she was wearing, not entirely unpleasant, but close. The enormous hood had fallen off her head, and her hair was really very badly matted and frizzed and chopped, little bright beads of water where snowflakes had landed. Around them the trees were scruffy, too, bare and overcrowded in what had been pastureland, the snow blowing through upraised branches, a few last, clinging leaves rattling. Seeing Eric, she unraveled herself from the bag handles and rubbed the twisted imprints in her fingers and hands.

Eric said nothing, but welling with anger—she'd no idea of the danger she was in—gave her one of his dress gloves, nice brown leather lined with warm fuzz. She took it quickly and thrust her hand into it, pride knocked back by the cold. He hefted all seven of her bags by the handles in the one gloved hand and she didn't protest that, either, though Eric got the idea she'd rather. Fifty or sixty pounds, easily, now that he felt it.

"I just thought," he said. He just thought some people needed to be protected from themselves.

"Storm of the century," she said. "As if they fucking know."

"Maybe just the last hundred years," Eric said.

And that was an end to talk. Down and down and to the river, at least a half mile, thirty minutes at her pace, then down a very steep approach to the flats along the river, then upstream another hundred yards in the protection of a row of riverside hemlocks that grew under a rocky slope, all but a cliff. The hemlocks blocked the snow and kept the path clear, a soft, six-century duff of fine needles and tiny cones and brittle twiglets fragrant and giving underfoot. The cabin was a surprise, a sudden apparition, brown as the trunks of the hemlocks. Except for the steep plane of its roof under the new snow, it might have been invisible, a rustic old place perched on stout cement piers atop a high rock outcropping above the coursing Woodchurch. Beyond the hemlocks were two of the biggest white pines Eric had ever seen, one then the next, partners over the river, trunks that four people couldn't hug: no logger had ever devastated this awkward spot.

So, she really did have a place to go. The young woman climbed three prodigious stone steps and pushed open the cabin's heavy front door, no locks to fuss with. Eric climbed after her and followed her inside, nice and warm. She hobbled straight to the antique cookstove, a Glenwood (so it said), a fancy thing all decked out with chrome scrollwork and numerous warming shelves and doors and vents and handles, lovely. She built up the fire with sticks of dead pine and a couple of moldering logs, all she had for firewood. Beside the stove, a vintage copper slipper tub with two washcloths hanging stiff—how would you go about using that?

No invitation, he hefted his load of bags to the top of a stout-legged butcher's block in the kitchen corner, slowly disassociated himself from the twisted handles. The gray of the afternoon permeated the place. The walls were beaverboard, and small sprays of snow had formed on the floor where there were cracks—not a shred of insulation, was Eric's guess, the whole thing open to the wind underneath, no kind of winter abode, the sprays soon to be drifts, interior.

The young woman shuffled around in her huge coat putting things right. So there was a basic competence. She filled a large pot with greenish water from an old joint-compound bucket, lit a kerosene lamp with a long match from a lobster-shaped holder bolted to the wall, placed it smoking on the table, bent efficiently to adjust the wick.

"Okay," she said in the sudden warm light.

"Nice," Eric said. Probably too helpfully he unpacked the plastic bags item by item, again depressed by her shopping.

Clearly annoyed by him, she reached to put things away in the rough-hewn cabinets nailed high on the kitchen wall, lined up her ramen perfectly, her mac and cheese, the big cans of beans. At last she shed the huge coat, hung it on a nail near the stove, plain that it had hung there for many years.

"I'm Eric," he said, noting once again the cut on her ear.

"Oh, for Christ's sake," she said and limped to gaze out the big window over the river, the only window in the place, blue light: the snowfall was nearly horizontal in the wind. "You'd better get moving."

He shouldn't have stared. "I'd like to help," he said. "Before I go." He felt strongly that she was his responsibility now, a kind of pro-bono client he'd taken on. He had nothing pressing to attend to otherwise, God knew, small-town lawyer with no cases, typical for November, or maybe a little less than typical: it had been a bad year all around. Also, Alison had missed their last several dinner dates. But he didn't like to think of that. Always hopeful, as Alison might say.

"No, really," the young woman said.

Eric noticed a ladder led to a loft above. She must sleep up there—no bed downstairs, only a couple of mission-oak chairs and small matching couch, cracked leather cushions, nice old furniture in the coldest corner of the place. He heard the wind picking up, checked his phone surreptitiously. No signal, nothing. The time was still only one o'clock, but sunset would come at 3:45, and in this weather dusk would drop fast.

He said, "What's going on with that limp?"

"Ankle," she said. "Pretty bad."

"We'd better take a look."

She sighed but shuffled to the couch, fell onto it, tugged her shoe off. It was a teacher's shoe, all right, kind of a felt clog with a negative heel, soaked through. Good wool socks, though, thick and green and fairly new. Whose charity accounted for socks like that? Gingerly she peeled her foot bare. The ankle was definitely swollen, a yellow-green bruise down to the toes, but none of the deep-blue hematomic color you'd expect with a break. "You'll want to keep using it," Eric said, old athlete. He took the foot in his two hands gently, palpated it gently, cool skin, toenails untended. Back before he'd flunked organic chemistry in college, he'd thought he'd be a doctor. "Light use," he said, "to keep it from stiffening up. And pack a little snow on it

for ten or fifteen minutes every so often. You can do that right
now, if it suits you. Maybe by the fire so you don't get chilled?"

"Okay, *Doctor*," she said, abruptly pulling her foot out of
his hands. "Don't you think you'd better get going? Like, right
now?"

"You'll need firewood," he said. "It's going to be a long three
or four days with this snow."

She looked at his loafers, his dress slacks, his natty sports
jacket. She wanted the wood, anybody could see that. She said,
"There're some boots and stuff in the shed." She pointed to a
narrow door in the corner, upstream. He'd assumed it was a
bathroom, but of course there was no bathroom. Behind the
door he found a rough shed, wind and snowflakes inside. Also
vintage water skis and slickers and broken fishing rods and
lengths of hose and every sort of summer thing imaginable, a little six-horse Johnson boat motor on a wooden trestle, rakes and
shovels and scraps of lumber and a workbench, plenty of tools
hanging and fallen, a thermometer nailed to the wall (fourteen
degrees), girlie calendar set forever to August 1965. The pin-up
was a chubby young woman with red cheeks and an inadequate
sweater buttoned strategically, no pants to speak of, but legs
folded demure. Funny to think that in real life she was probably about his mom's age, photographed in a less sexualized era.
He wondered where the young woman was now, those plump
shoulders, the cute chin tucked in, the finger to her lips, how
many kids, how many divorces, what illnesses, alive or dead?
He flipped through the calendar, couldn't stop himself. August
was the woman for him, all right, or would be when she grew
up, though of course by now she had grown up and then down

again, potent gaze. He could see why someone had saved her, and why she'd been banished to the shed.

In blue rain boots, a stiff yellow slicker, and a pair of pink fish-scaling gloves (very tough, not warm), Eric emerged from the shed carrying a bow saw and a dull hatchet he'd found, closed the door behind him.

His hostess very nearly smiled at the sight of him.

He said, "Pretty manly, I admit."

The joke killed any amusement. "And then I need you out of here," she said.

"Yes," he said.

"But thanks, okay?"

"Tell me your name?"

"Danielle, for now."

Four

OUTSIDE HE FOUND an open little woodshed, but Danielle-for-now had depleted the supply to a couple of uselessly huge logs, half rotted in any case. So Eric flapped in his rubber boots up and under the hemlocks, snapped off dead-dry branches and twigs, broke it all into kindling lengths over his knee, made several large bundles in short order, carried them hugged to his chest, tucked them one at a time inside the cabin door. Danielle was in the kitchen corner, paid him no attention, just put the last of her groceries away. She'd pulled off her bulky, practically knee-length sweater and he saw she was slender, not so blowsy as he'd thought, and except for maybe the hair and shiny, unwashed pants pretty much just a person you'd find anywhere in Woodchurch. Her shirt was big like everything else, an old flannel job misbuttoned. She was wet up to her knees. Make that soaked. Well, she didn't need him telling her to change her clothes.

Back in the pelting wind, Eric struggled up the path he and Danielle had come in on. Their footprints were already obscured. He found a dead maple standing nice and dry, maybe ten inches at the base, sawed it down more easily than he'd imagined, satisfying crash. He sawed off the bigger branches, sawed the trunk into manageable lengths, more sweaty effort, maybe a half hour's work in the dumping snow, more and more uncomfortable as his fish-scaling gloves got soaked, dragged the pieces down one then two then three at a time to the woodshed, climbed back up the hill and retrieved the branches, exhausting. He saw himself returning in a couple of days after the storm had blown through, saw himself checking in on her friendly, bringing fresh victuals, a packet of clean T-shirts, unless that was too personal, certainly a decent blanket.

Under the overhang of the woodshed's roof at least he was out of the horizontal snow, which had started to mix with flecks of stinging ice. He got himself set up and cut about half the wood into twenty or so logs of various diameters, only a few so big around that they'd have to be split. In the woodshed he found a splitting maul, and he enjoyed the work so much he just kept splitting till even the smaller logs were done. This gave the impression of a lot more wood and he brought it into her house in several trips, no sign of the young woman. So he filled the woodbox by the stove, stacked the rest against the wall, enough for a couple of days at least. Which, of course, meant a couple of days at most. After which he could come back with a chain saw and maybe a friend and do the job right. Or, maybe more to the point, a couple of social workers and a cop, get her out of there. You couldn't let people die just because they might get mad at you.

"Wow, sweet," Danielle said from up in the loft, disembodied voice. "That was above and beyond."

"My pleasure," Eric said. "Like a day at the gym. And there's more out there, too."

"Have some water—it's boiled. In the small pot. And then you'd better go."

He drank directly from the pot, the water still warm, faint biotic taste of the river, deeply satisfying: of course he was thirsty. She'd pulled the two mission-oak chairs up close to the stove and her clothes were arranged on them drying, meager items, pants and shirt and huge sweater, underpants. He stood there and stripped the sopping fish-scaling gloves inside out off his puckered fingers, found himself studying the underpants, elastic emerging from the band, side seam ripped, a picture of desperation. He hung the gloves near them. He could come back in a few days with a chain saw, yes, and also some provisions, even a load of clothes and bedding from the thrift shop. Maybe Patty Cardinal from the church would help him, jolly old Patty the volunteer organist and inveterate do-gooder, woman's touch, always wearing red.

"You're a masochist," Danielle said from upstairs, her face and naked square shoulders suddenly in view. The color was back in her cheeks. She'd tugged a big knit hat over her hair, looked at him from under the brim, one of those Rasta caps in the colors of the Jamaican flag. So maybe she was growing dreadlocks, fine.

"Referring to what?" he said pleasantly.

"To your masochism," she said equally.

He didn't want to appear to be lurking, but didn't want to appear to be hurrying, either, in case she had any further tasks she'd like done. If that were masochism and not altruism. Which was the joke he wanted to make. But did not. Because who knew what she was actually talking about. It really was time to get moving, the room and the day a notch darker, then two notches, and still the hope that Alison was coming, that Alison who'd broken their last several dates and hadn't been home for months was on her way back to Woodchurch.

Danielle said, "Keep the boots and stuff. You can't walk out in loafers."

"I'll bring them back, don't worry."

"Don't bother," she said. "Really, don't."

Five

His footprints and every sign of his miniature logging operation were completely obscured. He ducked under the hemlocks to where the path started up the hill. He hadn't noticed the outhouse right there, though he must have walked past it several times. Solid little building with a blue toilet seat bolted over the single hole, half roll of toilet paper, box of tampons empty, thick soft-cover copy of *Anna Karenina,* apparently much thumbed, faint stench of shit, which he was something like embarrassed to associate with the young woman. He anointed the depths of the pit with his own urine, only heightening the embarrassed feeling, an intimacy he'd just not ever thought of before in a whole life of using outhouses and wished he hadn't thought of now.

Up the very steep hill he climbed, lingering odd feelings, an afternoon of only half-appreciated charity behind him, plodded like making the last steps of a Himalayan ascent, stopping often to be sure he hadn't left the path, which was increasingly indistinct. The wet snow lay atop the ice from earlier in the week and in the rain boots it was slippery, not only heavy.

And yet he was full of the surest feeling that *this* was the night, the long-awaited Alison night, and that his patience had paid off, would pay off, Danielle-for-now's need and his response amounting to a sign. Of something. Karma being one's actions. And one's actions bringing destiny to bear. After Alison left, that time. For example. That time she'd arrived for the monthly visit they'd negotiated as a way to test their separation over the course of a year. The second monthly visit, after a very bad first one. Yes, that second one made a good comparison. She'd arrived early with her bike on the rack at the back of her sensible car, greeted him all bright and lively, a particular vivid mood of hers that he hadn't seen in years. "Rumble Pond!" she'd announced.

Rumble Pond was a full-gear outing: saddlebags, food, sleeping bags, bike parts, tent. They pedaled side by side right out of the neighborhood and out of town and up Dairyman Hill Road four stiff miles to the log-company gate and then on gravel onward, then no gravel, mountain biking on an actual mountain, the gorgeous little lake at the end of the ride, the hot swim, the isolated campsite. And he hadn't seen that game look on her face for years, not since the time he'd just shaved after work and she liked his smooth chin so much that she pushed him to their bedroom, fucked him hard (unheard of!), came to quick climax (unprecedented!), and bit that smooth chin (drawing blood!), just that one time, ancient history.

At Rumble Pond they'd made dinner excitedly working together, not like people who were separated but like the old kitchen team they'd been in the first flush of their romance. And after they'd eaten, well, instead of cleaning it all up right away they made love, first time in at least months, and the second-best time ever, as he thought about it, and he would think about it lots. She started it—kisses of unfamiliar depth, at last an acceptance of his real kisses and not the kisses he'd developed for her overly peckish tastes. And actual giggling and the ripping of his shirt buttons, okay? And a tumble on top of un-deployed sleeping bags and then upon the tent, complete inadvertent disassembly of the poor little thing. And her skin in the moonlight, unforgettable, as if it had grown soft in his absence.

They stayed up there that way three days, bike excursions east and west and north, a honeymoon like they hadn't let themselves have in Prague (that she hadn't let them have), stayed past their food, an extra day, giddy on the way back out with fasting and promises. Give her a month, is all she asked. They felt they'd solved the puzzle of their fractured marriage, one of those long algorithms from college math.

Tonight would be like those nights!

He felt a moral tug. Danielle had food. Danielle had shelter. She had firewood, now. But Danielle was alone, and with an injury, and very likely unstable. A small accident would be amplified. What if she burned herself or fell from her loft? He certainly knew of dozens of such cases, small-town law. That little girl who'd cooked to death in the back of her parents' van parked outside the Sugarwood Grille, hot August afternoon? Or poor Kurt LaFarge, who fell on the North Church steps in the snow one Saturday night, last man out after choir, broke his neck and froze solid, ambulance and police and sheriff and medical examiner still there as the parishioners arrived the next morning. Pastor Tony paid for that one, and unfairly: gross negligence. Eric might have done more for the girl, was the point. Danielle would need more water, for example. Or did ghosts never drink?

He trudged, made the road, crossed to the veterinary parking lot, climbed in his car and started it, sat a few minutes catching his breath. Really, that was a very hard climb in these conditions. His own pants legs were soaked, but the boots had kept his socks dry. The veterinarian—a crabbed old soul when it came to humans and a well-known killer of show dogs—looked out her window at him, the longest look, no expression on her face. He gave a short wave, and she disappeared behind the curtain so fast that he felt like a magician.

Findings: Ms. Danielle would be alone down there for several days. A life on Doritos and ramen noodles. At least she had wine. A blizzard called for a box of wine, simple as that, no need to judge. Alison was probably on her way, should really be on her way if she was going to make it. And then—no doubt she'd thought of this—maybe she'd be snowed in and he'd get to make her breakfast after all, maybe a few days of breakfasts, if the Weather Channel was right. Unbidden, a certain bra came to mind, gray satin. From back in the day. He felt his hand upon its clasp. He checked his phone. No calls, no texts, no tweets, no e-mails, not a word on Facebook, not from Alison anyway, not a peep from Alison, who'd done nothing but stand him up for months, if he admitted it. He stifled a wave of anger, checked Troy Polamalu's game stats one more time: fantasy football. Then the weather: the Winter Storm Warning had been upgraded to a Winter Storm Emergency. He'd never seen that designation. And a link to a checklist for disaster preparedness.

There was about an hour before the day would get swallowed by the storm and he was wet anyway and there was this terrible sense of responsibility, also the food he'd bought: she'd need everything she could get, and he had all he needed: Alison wasn't going to show, third month in a row, and who was he kidding? Fourth in a row. He was no masochist. He heard his father's voice: *face facts*. The snow was building, building. No more cars coming in and out of the veterinarian's lot, just the Mercedes with the SPAY plates. No cars on the road, either.

He retrieved his bags of groceries, left the expensive wine in, why not? He had beer at home. Plenty of daylight. The snarly old poodle of a vet was spying on him again, glowering out the window at him. He'd won the case for his client, that's all, had never thought twice about continuing to bring his dog to Dr. Mia Arnold, but then he hadn't needed to: poor Ribbie, living now with Alison down in Portland, another stab of anger.

A lot of anger, Alison had said sometimes, no matter how justifiably pissed he was. "A lot of anger, Eric." Heavy on the *K* sound in his name. Had he been angry on their bike trip? He had not. Had she returned? She had not. The bags were heavy, but not as heavy as Danielle's had been, and only two of them. More awkward, though: paper. He arranged them in the crook of one arm so as to have a hand free. His own footprints from a mere three minutes previous were already filled in, but no question where the path was through the roadside meadow. The forest, however, was decidedly darker, the balsam firs beyond the stone wall drooping with snow, the branches starting to block the path. He enjoyed tugging on them, watching the snow dump, the branches springing back skyward. This would be a place to come mushrooming in the spring, and warbler walking. It would be a lot of things in spring that it was not now. He and Alison could come here together: she'd always liked to explore vernal pools. She'd bend deeply from the waist—all that yoga— and examine the loops of frog eggs. She'd flip leaves uncannily and find a fire newt every time. She'd have zero compassion for Danielle, or less.

The pitch of the slope seemed steeper and the rain boots more hopeless and he slid and slipped his way down, proud of his balance, almost skiing at times, groceries at risk. The last stretch of the path coming down from high above the river and past the outhouse was difficult—the wind and snow hard in his face, ice underfoot. The hemlock branches, heavy with wet snow, were already brushing the ground, no obvious entry to the shelter they'd provided earlier. He skirted them, stinging snow in his face, ducked to the cabin and up the stone steps, hurried to push the door open and escape the pelting, a loud halloo so as not to frighten the young woman.

He failed at that:

"Hey," she cried. "*Hey!*" Then, "What the *fuck,* yo, get out!" She'd pulled the big slipper tub up practically touching the stove and stood in it, her naked butt pinkened from a scrubbing; anyway, she was in the act of dipping her washcloth into the pot of water she'd put on, and her legs were long and bare and awfully hairy and dripping, a patter of metallic beats from the copper tub, like a shower of pennies.

He turned away mortified. "Oh, my god, sorry! I just brought you this stuff. You'll need more food. And there's good wine. From the store. For you. If you want."

Danielle had a tattered robe instead of a towel, but at least she had that. She wrapped herself up in it. "You just come crashing in?"

"It's so windy, I . . ."

She climbed out of the tub in her pink-gray robe and marched toward him, sharp little fist at the ready. "Out!" she cried. "Get out!" And then she was pummeling him as best she could, one hand holding the robe, knuckles in his sternum between the grocery bags, which he didn't want to drop. He tried not to smile, blocked her hand between the bags. "Help!" she cried, pulling it back, punching at him wildly, little knuckles ripping the heavier of the bags.

He crouched to save the wine as the bag tore open, dropped the other bag in the process, cheese and scallions and peppers tumbling out. She took the opportunity to pop him in the chin a good one, even as the next wine bottles hit the floor clanking against each other, rolling away across the floor. He said, "Hey, okay, easy. I just thought you could use some more food."

And she popped him again, kicked at him. "You didn't think! You didn't think at all! Jimmy! Help!"

Jimmy? He fumbled on, the rest of the groceries hitting the floor, perfect mango splitting. He said, "That's raw-milk Parmesan. It's delicious, the real thing. I thought you'd like to have it. And some basics? That's excellent flour."

She kicked the bag, a puff of white.

"And all sorts of vegetables."

She tried to stomp the first eggplant, but it rolled under her bad foot and sent her off balance. She fell hard, clutching her robe tighter then diving at Eric from a mad crouch, catching a pocket of his jacket, which ripped half off. "Get out! Basics and all! Get the fuck out! You're so nicey-nice, you fucking . . . *creeper,* with your creeper *gifts.*"

Suddenly she softened, maybe at the sound of the word *gifts* as it flew from her lips, maybe at the realization that she'd ripped his clothes, maybe noticing that he really had brought food, food she really needed. Stiffly then, not exactly contrite, she said,

"You're crashing in here and grinning at me like a wolf and it really, really *freaks me out*." She was back to shouting: "*You have to understand*. Please, just go. And quit *smiling*."

Okay, he really was grinning. He killed it, said, "You were in a private moment. I'm very sorry."

She blew up, jumped to her feet, jabbed a finger in his chest, backed him toward the door: "*All*-moments-are-fucking-*private*!"

Eric backed away, step-by-step and to the heavy front door, defending himself with his hands, the young woman poking at him all the way, trying to get at his face. He yanked the door open to wind and snow, said, "I hope you have a corkscrew down here. That's nice wine."

"Go!" she shrieked, and pushed him by the chest.

He stumbled down the stone steps, fell into the snow at the bottom.

"I said *go the fuck away*!"

Six

Outside the storm was howling, a different kind of snow altogether, curtains of it blowing, already drifted to knee-deep in sculpted ridges along the ground, coming so thick and furious it was as if legions of dump trucks were emptying their loads in his face, in the world's face, misery: the jostling wind, the river coursing black below.

He pushed his way through hemlock branches and into their protection—a Mongolian hut of a cavern under there, still the ground bare and soft, cracks of muted light all around him. He barged through and back into the wind at the end of the line, the end of the cabin's little dooryard, but reluctantly: his socks inside the rain boots were no longer dry, squishing in fact, and the going was more slippery than ever, nothing for a path but slight depressions where his footprints had been only short minutes before. Still, he felt a lightness: he'd given away Alison's dinner, which amounted to giving up on her, admitting she wasn't coming home, never again.

He slipped on hidden ice—it was all ice underneath—dropped to his knees, the snow immediately wet through his pants. If this weren't such a short hike he'd be in real danger. No great loss, those groceries. Plenty of food at his house, in case Alison did turn up. Plenty more wine. Cases of good beer. He'd watch whatever movie and eat chicken-barley soup. He made good soup and froze it in batches. He put his head down and trudged. The dark was like an eclipse, sudden and thorough. One foot in front of the next, that was all you could do. He bumped up against a tree trunk, a really impressive yellow birch. Close by was another. A hundred years back, there would have been a barn here—yes, a large depression in the earth, great location over the river, when all of this would have been fields and farmsteads and pasture.

Fine, but the birches and the basement hole had not been on the path before. He followed his footfalls back—less than a minute old and already smoothed, as if each print were the basement of an old barn, nature closing in. He hurried, suddenly afraid, followed his tracks back all the way to the hemlocks near the outhouse, started back up the hill, paying close attention this time, allowing no stray thoughts. He saw immediately where he'd gone wrong: the branches of a white pine pressed down and covered the faint path. The radio had said record falls. But three inches an hour? He'd have to look at the Weather Channel when he got home.

With great attention he made his way up the long hill and to the road, which was still unplowed, the sky much lighter out of the woods, like a weight lifted off him. No car had passed recently, and no plow. The lights were off at the veterinary. The Mercedes was gone. And so was his Explorer.

He looked again and then looked all around, as if perhaps he'd parked somewhere else, somewhere he'd entirely forgotten. But, in the end he had to admit it: the car was gone. Already, efficient lawyer, he was rehearsing the phone call to Galvin's Towing. He fingered the keys in his pants pocket, reached for his phone. Which was missing. Or not missing, not at all. He knew exactly where his phone was: his phone had been towed with the car. His sports jacket was soaked through, snow from the outside, sweat from the inside, pocket pulled half off. It was four or five or more miles to town, an hour and a half at a brisk walking gait on a bright summer's day, so make it three hours in the heavy snow already on the road, face into the increasing wind, the new fresh snow blowing in devils all around him. No houses in sight. Only the veterinarian's buildings, closed up tight, even the dog kennels quiet, built out here in the boonies where the barking could bother no one, the boarded dogs locked in for the night, maybe some comfort in there, if he could break in. No, no: the vet had had to shut down the kennel after the lawsuit, a requirement of the settlement. Bitch had had him towed; he'd sleep on her desk! But no. He wasn't going in that place, not for anything.

No way around it, he trudged in the increasing cold for ten minutes, remembering houses around the big sweeping curve ahead. No lights in sight. Not a blink of light. Power must be down; it was always going down on these country roads. Around the curve was only one house, as it turned out, an old farmstead, faint light in the windows. Eric hurried up the long driveway and to the red-painted door. An elderly man answered, flashlight in hand, ready to use it as a club if this were death come knocking.

"Sasquatch?" the old man said, comedian. He was the ancient guy from Woodchurch Feed and Lumber, retired.

"Jack, I need to use your phone," Eric said, coming up with the name heroically.

"Haven't got one," Jack said, heavy Maine accent, swallowed syllables. Back in the dark house the bright voice of an excited weatherman. Jack would be the guy with batteries for his radio, of course, the guy without a phone. "Fastest ac*cum*ulation in the records," the old man said.

Mildly, Eric said, "I'd heard that predicted."

"By jeezum crow," Jack said.

Behind the old man in the dimmest possible light Eric could make out piles of cardboard boxes and high stacks of newspapers and cat-litter stations, whatever you called them, encrusted cat turds strewn all around, stacks of soiled books, folded lawn chairs, bundles of firewood, stench of piss like the breath of the house, clogged passages through all the junk.

But Jack wasn't inviting him in: "So much for all this hockey-puck of yours about global warming!"

"Hockey-puck," Eric repeated.

"They keep uppering the prediction. Now they says four feet!"

"Four feet!"

"Forty-eight inches! Just heard!"

No phone.

Whom had he been planning to call, anyway? He had had to let his secretary go months since, and she was still bitter. His best local friend, Carl, was in Nigeria for the year. Patty Cardinal, his church friend, didn't drive anywhere after dark: all these private fears. Alison, be real, Alison was on permanent leave, it increasingly looked, and two hours away in any case, down in Portland, three in this weather, finally living the big life she'd always envisioned for herself, cute condo, high-pressure job, and the company of Ribbie their dog, who spent all day alone. His own house, a tidy little place he'd owned before Alison ever moved in, was on the other edge of downtown, a good five miles away, maybe six.

Hardware-store Jack had all the time in the world, was introducing various cats as Eric stood in the open door, Tingle and Pete and Round-Eye and Pretty Miss and Little Hunger-Tum.

Eric's mind raced: his office. But that was no help, only slightly closer than home—four hours at the rate he'd been proceeding, and with the wind higher and the snow deeper every minute. The closest houses were at least two miles. A year back he might have called Jane and Bill or Drew and Sarah, these couples like friends of the marriage, but they had proven themselves aligned with Alison, or if they hadn't they'd been neutral and that had irked him and he'd backed away, isolating himself, Alison liked to say. He started back down the list of his acquaintances, lots of whom might be helpful. Or, what the heck, call the police: he knew them all anyway from his work. They'd come and get him.

If he had a goddamn phone.

Some hell creature shrieked from back in the packed bowels of Jack's castle. "Hunger-Tum!" the old man cried.

Seven

ERIC BANGED ON the cabin door this time, banged and called out. His own fresh tracks had already been thoroughly buried, and he was soaked to the skin, his wrists aching from falls, but he'd made it down and now it was dark, no going back.

He was too miserable to stand on courtesy: when she didn't answer (and why would she, even if she could hear his banging?), he took a deep breath, blew it out, grimaced, then shoved the old door, a desperate push. It fell open easily. "Halloo," he said, though she was only at the big butcher's block, hacking at something.

She spun, startled: "Okay, no," she said.

"My car was towed."

More than startled: "You're scaring me, mister."

"No, no. It's not like that."

"You're scaring me *badly,* mister! Get out! *Out!*"

He held his hands up to show them empty. Also in case she came at him with the knife she'd been using, which it looked like she might. Quietly he said, "I've got nowhere else to go. Don't be afraid. Please. You know me. I mean, I'm a nice local person.

I just need help as you did. I throw myself at your mercy. All the power's out up there. My phone was in the car." He knew he had to up the ante: "The fucking vet bitch had it *towed*. And that place is like a fortress—I couldn't kick the door in. I bruised my shoulder on it, I'm telling you, and I'm not exactly a shrimp. And I'm *freezing*. The snow is coming down like, like I don't know what. Like an *explosion,* like a building coming down, okay? There's not a car passing up there. Not one car. There's like one house and the guy in there is completely nuts. That's as far as I could get, all this time. And now it's *dark*." His voice broke, surprising him. Tears started to his eyes; he couldn't help it.

She'd been cutting oranges, or so it smelled. The lantern light was reflected in her eyes as if it were they that burned and not the kerosene. Her big bag of tortilla chips was ripped open and half spilled on the butcher's block. His groceries were on the floor where they'd fallen amid the ripped bags. She was still in the robe, had found her thick wool socks, still with the Rasta cap.

She said, "You made a big mistake. You think you're nice but you're not. What you are is you're an idiot. You're an idiot to help me, and you're an idiot to come back down here. Of course there are people up there. What do you want from me? What do you *want*?"

He looked to the stove, the beautiful hot stove.

She said, "Stay there. Right there. When Jim gets here? You're *grease*. Do you understand me? *Grease*."

"Let me just warm *up*," Eric said. He'd seen her soften. Just one tick, but something. *Grease*. That must be her husband talking. One of those solid guys on the road crew, say, or in Maxi's garage, tough and funny, shaved heads and rough tattoos, tender inside if you didn't cross them, though crossing them was hard to avoid. The fire had burned down but the air in the cabin was hot, at least in a layer starting at Eric's face. The floor remained frosty. He slipped to the stove without her assent and felt how wet he was, and likely how close to hypothermia. He couldn't think straight. If he'd been thinking straight he wouldn't be back down here. He pulled the rain boots off and poured puddles from them to show her how bad it really was. "It's getting *colder*," he said. "They said it would get colder and the roads would freeze and they have. And anyway I was scared for you. They're saying *four feet*. Apparently it really is the storm of the century. I was worried about your safety. I mean, I was truly worried about you."

She tapped the knife on the block. "Worried about me. Scared for you. Two stories equals a *lie*. That's what Jimmy says."

He pressed close to the stove, felt the heat on the fronts of his legs, the cold at the back. "Listen," he said, "I'm sorry. Relax, please chill. This is not better for me than for you."

"Chill? You chill, you liar." She turned the knife, held it weapon style, *Psycho* style, took a menacing step toward him.

He felt that grin rising in his cheeks, couldn't stop it.

"*You'll* smile," she said. "How does your car get towed in Woodchurch, Maine? Tell me that, mister. No one ever gets towed in Woodchurch."

Very softly: "You win a case against the veterinarian, I guess."

She wielded that knife, stalking closer. "You sued her? You sued the fucking nice old vet?"

Even softer: "A client sued her. She killed his dog."

She feinted at him with the knife. "You're a fucking lawyer?"

He shrugged, grinned harder, backed away from the stove. "Easy," he said.

She said, "You're not old enough to be a fucking lawyer."

He couldn't stop the grinning. Same thing in court when he wasn't sure of his case. "I'm old enough to be anything," he said calmly. "But, yes, a fucking lawyer. Okay? As small town as they get."

Keeping her eye on him, knife still poised, she reached awkwardly across herself and pulled the long iron poker from its hook behind the stove, came at him as he shuffled backward, back into the cold, back toward the door, her weapons really more comic than menacing.

He composed his face. "I'm just a nice person who helps others for small pay or even for free, or even gives away money, and wouldn't hurt a fly. And I've got no way to leave."

She pushed the tip of the ancient poker against his chest, rested it there, too heavy to loft for long. She said, "Why don't you call your wife?"

"She's not available. We're separated. It's bad. And it's very bad out there in the storm. I was frightened. And my phone, it's in the car."

Glimmer of compassion on Danielle's face, knife still poised.

Eric turned the ring on his finger, gazed at it, a poor thin thing from antimaterialist Alison, twenty-one dollars at Kay Jewelers. Danielle had seen it, good or bad. He'd never removed it for any reason, never since Alison had stuck it on his finger in her parents' church. More sadly than he wanted, he tugged it off, stuffed it in his pants pocket. He said, "An artifact, I guess."

"Okay, so now it's archeology."

"And even if she were home where she belongs, I'm not sure the roads are passable in any case. There's not a car in sight. Nothing's been plowed, nothing at all. Record rate of accumulation, they said. Please put the knife down."

Instead she feinted with it again, prodded him hard in the chest with the poker, once again indignant. "Who said? The pixies? The roads are passable, all right. Of course they're passable. People have big four-by-four trucks around here. Nothing stops them. Don't you have any friends? Aren't the plow guys driving around? The tow-truck guys? The ones who towed your car, for example? But you come down here? You hide the ring and think it's gone? I don't know what you think you're going to get out of this situation. Because you're going to get *nothing*, except your teeth beaten through your lips when Jimmy gets here."

Eric pushed the poker away from his chest, held it away from his chest, ready to catch the wrist of her knife hand if necessary. But she just kept the knife poised, fought to pull the poker back away from his grip. She wasn't strong.

"Easy," Eric said.

"Let go!"

"I'm not going to let go. You were hurting me. Kind of got me right between the ribs there. Easy now. Okay? You didn't see the road. You didn't see how much snow. That first wet stuff has frozen solid and now there's another, I don't know, almost a foot since you've seen it. Don't scoff. It really is a foot. Just since we came down. As for my coming back, I was afraid of freezing. I didn't want to come back down here. But there's no one around. No one. And what I want out of the situation at this point, and what I wanted coming back down here, the only thing I wanted—okay?—is not to die. I mean, that's how serious. A person could really die. I'm half frozen, and I'm stuck here, and it's because I tried to help you. I did help you. You wouldn't have made it halfway home without my help. Now it's my turn. Why can't it be my turn?" He couldn't stop the shivering, stood in the freezing puddle his office socks made, thin silk.

Danielle let her end of the poker go such that the heavy handle swung and hit Eric in the shin. She let the knife come down, too, scuffed in her nice wool socks back to the kitchen corner, resumed her position at the butcher's block, exactly the tableau he'd walked in on, went back to her chore—there'd been no interruption, Eric didn't exist—went back to cutting the orange, not in wedges but in slices, round slices like you'd do a tomato, every seed picked out with the tip of the sharp knife. Only when she was done did she return to the problem of him, gave him a long look, the new puddle at his feet seeming to get her pity.

"Okay," she said sharply, "my husband is an Army Ranger, you know what that means? It means if you do anything off-game he will kill you with his bare hands and he'll stuff your body into the outhouse pit and we'll fill it in with rocks and no one will ever know."

Outside the wind kicked up into a new intensity, whistling through every crack in the cabin, puffs of fine snow coming up through the floorboards. Something flapped and knocked on the roof. Eric sidled back to the stove on frozen feet. She'd moved the copper tub far from the fire. The unusably torn panties were draped over its edge along with her washcloths. Eric hopped around absurdly on the icy floor while trying to keep a serious demeanor—because it was very important she take him seriously, very important he not have to go back out into the storm.

"One minute it's a normal afternoon," he said shivering more violently for trying not.

"The floor is frozen. You'll have to dry your socks. I only have my one pair. Sit down. Take your socks off and dry them. Then we'll just see."

"Thank you," Eric said sitting. He rolled his thin, soaked socks off, put his feet up on a warm ledge of the stove, stinging relief.

She stabbed the knife into the butcher's block, brought him a slice of orange, watched him tear it and eat it, delicious, fresh, wet. She dipped a pot of water out of a plastic bucket on the floor, put it on the stovetop to heat, collected another orange in the kitchen, cut that up, too, slowly, methodically. He hung his socks on the edge of the tub, not too close to her broken underwear. She brought him more orange, plopped the slices on the chair arm, ate her own, looming over him, licking her fingers. The warmth started to move into his feet. He noticed how wet his pants legs were, soaking wet around his ankles and up to his thighs.

"How do you get your drinking water?" he asked, something to say.

"Just quiet," she said.

They watched the firelight through the stove vents as the cabin darkened. The wind howled and whistled. Something landed on the roof with a startling thud, a branch, no doubt, a branch from one of the huge pine trees above. Slowly Eric's shivering abated. He closed his eyes, felt his head nod, his neck go slack, his toes prickle and steam.

Eight

DANIELLE WAS BACK in the kitchen corner, hacking away with her knife at his block of Parmesan, light of a kerosene lamp. She'd dressed in grimy jeans and an overly large black T-shirt, those beautiful thick wool socks. She was even thinner than he'd thought. "Who buys such stale cheese?" she said.

"Well," he said. "A lot of people. It's not that it's stale."

"And disposable razors? Aren't disposable razors a waste of dwindling resources? I would have thought you'd be the guy with a little precious antique straight razor and, like, strop. And so much flour? What do you do with flour? Paper mâché?" No smile. The words kept coming, grew indistinct.

Eric sat up with a start. His pants were thoroughly dry. How long had he been asleep? His socks were dry, too, almost crisp. He struggled into them, said, "All that stuff. I was going to make dinner for someone." He yawned compulsively. "For Alison." And yawned again.

Danielle wasn't there. "You talking to somebody?" she said from above. "It's okay. That stove takes every stinking molecule of oxygen out of the air. And who is Alison? The one with the ring? Why would you make dinner for her, someone who treats you like that? And anyway, I never trusted a boy who cooks."

"I haven't seen her in months, actually. But we talk. I just talked to her last week. A few weeks ago, I should say. Or so." He yawned again. "We had a long talk. September, I think. We're separated."

"So you said."

"We meet once a month. It's a ritual."

She quoted something: "'A ritual to keep me from despair.'"

He laughed abruptly, said, "'Paper mâché.'"

But she was not to be deflected: "I don't understand people who break up and then hang out. I'm more full of hate and monstrosity. I mean, if the relationship was any good. But what would I know about that? I'm with Jimmy. And we don't break up, and we don't separate. And September is more than a month ago, mister. Are you awake?"

"We'd just have these meals."

"I swear you were snoring."

"You can't trust a boy who cooks. Where does that come from?"

"From boys who cook."

"Anyway," Eric said. "She'd relax and I'd relax and we'd get over whatever argument and it would be just like it ever was, only maybe fonder, you know, absence and all of that." A log collapsed in the fire, pushing hot coals against the very door. Eric opened it and tended things with her poker, so recently stuck in his ribcage. "Very nice, really. Maybe a way of acknowledging all we've been to one another."

"You mean you'd end up naked on the kitchen floor."

He felt himself flush, but because it wasn't true, and then he lied: "On the couch, in point of fact."

"Breakup sex. And then she could go home immediately after and not feel like she owed you anything."

Eric said, "But not since September."

"Not since before September."

He craned to see Danielle in the loft, but her voice was disembodied—nothing to see up there, only the beams of the ceiling and the footboard of an old iron bed by lamplight, Danielle shuffling around, hard at work at something, dressing maybe, or making the bed.

He said, "She had to go to work Monday mornings."

"You met on Sundays? Who designed that?"

"It was in our separation agreement."

"How long has it really been?"

"So that's why I bought all this food."

"I'm this close to feeling sorry for you."

Eric said, "There's such a term as 'breakup sex'?"

"Such a term, yes, very mainstream. They talk about it on *Oprah*. You should try it sometime. The term, I mean. The sex you've done. And where have you been? You don't have a TV, I bet. Do you even know who Oprah is? You never heard of breakup sex? You buy dinner for someone who isn't going to show up?"

His cozy little tent crushed under them in firelight on the pond after biking all day. He said, "I wish you'd be nicer. I'm feeling pretty tender."

"You mean pretty asleep," she said tenderly. And then she was climbing down the ladder from the loft. She came to him, right to his chair, same shining blue jeans, a different woman,

Rasta cap pulled down hard around her face. She said, "Sorry. Honestly. You were nice to me today."

He couldn't get off his trajectory: "Alison needs support that I apparently didn't give her. Which I don't even know what that means."

Danielle snorted: anyone knew what that meant. She said, "And then there's her secret boyfriend. He told her she had to stop seeing you. An ultimatum. Because he knew how much she still loved you. She'd come home to you all flustered and fucked by someone who knew something about her that you didn't and who she needed to keep just jealous enough to commit, to drop his other girlfriends, like four of them—just what he'd promised himself he wouldn't do, and just what she'd told herself she didn't want, some fresh marriage when she'd finally got free. Her therapist is all over her. She'll dump this guy in another couple of months, you know—but the connection with you, it's, like, *snap,* and that was the unspoken plan, the work of her subbrain, back in September though from your face it's more like July. So for you, of course, it's: Now what?"

She put one of his logs in the fire. This took some arranging. The firebox was already pretty full, roaring nicely. The wind had died down. The window was black dark.

He said, "You'd make a good summation in court."

"Well, don't expect me to swoon over your rock-hard cheese and packets of whatever. Yeast?"

"I was going to make pizza. For Alison."

"At home. Which is where you should be, liar, eating by yourself." She limped to the butcher's block, hacked some more at the cheese. And then she said, "You need to walk out, now. This isn't Mount Everest. You'll make it. You're all warmed up."

"I won't make it. Please."

"You can take the old coat. It's like a tent. You could live in it."

"Then you wouldn't have a coat. And coat or no, it's dark out there, it's snowed deep, Danielle. Please. I'll make dinner for you, a boy who makes you dinner. I won't drink any wine—you either, no drunken incidents. I'll sleep on your couch there. I'll leave at dawn. I just can't leave now. I will die if I leave now. And I mean that literally."

"Oh, tell me about it. You really couldn't break into the vet's?"

"I crushed my shoulder on that fucking door. I ninja-kicked it over and over again. I ran at it like a linebacker. More than once. I really tried. She's got like *security* doors."

Danielle's posture spoke plainly: she didn't believe him. "You'd do great in Afghanistan."

He must have grinned.

Because she was suddenly defensive: "It snows there, too, you know. It snows a lot there, though you think it's a desert. That's where Jimmy has been."

Jimmy. Eric hugged himself. The shoulder really was sore. He said, "In fact, I *was* there. In a manner of speaking. At least in the Persian Gulf. Off Iraq. Between wars. Navy. Fairly luxurious by Army Ranger standards, I realize. Just basically standing on a ship."

"Navy?" She looked him over critically, not entirely unmoved (judging by her posture, once again, all his years of sorting jurors). Yes, Navy: Navy ROTC at Amherst, then law school, all paid for by the military, then five years in, the minimum, two as a shipboard ensign, three as adjutant spokesperson and analyst on environmental matters at a time when the chiefs of staff wanted real reform, safely between the two Gulf wars. And good things had happened, lots of good policy shifts of which he was part, acknowledgment of global warming, for one thing, a series of desk jobs, all compensated. But he didn't say any of that, only shrugged.

She didn't care, said, "Let's have a look." She marched to the front door, the one door, pulled it open to a shocking wall of snow, no opening at all, a perfect print of the door with its cross-bracing and big hinges. She punched the top of the drift and made an opening to heavy wind. A plume of dense snow blew in and then a cascade of fine snow off the roof, like two storms. She punched again and broke the opening wider, just more weather to let in, more night. She thrust her face into the wind. Then she shuddered, shoved the door shut, leaned into it, forced the wood-and-leather latch closed with a few punches of her tight little fist.

"Navy," she said disheartened.

Nine

ERIC MADE HIS famous pizza dough: flour and cold water, salt, couple tablespoons of the good Tuscan olive oil, two teaspoons yeast, very simple. He liked to cook and, like a lot of people in Woodchurch, where there were no real restaurants, he had gotten pretty good at it during his time with Alison, constant dinner parties. The old cabin stove had a smooth firebrick floor to it and you could move coals around the oven compartment wherever needed, make room for a pizza, perfect. He fed logs and sticks in, gradually brought the temperature up to very hot—pretty pleasant in the snow-swept interior of the cabin. The stovepipe rattled and creaked and pinged with the snow and ice flying into it above the roofline, but no danger of its falling—it had been beautifully installed, someone with great skill, also time on his hands, 1930s no doubt, the last era like this one. The cabin that had seemed so rustic seemed more sophisticated suddenly, craftsmanship and materials better than any you'd find in many a contemporary house.

Danielle was into a second hour of a nap up in her loft, had climbed the ladder in a huff after yet another discussion of Eric's motives, which, interrogating himself repeatedly, he still found benign: she was a puzzle and interesting to him in the way of puzzles, but he felt no further attraction to her, romantic or otherwise, and of course nothing of the violence she seemed to imply. She didn't know him. She only knew assholes. She was married and furious and her hair had been rudely chopped off and that was that. But more than a puzzle, a kind of story problem, that intelligence lurking, the fineness back there in her eyes. Something he could do: dedicate the evening to showing her that they could be friends, that in the months or even years to come, he could look the Army Ranger in the eye, shake his hand, be his friend, too. That there were people willing to help you, and no strings attached. If he was anything, he was a guy who wanted to try and help get things sorted out.

Shit, the tomatoes. The tomatoes were at home, last produce of his neighbor's garden. He pictured them on the kitchen windowsill in sun, carefully ripened post-season and ready for saucing, saved for Alison. Quietly as he could, he searched Danielle's cabinets for tomato paste, tomato puree, canned tomato sauce, anything. But no. He thought a while, things he and Alison had eaten in Italy, remembered all the various pesti they'd encountered, few to do with basil. Breakup sex. And here he'd thought it was get-back-together sex. What did he know? He had bought kale, and so he fished it out of one of the bags, washed a couple of the big leaves as best he could in the bucket of river water, borrowed a smooth river stone someone had long since put on the windowsill, mashed up the green right on the butcher-block table, mashed in garlic and olive oil and Parmesan and salty sunflower seeds from an ancient snack bag he found, working a little angrily: Danielle wouldn't recognize the genius of his invention any more than she appreciated his kindness.

But, oh, the pesto was very green and bright. He would spread it on his dough once the yeast had done its work a time or two, then barely cover it with shavings of Parmesan. Unaccountably angry, he pictured Jim in dress uniform, Danielle back to health on Jim's arm, both of them thankful for Eric's help, she'd see.

The next sauce was prettier, making use of the bright red peppers he'd picked out at Hannaford, best of the lot, which he oiled and roasted close up against fresh coals, then plunged in her bucket of cold water and peeled, finally mashed smooth in olive oil and garlic. He sliced one of his large onions very thin, sliced one of his eggplants a touch thicker, left the pieces in a puddle of olive oil in a pie pan.

He wouldn't drink wine. He'd promised Danielle that and she'd been glad. Her history wasn't hard to read. Alcohol factored in. Likely worse. He conjured a brutal father. But Eric's teetotaling didn't mean she couldn't have wine if she wanted, and both pizzas would go perfectly if differently with the Côtes du Rhône he'd bought for Alison, all to be presented in the most understated way: he wasn't trying to seduce Danielle and there shouldn't be any room for her to think so. Thirty-four-dollar goddamn bottle of wine. It was Alison he was angry at. That's where the anger was coming from. You were supposed to go ahead and feel it.

This was hard for Eric to do, to feel appropriate anger, and knowing that it was hard was a pretty big spurt of growth for him, if he could find a way to give himself credit. Alison had set up the couples counseling and had never attended. So, in effect, once a month, Eric was in therapy. Feel your anger. Give yourself credit. The day would come when the separation would be over. They had a no-fling agreement, which helped with his jealousy of her new life. The separation would be over and either she'd be back or they'd be divorced. And if divorced, then he'd be dating, a strange concept, and painful, yet attached to a kind of excitement. Not that there was anyone in Woodchurch you'd ask out. He tried to recall the feeling of falling in love. Chocolate was supposed to imitate that feeling. Polyphenols related to caffeine, apparently. He'd been web-surfing an awful lot. Scholarly inquiry gone awry. Long articles from scientific journals. Videos of brides dancing with their comical fathers. When he should have been sleeping. With Alison. Who did not live home anymore and who did not attend the couples therapy sessions she herself had arranged and who did not come to their monthly dinners, so it seemed, and who, lately, didn't answer e-mails or texts and certainly not phone calls. Nor the letter. But that just shouldn't have been sent: tear-stained legal bond, plain begging.

Once he'd got his sauces made and once the dough was rising nicely, he positioned another pair of logs in the firebox, one thick one from the trunk of the dead maple he'd cut up (way back eons ago, when he still belonged to his real life), one split of birch to keep the first log burning hot. And then he thought to read. Normally, daily, pretty much to the point of obsession, he'd be surfing the Internet at this hour, chasing down some thread of inquiry, sliding through apps on his iPhone. He felt a hunger for that familiar keypad, a kind of mental reaching for his phone even after he'd managed to stop patting his pockets for it. He especially wanted to check the weather app, he told himself, see what the storm had wrought, see what was still

expected of it. This was not about Alison, not about whether or
not Alison had thought to check in. Talk about appropriate anger. He felt it, all right. His shoulder ached, and he felt that, too.
Let the shoulder stand for everything. He'd smashed it into that
door at Mia Arnold's repeatedly. He felt lucky it hadn't worked.
Imagine facing Mia Arnold in the morning!

He could see the corner of a full bookshelf up in Danielle's
loft, but of course there was no way to get near that. By the
mission-oak couch in a matching oak cabinet (fine carpentry,
old-fashioned click of brass), he found board games and puzzles,
also a copy of Thoreau's *The Maine Woods,* a book you'd find
in many a summerhouse in the North Country. He settled in
with the kerosene lamp to read about the mountain Thoreau
had called Ktaadn. *"Contact!"* he read, the old leather cushions
crunching under his every movement, horsehair in there, hard as
rock. But quickly he was absorbed: Those canny young men! A
century and a half away! Traveling by bateau from Bangor and
all the way to the mountain, paddling, carrying, retracing their
steps, forging ahead, seventy-five miles or more! He picked up
his feet, folded them under him—the floor was all the way icy,
but he realized the wind no longer rose up from its many cracks,
not at all: the snowfall had already been sufficient to form an
insulating barrier. Thoreau's wonderful figures of speech, the
freshness of his mind, the architecture of his thoughts, his people! Eric had forgotten all that.

"Contact!"

He reached for his phone to look up more about the storm.
Of course there was no phone. He read a little more Thoreau—
competitive young man leaving his companions behind to summit among the rocks of the great mountain. And again checked

for his phone, which might have been amusing if it weren't so pathetic. He opened the cabinet again, that satisfying click. Awkwardly (trying to avoid putting his feet on the icy floor), he pulled out one puzzle then the next, settled on a large one—1000 PIECES—thick, flaky cardboard probably produced in the 1950s, large photo of Lichtenstein Castle, which he knew to be in Germany.

He and Alison had met as teenagers at a Future Lawyers of Maine retreat on Lake Damariscotta, a high-octane weekend culminating with a moot court. They'd been on the same team, she two years older, very impressive, commanding, intimidating. Years later—they were both already real lawyers—he was solo hiking the Piazza Rock portion of the Appalachian Trail near Saddleback Mountain and recognized her struggling into her backpack in front of the shelter near the massive cantilevered rock. She had no memory of him till he reminded her of a quip he'd made in moot court after she'd warned their team to defer to the bench: "The judge is, like, fifteen."

Hiking, she was with a group she didn't like from the office she was tired of, a tax firm in Boston, and walked with Eric hours to the top of the mountain—an incredible granite bald with a view of heaven. Her group was walking out via the ski slopes and so he did, too, and accepted a ride back to his car. The next month, after increasingly warm phone calls between them, he visited her in Boston, tiniest apartment imaginable, Beacon Hill. She met him in front and rode with him to park his car, the shiny VW Golf his father had given him for graduation, pretty small. Still, they managed to get half their clothes off and declare their love and make love in a cheap parking garage she knew. Then again at her apartment in her fresh sheets and with her doleful old dog Bruno watching. They had a natural fit, they agreed. Much later she'd deny saying anything of the sort. He'd found her overly starving and frank and perverse but of course didn't say it, barely allowed himself to think it, later got over it, got into it, got hurt when she backed away, and backed away further. The jigsaw puzzle had a smell to it that was the smell of that apartment. Dry cardboard, whiff of decay, whiff of mold, and a kind of perfume: old bar of travel soap tucked into the box, probably someone's effort at mouse proofing.

He dumped the thousand pieces on the coffee table and searched out the edges. The soap wrapper said Hotel Myron, Milwaukee. Earlier vintage even than the calendar in the shed. A series of thuds hit the side of the house, like car doors slamming in the driveway, if there'd been a driveway: snow bombs off the high trees all around in the wind. The front window out onto the view of the river was picturesque in the lamplight, a skein of snow stacked in its lower edges and across the bottom occluding a quarter of the big pane of glass, not that there was anything to see in the dark.

Alison's body was. It was. It was hers, that's what it was. She lived in it easily. Sumptuous, full, tending toward plump, bigger toward the bottom, Reubenesque. The sandwich, not the painter, as her unkindly father had once observed, not joking. That next morning, the Boston morning, she standing in the doorway to the minuscule kitchen, her back to him, intent on a phone conversation. Bent to a phone conversation. Back when phones had wires. Something she didn't understand about young men in love: her body that morning as she talked on the phone was easily the most beautiful vista he had ever encountered. That included all the great wonders of the world—Grand

Canyon, Great Wall of China, Costa Rican rain forest, everything. The sight of her naked in that doorway and bent to the
phone conversation—it was in his collection for life, one of the
small number of visions a person can call up at will and see with
the kind of clarity not even the present moment ever offered.
And that morning she'd hung up the phone and turned and come
to him in her small bed.

He got the border all built, sky and garden, and was starting
on some of the castle turrets when he heard Danielle cough and
sigh and stretch. She must be as ready for dinner as he. He left the
puzzle as it was (hearing in his head Alison's voice making fun of
him for starting it), found his dough nicely expanded. He gently
divided it, caressed it, shaped it into two balls, then back to the
puzzle. While the dough rested he got the entire roof outline of
the castle—not too difficult, all this pointy architecture against
the blue, blue Bavarian sky. Danielle was stirring in her blankets,
rustling, sighing, yawning. She wasn't in any hurry to get up, it
seemed. He didn't think Alison had ever taken a nap, someone
who hated vacations unless they involved extreme sports: deep-
water scuba, cloud-trekking, kickboxing lessons, breakup sex.

Hurrying, he added wood to the fire, banked his beautiful
coals—very hot in there—then searched the shelves and cabinets
and half-broken drawers for candles, which he found, a box of
votives. He lined up four of them on the butcher's block and put
a wooden match to them. Still not enough light, which was all he
was seeking, certainly not atmosphere, if that was what Danielle
was going to accuse him of. In the lambent glow he dredged the
eggplant slices in flour, slipped them into the oven in their pie
pan, patted out the dough balls with his palms on the floured
butcher's block, the only real work surface. And, oh, it was a

good thing he had something to do, Danielle out of her bed now and apparently dressing, subtle zipper sounds, several different pairs of pants coming off and on, soft humming. He twirled the first circle of dough up on his fists, thinning it, not really showing off, as of course she wasn't paying any attention and would only mock him in any case, twirled the second circle even higher, let it land on the cutting board he'd improvised—just a well-worn piece of plywood he'd floured heavily and that could serve as a peel as well. He spread the brilliant red-pepper sauce thinly on the dough, grated a layer of Parmesan, placed the slices of onion, drew the eggplant out of the oven and apportioned it neatly. One more shower of Parmesan. He floured a peculiar antique cake knife (handle real ivory, it looked like) and used it to loosen the dough on the plywood. Finding everything ready, he jerked the pizza off the board and onto the hot oven bricks, clanked the door shut.

Quickly he prepared the second pizza—kale pesto, drizzle of olive oil, layer of cheese. Had to be quick because the first pizza was ready, less than five minutes, rage building in his breast. What good did it do to feel it? That's the part no one ever explained. He used the knife and a pair of antique canning tongs to pull the first pizza out, piquant, poignant, fragrant, bubbling hot, simply plunked it on the table where they'd eat. And quick slid the second pizza in. Alison had carried him across their threshold, what had formerly been his threshold alone, funny enough, that solid build of hers, her serious kisses.

"That smells good, mister," Danielle said from above.

He felt an angry shout at his throat, a confusion of women, he knew. "Come and fucking get it," he said grinning.

Ten

A HEAVY GUST set the windows whistling and seemed to pick up the roof, anyway, the storm made itself known, a chill wind straight through the inadequate building, an insistent banging and clanging, probably a section of the metal roof coming free. High winds made it a true blizzard, sudden image of himself lost and trying to survive the night in the woods up there: it could have been that way; it really could have been that bad.

"Nice candles," Danielle said.

"Probably literally a dime a dozen."

"But they've only got so many here. I should have bought some. And you really shouldn't be using them up, fucker." Said kindly. She put one of his logs on the fire, added a stick of kindling—they owned this fire together, the gesture said. She left the stove door open for a little more light, just as he would do. Her build was more arms and legs than he'd thought—all those loose clothes she'd been wearing—fancy mall jeans now, fake silver filigree on the thighs, once tight cloth covering her no longer secretly furry legs. Her hair she'd tucked under her Rasta cap. Her top was a kind of T-shirt but pleated a little in the bodice and with a wide neck that showed two sets of camisole straps, nothing warm enough. She was way too thin.

Eric blew out two of the candles, feeling petulant though she was right. The cabin fell a shade darker. Maybe he was just hungry. Still Danielle seemed pleased with him, retrieved the kerosene lamp from the puzzle table, lingered there a moment inspecting his castle roof, no comment, not a tease, not a word. The set of her shoulder was provocative, one strap pink, one strap black. Ghost, he shouldn't forget, a wraith with a collection of words she spent quiet hours interchanging up in her loft, all that shuffling and muttering, zipper sounds. And of course there were the ectoplasmic, unreadable glances.

She stared at the pizzas like they were exhibits at a foods-of-the-mortals museum. "Nice," she said.

"That poem was really good," Eric said. "About the snow."

"It's Emily Dickinson."

"Oh. I should have known."

"It made you like me."

"She was a kind of hermit, right?"

"Not completely. She fucked some minister that came to visit."

Eric flinched, then laughed, but too provisionally. "I think that's in dispute. That it was maybe more spiritual than physical?"

Danielle shook her head: Eric didn't know shit. "Whatever," she said. "But I like to imagine it. This ray of light in his life. Poems in envelopes forever after. With like blobs of sealing wax."

"Can you recite any more?"

"I got a C. Actually. But there were a lot of them about flowers. And a lot about death. A lot."

Eric reached for something to say, something beyond his flinching. "Another hermit was Thoreau."

"Not really. Not him. A hermit, I mean. We studied him, too. Severely boring. He lived in that shack of his but he went into town all the time for meals and such. It was only a mile or something. My teacher said. She wasn't a big fan. She called him Henry David."

"Another person who never took a lover."

"How do you know? I think she did. I'm sure she did. Always disheveled for this, like, afternoon class, yo, and her lipstick smeared."

Eric grinned, all he could do not to laugh out loud. He said, "I meant Thoreau."

But Danielle didn't see the joke: "Oh, well. Henry David. Not exactly Larry Flynt. No, no. There *was* a woman. Like, his brother's girlfriend. And she dumped the brother, so your little friend asked her to marry *him*. And she said no. And—this was in his diary, too—he wrote a poem about her. In his journals. And I remembered it and said it in class."

"Quite a class," Eric said.

"I loved that class. We talked about anything. And Henry David, he's all heartbroken, and not even poetry is working, so he wrote down something like that the only remedy for love was to love *more*. Like love was a disease that cured *itself*."

"He was quoting Ovid!" Eric said, proud of himself. "*The Cure for Love*. I read it in school, in Latin class. It's racy. Mr. Tims used it because it would make us work harder, finding all the naughty stuff."

"Ovid, *pfft*," Danielle said.

"The Larry Flynt of his times! He said the cure for love was to go find more lovers. Among other things. Like focusing on your lover's flaws. Or farming."

"Another ancient fucking asshole, and talking only to the males. Yoo-hoo, over here."

"Okay," Eric said quietly.

"And that quote is the only thing I like about Thoreau. Eric. And you wreck it."

"No, I'm sure Henry meant it. Really meant it, that he was in love."

"He told his sister when he was, like, on his deathbed, that he had always loved that woman. That he never stopped loving her, all right?"

"Okay. Shh. I didn't mean to upset you."

"He *never fucking stopped*. More *love*. That's what he said. And that's what he did."

"Okay. You're right. You're definitely right."

"*Love*," said Danielle.

They thought about that, the ideal last word.

After a while, Eric found a couple of plates and an absurd old meat cleaver, whacked the pizzas into big slices.

Danielle, meanwhile, still visibly riled, retrieved one of the bottles of Côtes du Rhône. She picked the foil off, gripped the bottle by the neck. She said, "This is how they do it in Kabul." She raised the bottle high, as if in salute, suddenly slammed its concave bottom on the butcher's block.

"Hey," Eric cried.

But the cork had emerged perhaps a quarter inch. She slammed the bottle again, gained a half inch more. She flashed a sly look, seemed to be cheering herself up. "Hey, yourself, yo. Jimmy does it on fucking concrete and the cork pops right out."

"He must smash a lot of bottles."

"Almost never. But sometimes. Every tenth one, say. It's like Russian roulette."

Was she kidding? Impossible to tell. Slam. Another half inch. Slam. And the cork was ready for her teeth: mighty twist and tug, then caught in her smile. She found two thick old jelly jars, filled them neatly halfway, handed one to Eric—all his promises about not drinking aside—spat the cork at his feet.

"To the U.S. Army," she said.

"To the Armies of Light," Eric said, peacenik, and no Navy partisan, certainly not taking that bait.

They took short sips regarding one another, eye contact he was forced to break: that was no ghost back in there. He put slices of both types of pizza on their mismatched plates. Danielle stood across the butcher's block from him, hip cocked. She bit the first slice as if she were biting him: red peppers, fragrant onions, flavorful eggplant, the beautiful raw-milk cheese. He tried not to seem like he was waiting for a compliment, but bit his own slice, the strange, sharp sweetness of the peppers. The crust he'd made was delectable, he thought, browned and tooth-some from the heat of the firebrick, touch of maple smoke, yet soft enough under the sauce, damn.

"I don't know," she said.

"You miss the tomato thing?"

"Oh, no, this? This is good. This is very good." Then she seemed to pay attention to what she was tasting. "Fuck *me*, mister, it's really good." She took another bite, chewed thoughtfully.

The Côtes du Rhône handled the peppers and the rank and randy cheese pretty darn well, he thought. He saw his puzzle outlined on the table, the sky above Lichtenstein Castle on some specific day in the 1950s, a specific day with its specific clouds captured forever and cut to pieces. Alison, too, liked his pizza. He'd gotten good at it for her.

"Mister!" Danielle said, biting into the next piece. She seemed to mean it in the positive, bit again, repeated the other compliment: "Fuck *me*." She slugged her wine. "This is major," she said after a while. "Majorly major."

"Oh, well," he said, his real smile, access of warmth.

From her that hot glower, that sudden, withering glance.

They fell into eating, most of both pizzas, most of the bottle of wine (Eric going easy), not another word between them.

Eleven

"WHAT KIND OF lawyer are you?" Danielle asked.

"Oh, small-town," he said. They had repaired to the fire. Sat, that is, in front of the old Glenwood in the oaken chairs with the crisp-sounding cushions, the empty bottle of wine balanced between them on a log she'd upturned. "Wills, estates, divorces, deeds, property disputes, property tax, petty lawsuits, petty crime, vandalism, auto theft, occasional felony this or that, a lot of drunk driving, more than you'd think. Drug cases galore. Add the odd assault case. And domestic abuse lately—the police have finally got their radar up about it."

"And you defend the abusers?"

"It has never yet come to that. What I do is make a plan with the abuser to get help, to quit drinking, to quit substances in general, to sit in therapy, to take anger-management class, to enter family therapy with the partner if she's willing—and generally she is—all that kind of thing, which you bring before the judge and D.A."

"Who are both friends of yours, of course."

"In a manner of speaking, yes, friends of mine. And we try

to come to a solution that benefits the miscreant, the family, the community."

"You sound like a public-service announcement. Do you get guys coming back? Like these unloved kids who have to repeat fourth grade till they're sixteen and can finally fucking quit?"

"No. No, no. I won't take them for a second offense. There's an office for that in Augusta—that's all state court, state prison, I mean by the time they fuck up that badly."

"Unless they have money."

"Sadly, yes." A public-service announcement! He tried to loosen up, failed: "The level of education does seem to play a role. Both in money terms and in terms of violence."

"Like the mother-in-law answers the door and says, 'Oh, there was some shouting, but they've made up now.' And meanwhile the poor wife is back there with a broken nose and a hairy hand over her mouth."

"Something to tell me?"

"So that's where all the cash comes from? You taking care of the good old boys?"

" 'All the cash,' ha. And good old boys? I'm not exactly, like, Foghorn Leghorn."

"All this high-nose wine and cheese. Follow the cash. And don't look at me like you think I won't know who Foghorn Leghorn is."

"Listen, Danielle. I buy very little fancy anything, believe me. The cheese and the wine, that was for a special occasion. And I hope you're enjoying it. The money isn't really anywhere. The money in a small practice is only in keeping busy, lots of little matters constantly. Which I've had almost none lately."

"And you had to go to law school for this?"

"Vermont Law. A great, obscure program. I was interested in environmental law, and that was the place. Still am interested in environmental law, though there's not much of that in Woodchuck. I've spent a lot of time lately advising the Maine legislature. Friend of the chamber, it's called, no cash. It's not a great period for environmental law. Jobs. People want jobs and it's widely been spread that environmental legislation kills jobs, not true."

"I'm still thinking of those domestic abusers you get off scot-free."

"I'm still doubting you know who Foghorn Leghorn is."

"He's that, like, *chicken*." Flicker of a smile.

She got up and found her box of red wine and slammed it a couple of times on the butcher's block for a joke before opening it. Or maybe not a joke—she didn't laugh. She poured his glass full from behind and above like someone taking a piss, foamy stuff, poured her own, used the box to push Alison's bottle off the upturned log; it clonked on the floor and rolled until it was under the Glenwood. And she sat, maybe slightly closer to him. The storm lashed at the little cabin from all directions, total disorder. One of the hemlocks had apparently drooped under its load of snow and was resting on the roof, or anyway something was, ominous scraping and clawing sounds in the wind.

"Mister-mister-mister," Danielle said affirmatively.

Eric sipped the wine. It was as thin and fruity as juice but not actually terrible.

Danielle slugged hers, pissed herself a refill, adjusted the fire. She was tall in her trousers, as Eric's father liked to say, tall in general, the fitted T-shirt having been fitted to a more fulsome figure, one she no longer posessed. Eric was on the tall side, too.

His last dinner with Alison, who was on the short side, had been almost six months before, he had to admit. The last time she'd kissed him, too, six months, perhaps even planned as a last kiss, a theory he'd developed and revisited in constant retrospect: Alison had come to say good-bye. Eric recalled the kiss very clearly, the abrupt end of one of their dinners, which had until then all ended sexually. "All" meaning the bicycle camping, only that. No shouting or anything, just Alison standing with an apology, kissing his mouth very hard, then taking her coat and leaving, nothing but the grinding sound of her car starting.

"Tell me a story from lawyer land," Danielle said. She hefted the wine box and dispensed more for both of them, pulled her chair in closer to the stove, which meant pulling it slightly again closer to him, elaborately folded her legs under herself and sat. She regarded him, not neutral, leaned to rub her ankle. "Look at us sitting here," she said.

Eric said, "It's pretty benign."

"Jim would *frenzy,* 'benign.' And how you stare at me?" She patted her own chest.

He couldn't help the grin, a different type altogether. He said, "I was looking at your clothes. I'm interested in clothes."

She patted her own butt.

Guilty, that was what kind of grin. He said, "I don't care about your posterior."

"Liar again."

"I particularly like those pants."

"Well, then I won't take them off." She handed him a half slice of the pepper pizza, her bite marks in it, last piece. He took it and bit her bites away and kept going and it was good to the last crumb of crust.

She poured more wine. How much did those boxes hold? She put a stick in the fire, and a large split, poked it all expertly into the coals, maximum efficiency. She'd have run out of wood about now, Eric thought, imagined her trying to collect more in the dark, remembered the door, that the door was utterly blocked, so much snow against the house now that the storm seemed more distant, the wind intense but removed. No particular reason, he thought of a visit to La Jolla, where Alison had grown up, the two of them in law school far away and not allowed to share a room in her parents' big house, views of the ocean. An outdoor deck connected the entire second floor, though, and he crept in the damp breeze at three in the morning past her dad's library. The old man was a judge, took the law very seriously, but mostly as a cudgel against those who would mooch off the state, long discussion at dinner, more like a lecture, with Eric adding sour notes. Alison's father was a humorless tyrant, and for the first time Eric knew that when Alison said she hated the man it was no figure of speech, though she loved him as well, a hundred stories of childhood joys. The deck was high—they lived on a cliff—and a light was on downstairs, Eric basically walking on top of the parents' bedroom. He found Alison's sliding deck door unlocked, slipped into her bed beside her, snuggled up, pressed close—she slept naked on the hot night—woke her with his ardor. "Buy me a ring," she said as they began to make love, and said it again, and again.

"Tell me about Jim," he said.

Danielle said, "Like, what about him?"

"Does he cook?"

"You're funny." The lamplight was in her eyes again, her pupils enormous, vestiges of beauty there, that fund of intelligence.

"What does he do?"

"Army Rangers, I told you." A fund of disdain, as well.

"Still?"

"Yes, still."

"But he was a teacher with you, I thought you said."

She turned back to the stove, clearly bugged. The Rasta cap was dirty, gave an outline to her profile, a girl on a coin. "He was in the reserves. He got called up. He was on the bus within a month. Ask me something more interesting."

"Isn't 'frenzy' a noun?"

She was glad for the joke, quick glance, quick grin. "No. Not always, mister. Sometimes it's something you can do. Certainly something Jimmy could do." She swallowed the last of her wine dramatically, filled her glass yet again, ignored his pointedly, took a long time, seemed to think past their conversation, anyway disappeared.

Eric filled his own glass.

"No drunken incidents," Danielle told him.

"Jimmy," he said.

"Jimmy is pretty broken-glassy around the edges. Especially on duty. On duty, he's all edges. There's nothing else. And he's sudden, sudden. He finished college in three years because four was just too fucking slow. He's a marksman in a strike unit, which in case you squids don't know is how the Rangers operate."

"Like the Navy Seals."

"But without the fishes. It's six guys: marksman, translator, doctor, munitions, navigator. And they're all warriors, every one."

"That was only five."

"I forget the other. Strategist, maybe? Doesn't matter, it's secret."

"How about off duty?"

"A total player before I got hold of him. Pretty short for a dude, like my height, and stocky, 210 pounds and just one big muscle. He cried the morning of his deployment. His hands are like this big, Eric." Really big. "And that's not the only thing!" Even bigger.

"But really."

"He's jealous. He's a country boy. You flinched! But I'm serious. He's like one big hard dick. Jealous. Very jealous. You flinched again! He's from up there, you know. Presque Isle. His family is Frenchie. His mom still speaks Québécois. They go out to cheap restaurants and eat fucking *poutine*. *Poutine* is disgusting. Like French fries with cheese and gravy, *what*? He will squeeze your head like a pimple till it pops when he catches you."

"Catches me what?"

"That pizza, mister, that was super. And that was a great bottle of wine. He would kill you for the greatness of the wine alone!"

"We'll be friends, he and I."

Danielle shook her head: No you won't.

Twelve

So, DURING THAT visit to her parents, he'd bought Alison a ring, using his new American Express Gold card, which they apparently offered to all employees at law firms, his first plastic. And it wasn't a real diamond but a cubic zirconium, cut big and with a bluish cast, gorgeous, and under two hundred dollars, still a bite at the time. That way they could get a huge stone, get a gasp out of Alison's mom. Her dad was furious that Eric hadn't asked him first. And though it was all couched as a joke, Eric and Alison found themselves mooning at the seal pier and making out on the beach along with the teenagers (blue balls, the works) and sneaking back and forth up and down the deck till dawn, all contention gone, all irritation aimed at the old man: they were engaged.

At length, Danielle said, "I grew up Jersey shore. My father was a fireman, actually—now he's Homeland Security. He will help Jimmy kill you. His brother is a dentist. Just look at my teeth."

He looked at her teeth, which though bared rather angrily

were ultrawhite, very straight, maybe a size too small. She said, "Jim's father isn't Homeland Security, you can be sure of that— he calls Homeland Security the Obama Squad. He's more like End-Times Jesus Survival Militia. He's a darkling, put it that way. I don't know what he does exactly. Jim doesn't even know. Or maybe he does. They sell stuff. Jim grew up in a yard sale, basically. His mother is this little rock-hard gargoyle lady. She won't smile around me cuz her teeth are bad. I mean really fucking bad. She won't even laugh. She works at like the chicken-processing plant. You can say the funniest thing and she's just like. Talks with her hand in front of her mouth and swears between her chicken-fat fingers, cunt."

"And you were *living* with them?"

"Flinch."

"Your teeth are terrific."

"Weren't you going to tell me a story?"

"Where's he stationed? Jimmy."

"No, really—you." Pink strap, black strap, like ribbons across both shoulders. "I want to hear about one of these abuse cases. The guys you represent."

"Or do those strike units just wander around?"

"Top secret. Afghanistan, supposedly, but he's in Pak."

"Pakistan?"

"Quiet, dude, fuck. Nancy Pelosi'll drone us. Now you, you talk."

"Um. Domestic abuse cases. Okay. They are usually quite hostile, though I represent them. One guy urinated on my shoes in the conference room at County. Took me a minute to get what was going on. Suddenly my feet were hot and wet."

"I've had dates like that!"

Eric laughed, and she laughed, too, progress for their friendship. He said, "There were women, as well. One, she'd dropped a cinderblock out the window onto her husband's head. Coma."

"Who keeps cinderblocks upstairs?"

"I guess it was shelving. With boards. Which they'd already knocked over. Fish tank and all."

"She went to prison?"

"He woke up and recovered. I got her put in a program for six months—rankled her that he just got off free, when he was in the wrong, whatever the argument was they were having, something about who had drunk all the Drano."

"Dude, no."

"No, I'm kidding. But whatever it was, the cinderblock was just deserts, in her opinion. And then they got back together."

"Okay, that's pretty good. But I want a story with, like, *trouble*."

He said, "Hmm. A cinderblock isn't trouble?"

"I mean where you almost die after a client bashes you and ties you up and puts you in the trunk of his car but then you come back from the very precipice of death to fashion a device that helps you escape, and so on and so forth, et cetera."

They drank their wine. Danielle put a log in the stove, a single stick of kindling to help it burn. This brought the light up several notches quickly. She drew her chair in closer to the fire (the cabin suddenly full of air, the wind roaring outside, all those thuds on the face of the house), which meant closer to him. He saw how much she wanted his company, any company. She was drinking this conversation like she drank the wine, biting it like she bit the pizza. Soon she'd be slicing into him, and it wouldn't be pretty.

He said, "My wife is a lawyer, too."

"Your ex-wife, you mean."

"My not-quite ex. Or my maybe not-ever-going-to-be ex."

Danielle went all Disney princess: "These gorgeous pizza dinners. Which hardly seem fair on your part, *dollink,* all that expensive cheese, so romantic. And the candles, golly-gee. And the Frenchie wine. She doesn't have a chance, this princess-bride of yours!"

"She worked in the state attorney general's office. So I would travel down to Augusta sometimes. . . ."

"No, not sometimes, you'd go on a regular basis. Like every Friday."

"Every Wednesday, in fact."

"Not that your predictability matters, mister."

"You asked for a story."

"With trouble in it, don't forget. I don't want to be the only one."

"Well, so, on one of those Wednesdays I was coming down the long hallway in the state building and far at the other end of it she was there talking to William 'Bix' Brighton, Republican state senator from Jackman, long married, long in the tooth, and just the angle of their necks and just the tension in her posture, the way they were leaning, the air between them: I knew."

"A *Republican.*" She took his glass brusquely, filled it to the rim with wine, splashed it back at him.

He sipped defensively. "Don't taunt."

"Well, I know what's next. At dinner you didn't say a thing, and later you fucked her for the first time in like forever."

He flinched. But it was true.

"And it was like nothing you ever."

"She hadn't kissed me in a long time, not like that."

"Not ever, mister. She'd *never* kissed *you* like that."

"She was kissing him, you're saying?"

"And of course kissing wasn't all. She did things you'd only dreamed of."

"Not so much. Not with me. But there was something about it."

Danielle thought about that for a while, seemed almost to drift away. A pop in the fire brought her back, or anyway, she spoke as if she'd never left: "And then everything continued on as ever."

"As ever?" As ever. "So much that I started to doubt my intuition."

"Until."

"Until all offhand she announces one fine summer morning that Bix and his wife have invited us to their camp for a week coming up, the same week, as it happens, that Alison knows very well I'm going to be in New York City, can't back out. At first I'm equanimous about it. Faint frisson of mistrust, maybe. But then. It's eating at me. Doesn't feel right. The way she told me about it, first thing in the morning like that. The new bathing suit. The new haircut."

"The bikini wax."

He put his glass down. "Jesus," he said. The woman was clairvoyant.

"You saw her in the *shower*."

Quite true, sadly. "So. As if in innocence I call the senator's wife to thank her for the invitation and express my regret that

I'm not going to be able to join them at their lake house for a week."

"And of course . . ."

"Of course she knows nothing about the week at their lake house. She's perfectly calm, however, just declares there's been some mistake. He's neglected to tell her, is all. But you can hear it's happened to her before. And after a few days Alison tells me she's decided she just doesn't feel like going for the week up there and will cancel. But it's got into her head, she says, to go somewhere, so she's thinking of going up to Montreal for the week, just to look around, you know, just on her own. So the next Wednesday I go down early to Augusta and straight to the senator's office, which he shares with two other senators, by the way, and he's not there, no one there. So I go to her office, hellos to all the ladies working, you know, increasingly bewildered—I've once again convinced myself I'm wrong."

"Bewildered," Danielle said rapt.

"And Alison's not there. Ginnie the receptionist says there's been a case that morning and Alison is due back from Portland any moment. I'm abashed. So much so that I decide to leave altogether, come back when I'm supposed to, and go down to the parking lot to wait."

"You have a nice voice, yo," Danielle said abruptly, her face bright. "You have a very nice voice, when you forget to be saving my life. What is a 'frisson'?"

"Just a hint of something. Enough to make you shiver."

She shivered. "How about 'equanimous'?"

"Even tempered, calm, accepting."

"Not really you."

"Hey."

She gave him the ghostly stare, said, "But a nice big word to hide behind."

The wind had stopped. The sudden quiet was a roar of its own. The fire dulled a little, absent the constant blast of fresh oxygen. The room grew perceptibly warmer. "No one's hiding."

"And you say you were *aboshed*." Mocking him.

"I'll try to forget I'm saving your life."

"No, mister, that part's over. Now I'm saving yours. Remember?"

His voice was nice, she'd said. He was good with juries, judges, too. You didn't fight them, you leaned into them, like leaning into a turn on a bicycle down a sandy hill, one foot out, just in case. He said, "There's a big park on the Kennebec River below the capitol. The ice going by us right now will end up down there in a day or so. I had an hour to kill after my mistake and I was full of emotion, of shame in fact, and remorse. It was a fine day, though, and all the negativity kind of lifted. I like the trees there—they've planted them strategically and there are all these varieties and they've grown without competition and each species takes on its perfect form, especially this one particular spruce tree, one I'd often admired from the road, this absolutely perfect huge cone of spiraled bluey branches, and the kids have made something of a fort underneath where the limbs spread across the ground and back in there under the branches there was this commotion, people trying to get dressed . . ."

"Your wife and the senator!"

Saving his life.

Thirteen

Once Eric and Alison were engaged, and once they were back in her little apartment in Beacon Hill, no more Pacific breezes, no more kinky trysts over the heads of her parents, the discussion turned to where they'd live. Alison had battled the fierce sexism of her office in Boston, the genteel old partners treating her like a secretary, the sleek new partners undercutting her at every turn, knives out always, but she was in possession of a sword, as it turned out, maybe a battle-axe—that level of skills, unmatched weapons—and was damn good with them, positioned herself to become the first female partner in the firm, and the first female partner in the constellation of old practices at the heart of legal Beantown. Which gave her no joy—the men would not change just because she was there, and there were any number of firms all around the city where she wouldn't have had to fight so hard, women having won so many battles already. Her father, humorless as always and full of advice, said she had a Rosa Parks complex, dour admonishment.

Eric had always been aimed at private practice and small-town law and after his hitch in the U.S. Navy conducted a methodical

search of the villages of northern New England, making a list of
ten that were underserved and settling on Woodchurch impul-
sively when he saw the county courthouse, which was tiny and
yet stately and occupied the very center of town as if it were a
brick church, and even sported a bell tower, the bell visible from
all around town, copper-oxide green and uncracked, perfection
of form, a gift of the French in commemoration of this or that
Woodchurch hero on the occasion of the town's incorporation in
1799, history that interested Eric. Within two weeks he'd found
his house, shockingly affordable, and within two more he was
moving in, the parlor as his office, shingle on the walk out to
the mailbox, all but a scene from his fantasies. His Navy service
brought an immediate raft of clients, the powers and movers of
the town, who would eventually drift away from him as they
sniffed out his liberal views. Which views hardly mattered when
it came to deeds and wills, the bulk of his early work, along with
a divorce or two, but seemed to block the environmental mitigation work he'd counted on, the chance to affect corporate and
private policy as actually practiced (often in the face of the law)
in this crucial corner of the working forest.

After their first series of dates he'd brought Alison back to
that house, showed off his office, introduced her to Woodchurch.
And she'd mocked it, and mocked him: the country barrister, she
called him, certainly not her fantasy. But suddenly, now that
they were engaged, or at least acting as if they were engaged
(that zircon like a searchlight), cramped in her apartment, it
gave her great pleasure to think about refusing the chauvinists
at her firm when her elevation came, leave them in the lurch, a
few public statements to go with the abdication.

That plan was never tested, however, as the partnership wasn't offered, some young buck five years junior and of brief tenure in the firm leapfrogging ahead of her on the pretext of her first poor annual evaluation ever, bullshit. Disillusioned, disheartened, discombobulated, disempowered, somehow desexed, she came to Maine. Even winning her lawsuit against the crusty old firm didn't help, famous case or no, and didn't bring back her ardor. But a new vision did: Eric would be her partner, of Eric she would make a rural star, and then she'd hitch a wild ride, one that would eventually take her back to her rightful place in the city. He saw now.

"You're an addict," Danielle said, patting at herself in imitation of his search for his phone. "'Is there a text from *Alison*?'" Scathing imitation, this ghost who'd never met the woman: "'Can't you just be in the *moment*?'"

"Uncanny."

"Probably she's waiting for you at home right now. Big Coach purse, right?"

Right, thick leather with vestigial buckles as adornment. Evenly, he said, "I'd like to hear more about your teaching. Is that how you and Jim met? Teaching?"

"Does she still have her own key?"

"It's still her house. Or half her house."

"She just doesn't come home."

"You and Jim. You two worked together?"

"Where does she live in Portland? She's got her own place? Is she working again in Portland?"

"She's starting her own firm. Or anyway, that's the plan. She has a condo."

"Sounds permanent."

Eric rubbed his shoulder—it really was sore. "Well, won't matter where she lives. Everything here is statewide."

Danielle typed at an imaginary cell phone, some kind of urgent message. "Even the marriages!"

Sharper than he meant: "That's enough."

"Okay, Counselor." She pulled her Rasta cap down harder over her ruined hair, an abused doll. "Why are you so curious about Jim? I'll tell you about Jim. We had the same placement in what-do-you-call-it—practice. When you're placed in a school as a student teacher. Before you graduate, you know. Practicum. It's part of the certification process for teachers in Maine."

"I thought it was part of the degree program. Isn't certification later?"

"Whatever."

"No, not whatever."

"The state placed me up in Houlton."

"No, Danielle. You're placed by your program. And Woodchurch College wouldn't place anyone in Houlton, would they."

"You are a dick, you know that?"

"I mean, why would it be something to lie about?"

"Because."

"Because you weren't a teacher?"

She crossed her arms across her chest and looked fierce. "I was a teacher," she said.

"But."

"But nothing. Just not like Jimmy. I was part of a special program, all right? Is that all right with you? And what do you know about it, anyway? I thought you were a lawyer, not a teacher."

"Danielle, I'm sorry. I don't mean to grill you. In small-town law you learn about a lot of things, that's all."

"I'm not your client!"

"Don't cry."

"I'm not crying." The tears made tracks then runnels in the dirt and soot on her face. The wind howled again, the stovepipe rattled. She wiped at her face with her hands, then with the hem of her shirt, exposing her belly, gaunt.

Eric wasn't good at this: "Shh."

"I was a substitute, okay? Where Jimmy worked, okay? If that's good enough for you. We actually met at a church thing. And I followed him up there."

"Okay, I'm sorry."

"You're drunk. And you just get more aggressive."

She was right, he realized. About the being drunk.

But she'd drunk more than he: "Jimmy, he's really funny. He likes to pull pranks. Once he sent his whole class to the principal's office, one kid at a time till the whole waiting room was full and Mr. Jenks was like."

"Shh."

"The kids adore Jimmy. Even the ones who weren't athletic, even the schlumps. He'd let them pat his fuzzy head. They'd trace the tattoos on his arms, you know? Something about the tough guy with the kids all around him, very fucking sexy."

"Shh."

"He's got like tree-stump legs with this long, long middle. We lived in this crappy old three-decker house full of tiny efficiency apartments. We'd sit on the steps with bottles of beer. He was too big to be indoors."

"And you'd wait for calls to substitute?"

She cried more privately, not much drama to it anymore, a lot of moisture. Eric took her empty mug from her and stumbled to his feet and found the bucket and brought her water. She took it in both hands and sipped as he flopped back in his chair.

"Thank you," she said. "I think I want Advil, too." He got the bottle, broke the seal, plucked the cotton out, handed her two, which she gobbled. Handed her one more, what the hell. That ankle.

"Thank you, Nurse."

"You are most welcome."

"Treat me so nice."

"My pleasure."

"It will get you nowhere."

"That's where I am right now!"

Slightest smile.

"So. You and Jimmy. You'd already met. When you went up there."

"His old man. His father. They had a tent thing. A revival. They would go to colleges. It looked inviting. And students can sign up. And pledge money and stuff, and make vows to the Lord and vows to help them find more college kids. There's music. And they had pizza. And you could get baptized. Behind a curtain. I don't know what got into me. I got in the line. And then Jimmy's father says—"

"He's a preacher?"

"I don't know what he is. He sees me there in my shorts and legs and halter and stomps right to my face and says, 'Satan is *with* us tonight. I have *seen* the face of Satan!' And I mean, uh-oh, he's talking about *me*. He's like, '*Satan* is *in* this *tent*!' And Jimmy, who I don't know except he gave me the flyer earlier, comes up to me and starts shaking me and then he's actually slapping me, and of course I'm shrieking and carrying on, and cursing and spitting and scratching and trying to get away—I wasn't so tough then—so it looks very real because it is very real, and he's dragging me back behind the screen and back there he starts laughing and he whispers that I'm great. And I keep screaming and he tugs me into their van and he's got, like, tequila and he gives me a shot and I calm down and he closes the doors and gives me another, and he's like, 'Go for a drive?' and, Eric, I fucking *go*. What about *that*? It was because I loved that they found out *Satan* was in me. Don't check for your fucking phone. And so, he drives me down to the lot behind the movie theater on the river up there and I had never been kissed like that. I mean, *kissed* isn't the word. I was schlooshed. I was eaten alive. You know bedbugs? I learned this in the public health class at the college. Disgusting. Every time I even see a white van I think of them. I don't mean there were bedbugs in the van. I just, I mean there's this fact I learned that the females have no, you know, no receptacle for the male's penis, which is like this *blade*. So the males just stab it in through the female's shell anyplace, and somehow that works. What I'm saying is that Jimmy was like *that*. It was freaking rough. I liked it. More or less. Or anyway that once." She pulled her shirt hem up and over her face, hid there, her camisoles riding up, too, wiped her eyes. Her belly was concave, her navel an impossibly neat slit, piercing visible, no jewelry in place.

Something cracked sharply outside—then a branch came down, muffled clout on the roof. Those gargantuan pine trees above. At the sound, Danielle emerged from her shirttails, listened closely. They both listened closely. She leaned and plucked her wine box off the floor, a practiced motion, drained a little into her mug, shook some last drops into his, tilted the box just so, got another splash out for him, then a little more. As she poured, the chimney stack began to vibrate, the wind around them to howl, the air in the room to shudder in their ears. The vibration only grew, the very walls of the cabin flexing and drumming, metallic hum from the stovepipe. If that were torn away, they'd be in terrible trouble, a room full of smoke and fire and cold wind. Eric planned in his head—you'd have to bank the fire fast, recover what pipe you could, redirect the stack somehow, perhaps just straight out the wall, which would mean making a hole. He felt he'd seen a keyhole saw in the shed. With a keyhole saw you could do it.

As the wind peaked, something big smashed onto the roof. The cabin jerked with it—that heavy. They both jumped, cried out, reached for each other, held on tight.

Sudden silence.

"Talk about being in the moment!" Danielle cried.

Fourteen

LATER THEY SAT on cushions on opposite sides of his puzzle, looking for flower pieces, and there were a lot of flower pieces to find, a jumble of them to be piled in color groups, all the castle gardens foreground. It was way too cold in that corner of the cabin, and so Danielle had put the big coat on. The smelly coat. Eric was just shivering, his ruined jacket over his lap, but something about the project being literally between them had tamped down the emotion.

"I always wanted to live in a castle," Danielle said. "I always wanted stone walls."

"My house is stone."

She made a face: So what about his house? She said, "What insect would you be?"

"In the castle?"

"In bed. With Jimmy being the bedbug."

"Huh. I guess I haven't thought about that."

"Dung beetle? Get the job done?"

"Something nicer. Luna moth. Or maybe a luna moth caterpillar."

"So slinky and silky soft. And green."

"You've seen 'em. With these little horns. How about you?"

"Black widow?"

"Fair warning. I'll tell the fellas."

"Jimmy'd be gone three and four days every month, which gave me time to think. Army Reserves. And do you know what I thought about? I thought about how I was going to get rid of him, that's what I thought about. That and resting my various fucking sphincters. Flinch." She began assembling a patch of puzzle roses—quick, deft fingers. "But he comes back Sunday night late with, like, mud in his hair and a big scrape across his cheek, forehead bruised, uniform all ripped to shreds, and, well." Behind the roses as she built them was a patch of garden wall, and that was the clue they needed, together adding her chunk of the puzzle to the section Eric had been working on. She moved onto the daisies. "This one time? Coming home? He's bought an engagement ring somewhere. He drops on his knee. He says he's felt he's loved me forever. Not 'I love you' but 'I feel I have loved you.' He hadn't mentioned about love before. Took me by surprise."

"Well," said Eric after a pause to search for more red. "Really, it's nice." He continued work on the wall with the roses, methodical, absorbed.

She pressed daisies together, piece by piece, unnervingly quick. The wind was quiet. Everything was quiet, muffled. She said, "I dig talking with you. You sit there and listen. And you haven't said one single stupid fucked-up thing for a while. Plus you flinch like a nun, which is trustworthy. And no hard-on, though you're definitely a dick."

He flinched. Not so fast on the hard-on. Her camisoles up around her face, the perfection of her navel in the devastation. And of course the wind picked up again, and continued to mount. He said, "I like talking with you, too."

"Ask me questions. I like when you ask me questions. I like that you listen."

"Well, here's the main one. How did you end up down here? In the cabin, I mean."

"Professor DeMarco. It's hers. Or like her husband's family's. She said I could use it. I'd been talking with her on the phone and texting and so on and e-mails. She was always trying to get me back in school. Nice to be loved, yo."

Eric said, "Well, yes, it is."

"You take everything so *seriously*. Daisies. Over there. I see some over there." She looked a child suddenly, collecting her pieces as he picked them out for her, talking away: "She said if I needed I could come stay as long as I liked, stay the whole summer. She knew how hard everything had been with school and with Jim deployed. I thought I was going mental. She thought I needed a rest. And so I did come and stay here. She walked down twice to visit and she was pretty nice, but maybe a little overly, like, weird? We swam in the river. We talked and talked. I mean, it was nice. She was really nice. She swam naked, and she's unbelievably fat. And I was supposed to go back to Presque Isle and be with Jim's family and substitute teach again on some fucking random calendar date, and she and her husband came exactly then and helped me carry my stuff up and load my car. They were going to stay here. I just couldn't go *back*. Not to Presque Isle. Not without Jimmy there. I stayed on the road for

the two weeks the DeMarcos were down living here, slept in
the car, drove up to, like, New Brunswick, Bay of Fundy, some
campground up there, pretty dramatic, ate wild fresh salmon
this craggy dude would catch and sell on the beach but that
he just gave me free. And don't think I fucked him, because I
didn't, not really. And I avoided everyone else. I barely noticed
the beauty of the earth. Then I drove back down here, broke. So
I sold the car to the dealer over on High Street? Moody's Used
Vickles? And then I came back down here to live till I could
figure out the next thing. But I didn't have a single dime to rub
together, as my father would say."

"How do you not really fuck someone?"

"You just really don't fuck them. Not for a fish."

"And you came down here."

"Yes, back down here."

"But you'd sold the car."

"Moody gave me like two thousand bucks for it, enough to
pay it off and still have, like, three hundred dollars, which went
faster than you'd think, like two trips for groceries and this trip
today."

"And Professor DeMarco doesn't know you're here."

"Professor DeMarco doesn't know. But she wouldn't care."
Danielle made a Professor DeMarco face, hunched down, spoke
in a high falsetto, what might have been comic in another setting: "She'd be *so worried*."

There was something he'd very much wanted to tell Danielle
while she was talking about Jim, but he couldn't quite get it
in his head again as another gust rocked the house. So instead
he said, "Maybe I can get you your car back, or at least a better deal. It's not actually illegal to take advantage of people in

distress, but it's not hard to embarrass someone like that, like Myron Moody, get a positive result."

"You know him?"

He knew him.

Danielle pulled her Rasta cap off, scratching her head unhappily. Her hair was really very dirty and matted and clumped, not in dreads at all, the only style being neglect. "A positive result," she said. "A positive result." She was the girl from the grocery store checkout line again, lost in that coat, suspicious, that huge, smelly coat. "Fucking freezing," she said, pulling it around her. She used the table to help her stand, pushing it toward him roughly, displacing the puzzle, one of the flower piles landing in his lap.

"I'm not drunk," she said. He noticed pine needles on her neck. And a phrase came to him, as if in a headline: YOUNG WOMAN ABANDONED.

He struggled to his feet, too, followed her to the stove. She shed the coat, put it on its nail. Her skinny jeans, Eric noted, weren't skinny enough to keep up with her anymore, hung off her hips (and would have fallen right down except for the heavily studded leather belt, which was like something from a tractor supply, or more like torture chamber), a pocket worn to threads by a cell phone that was no longer present, the seat worn by a full fanny gone missing. He'd like to feed her. He'd make her huge meals. He'd like to take her shopping, or let her take him. The smokestack shuddered, the cabin groaned, the wind spoke from every corner, these long gusts that only grew.

She turned on him angrily: "Like I'm something you brought home from the shelter. 'A positive result.' You think I'm a *rescue*." And before he could protest she collected the oil lamp, lurched to the ladder, climbed unsteadily. "Dick!" she said. "Lawyer! Phone addict! Loser! You can stay down there and ponder the legalities." She shuffled and clanked and thumped up there a long time as Eric built up the fire. Then she threw down a blanket, next a pillow, finally pulled the ladder up behind her, blew out the light.

Fifteen

ERIC WIPED HIS teeth with a piece of paper towel, carefully getting to all the corners and swishing with boiled river water, taste of the very slime on the rocks, like summer. He picked up his bedding, what she'd thrown down, a lumpy pillow with no case, but a nice thick wool blanket, army green. The mission-oak couch was too short to lie on, so he tossed its hard cushions on the floor between the puzzle and a growing snowdrift blown in through merest crack, beautiful, depressing, a long, scalloped sculpture. In faint firelight he added the cushions from the chairs, made himself a little pad on the small carpet and lay down in his clothes, covered himself. Field bed. Too cold. He got back up, folded the blanket into a kind of sleeping bag or taco shell and climbed back in, much better. The pillow smelled of smoke and Ben-Gay and cough drops and mildew: the stench of isolation. His shoulder was very sore, now that he thought about it. He was the one who should have been taking Advil.

He woke abruptly in the night—the wine like a rat in his head—minutes or hours later, he couldn't tell. He was freezing, though, that was sure. He pulled the blanket tight as he could, hopeless. The temperature outside had plummeted as the guy on *News 5* had predicted, and so had the temperature inside. He turned this way, turned that way. The horsehair cushions crackled under him. He had to piss like a race car (as his father used to say). His head began to ache. His mouth was dry as hemlock twigs. He got up, thought to go outside, remembered the snow chest-high and who knew what drifts, crazy, the door entirely blocked. The wind had picked up again. Alison hated it when he farted. He peed in a pail he found with the pots and pans, emptied it quickly at the drain board, put it back. He'd have to swab it out with snow in the morning. Somewhere outside, of course, after he'd dug them an escape route. He built up the fire—maybe it had been hours—then moved his whole sleeping arrangement close to it, but on the floor it didn't matter: perfectly fucking freezing. The wind was howling again, raging, suddenly shrieking through all the boards of the house, clattering the loose siding, dragging laden branches across the drifts on the roof, thumps and screeches and odd, muffled snaps, the cabin filled again with living air, dry and sharp and just very, *very* cold.

Upstairs there was a rustling and a private sigh. Then the wind, again, building.

"Eric."

"I woke you," he said.

She said, "I haven't actually slept."

"I did. Some anyway. Maybe a couple of hours."

"Uh, no. More like a couple of fifteen minutes. You snore. Are you frozen?"

"I'm okay. I'll be okay."

"It's warm up here. It's fine up here. You'd better come up, mister. I'm in my sleeping bag. Bring your blanket. But don't get any fucking ideas."

"Don't worry. I haven't had an idea in months."

"You had an idea earlier."

The ladder came down, seemingly on its own. Danielle struck a match, bright as sun. Then the lamplight. He gave her a moment to get back in under her covers, climbed the ladder dragging his bedding behind him like Linus. Simple truth: heat rises. Danielle in her Rasta cap helped arrange his blanket, carefully folding it to open away from her. Something startling in the shapes her clavicles made, not that he was looking. She'd startled him all day with her strange, retractable beauty, like a cat's claws.

"There," she said.

"Thanks," he said.

"But take off your shirt."

"Better not."

"Just take it off."

He unbuttoned it, pulled it off. Good idea, preserve some small corner of freshness for morning.

"Your shoulder," she said.

It was bruised, he could see, and pretty badly. He shrugged.

She said, "You really did try to smash down that door."

"At the vet's, yes. It was armored in some way. I hurt my foot, too."

"It's all the dog drugs they have in there."

"Heartworm."

"And take off your pants."

He did, and then his boxers, too (a kind of bravado), and slipped quickly into bed as she looked away. She blew out the light. He settled in with his back to her and they lay a long time like that, close enough to feel the heat between them.

"Who *sent* you?" Danielle whispered seriously, suddenly.

"Oprah," Eric whispered back.

"Would you please," she said.

"I'm sorry," Eric said.

And they were silent. At length, she whispered, "I was smart to go for groceries. Somewhere in me I just knew." She turned on her side behind him, put her arm over him, placed a hand on his chest. "I'm going to bite you."

"Well," he said.

"If you come here," she murmured, pulling him closer.

"Really," he said. "Better not."

"We saved each other," she said, oddly fervent, bubbling like a pot in a way he could *feel,* and not just through her hand. Heart-to-heart, as his mother used to say, soul-to-soul, too mystical for his taste.

They listened to the storm, the muffled hits of who knew what on the roof.

She kissed his hurt shoulder.

"I don't know," he said, aroused.

"But what?" she whispered, biting him, ten little bites across his bruises, rising up behind him and over him to bite his chest. She kissed his neck, stroked his belly, kissed his ear.

"No," he said.

"Just what I was thinking," she said. "No way."

"We will be fine friends," he said.

"You sound like Winnie the fucking Pooh," she said gently, resting her cheek on his shoulder.

"Black widow," he said.

"That's better." She bit him once more, maybe a little hard, patted his chest, reached suddenly to grab his erection, which was straining, moment of no return, moment that best intentions fled. "Mm," she said.

"No," he said. He had a responsibility.

"Just checking," she said, giving a hard squeeze. Then she let go, patted his belly, stroked his chest, kissed that shoulder once more. "You're nice," she said. "And you are very strong."

"Not really," he said.

She bit him hard. But she was done, whatever her project was. She bit him once again, more gently, then kissed him tenderly, kissed that shoulder sweetly, kissed it again and again, leaving it wet, finally turned away from him. Shortly her breath came even, came slowly, came deep, a secret reserve. Carefully he turned and watched her in the faint light, the light of the fading fire, made out the barest lineaments of her face, something important there, he felt, something deep, too, the wind crashing outside, something he couldn't quite fathom, something terrifying, as in, tie yourself to the mast, the wind mounting higher, relief at a narrow escape—that was part of it, too. He couldn't look away. The way she had contained him, the way she had parried him, the arc she had made of the afternoon and the evening, all designed, he felt now, felt the strength of her, the hidden power of her, the thing visible in her face, where in the grocery store and just after he'd only seen weakness, a reflection he now realized, her way of showing him *himself,* the loose roofing or siding or whatever it was clattering, all of it a kind of tide washing over him, that he was nothing, and fear, and sleep.

Part Two

Sixteen

IN HIGH SCHOOL, back in Indianapolis where his parents still lived, there'd been kids in couples all around, but Eric was part of a bigger unit, a tight circle of friends, almost a group romance, in that the crowd identity seemed to preclude any coupling. Jane "the Brain" Gilmore was his crush, but Jane was in love with nutty Randy DiBiase, great guy, and Randy (like everyone else in the universe) was hot for Leslie Armour, but Leslie, poor kid (she'd later die in a car wreck), only had eyes for Trip Morton, who, it went entirely unsaid and unremarked by anyone till at least a decade later (though it was obvious even then) was hot for Eric. This circle kept things tight and let no new faces in and went to movies en masse and to the proms and socials in ever-changing pairs and even lingered in basement playrooms all but making out as they circled around each other clear to graduation.

And that might have been it for high school romance, but the summer after junior year, Eric's parents, Glad and Bob, visited Antarctica on an extended research trip (they were both climatologists). His choice from all the pamphlets they'd provided was tall-ship camp, a two-month program sailing out of England. Shipboard, he'd met Iskra, who was the daughter of a Russian diplomat in the British Mission and hadn't a trace of American inhibition around the subject of sex. She liked him and claimed him and insisted on walks whenever they hit shore and on the third of these adventures he just took her face in his hands and kissed her (she'd been talking obscenely about various types of body kisses), just enough of a laugh beforehand that he could claim it was a joke if she weren't interested. But she was interested, all right. They'd made love on a carpet of pine needles behind a Mediterranean graveyard, his first time. Which she had no problem detecting. A great teaser, Iskra. A great lover, too, vast fund of experience. That was seven great weeks of immersive learning, all right. She didn't write to him from the embassy, despite ardent promises, and his three letters to her came back undeliverable: sadness.

And hunger, sexual. He didn't have a proper girlfriend till college, and that was Cindy Izquierdo, who was Catholic and Mexican American with the strictest parents Eric had ever heard of and had her own very strict ideas about the proper progression of physical love, which found its finish line in marriage. She was a monstrous kisser, however, willing to smooch four and five hours at a stretch, the two of them talking into one another's mouths, entire conversations about far-reaching subjects lip-to-lip and with a trick or two tucked in her bonnet to keep her honor while honoring his ardor, and good at arriving, as she called it. Did he love her? He hadn't thought so—at least not in the way she meant—didn't think so while their romance was going on, a full year at the University of Chicago, though he occasionally said so, as it lubricated her desire. He didn't think so till sometime about three weeks after he broke it off, eliciting buckets of her tears, passionate girl. And then when she took up with his roommate, Brian Flynn, he really thought so. He still thought so, thought about Cindy often. She'd worn a gold chain around her ample hips; you only got to see it rarely.

And then of course there was Alison, who'd bit him exactly once on the chin.

He couldn't think of a way around pulling snow into the house with the hoe he'd found in the shed, so that's what he did, pulled snow straight into the cabin, trying his best to keep it neat, piled snow on the wooden floor and then more and more on the rug. The shoulder was very stiff. He had to make his way out, and he had to convince Danielle to leave, too. He'd had cozy feelings for her as he woke, and cozy wasn't good.

Danielle, dirtier than ever, was busy at the stove pouring water from one vessel to another and finally to the teapot. She shifted from foot to foot in her big wool socks, built up the fire. Their two mugs were on the counter still, stained burgundy from the box wine, which is how Eric's brain felt. She wore her cap and the same old clothes, those thick socks, posture slumped artfully, or so he now thought. She'd awakened before him and descended alone, had been grumbling and cursing to herself since, not so much as a glance in his direction when he finally climbed down, though spears flew and he felt them in his chest and neck, heavy hand-carved things with legends written up and down the shafts. Her kiss was on his shoulder like a burn, her bites like the letters of a secret alphabet. And something coursed through him, an elixir still potent, labeled with runes. Danielle muttered, more curses.

She'd get over it. He shuffled in his own thin socks to the

stove beside her, warmed his hands a minute, stole her empty coffee cup, dipped a cup of warm water from one of the pans on the stove, drank it, dipped another, drank that.

"Don't hog it, yo," she said.

"We can melt snow."

"Okay, melt snow. Like, before you leave, okay?"

Her kisses, if they played in her mind, played on a different channel. He said, "Let me have a look and see what kind of odds we have here. Of getting out, I mean."

"You have all day—you can make it easily. Don't you see? You actually *have* to go."

"We burned a lot more wood than I would have thought," he said.

"We're still burning wood, yo," she said. "And you can find more of that, too. And then leave."

"I'm for leaving, don't worry. But I can't leave you here alone."

She glowered, fumed, attacked a box of Pop-Tarts, tore it nearly in half getting to the subpackaging inside, used her teeth to free two of the things, slabs of dense-looking cake infused with a jellylike substance and slathered in icing. She slapped them on the stovetop to warm. Yo. Give her some space. Try to maneuver near the Advil.

The big window over the river was barely a window anymore, frosted like a Pop-Tart and draped heavily with snow, just a whale's eye left open in the middle to peer through, a sobering view. The snow out there was deep, very deep, a heavy drift wave like the purest sand dune mounded clear up over the windowsill, eight or nine feet deep off the ledge, maybe more, no color anywhere, only white and black and every shade of gray between. And the snow was still falling, still driving, in fact, still cascading from the roof, the river black just below and carrying rafts of snow and tremendous pans of ice and drinking every flake that hit it unto trillions, rising, rising. Eric rubbed the frost of his breath from the limitless porthole and, gazing long, admired the birches bowed in fair arcs on the far bank, balsam firs like court ladies in tiered dresses, green emerging only darkly from the strange humps where whole jungles of alder ought to be.

The Pop-Tarts didn't smell bad. They didn't smell bad at all.

He boldly found the Advil, took a couple, minimal sip of water from his hand as she watched critically, then skated back to the task at the door, a solid half hour with hoe and crowbar and storied shoulder to carve out a passage he could climb through, not a shovel in the place, a four-foot-thick wall of snow that must have fallen off the high-pitched roof. When he got through to the air outside, he admired his work a moment, like looking through a wind tunnel. He found the rain boots and tugged them on, bumped past her for her coat.

"I have to shit, yo," she said miserably.

"I'm sorry," he said in general, though—forced intimacy—the specific problem was the same for him. He tugged on the useless fish-scaling gloves and clomped to the burrow he'd dug and painfully slithered out there into the storm. A long drift of unimaginable dimension had buried the dooryard, buried the funky woodshed up to its high shoulders. Eric found his footing and battled his way forward—snow filling the boots and rising up his pants legs. Even so, it was gorgeous out there, exhilarating, everything flowing and shifting and drowning and blowing, the trees oddly still, plastered down with the early wet snow now frozen hard. The breath froze in his nostrils, too, and new snow filled his hair.

"Okay. I've really got to go," Danielle called, suddenly tumbling out of the tunnel he'd made—nothing of the cabin to be seen. She swam to him through the deep snow, leaned on him abjectly, the smelliest blanket wrapped tight around her, that Rasta cap pulled down over her ears, hands bare.

Eric pushed his way through the snow with her practically riding his back, bashed at the hemlock branches ahead with his hoe but couldn't get them to drop their snow load, simply dug his way through the fragrant boughs by hand till he and Danielle were able to squeeze into the dark cavern beneath. Under the hemlocks they ducked along beside the thick trunks, an eerie passage on nearly dry ground, she in her socks and big sweater. Eric broke through at the end of the line, dense layer of ice, then hard-packed snow, then deep powder. The outhouse was just where he'd calculated, buried up to the half moon. He pulled snow away with his hoe and kicked it clear with his rain boots till he could push the door open without filling the space in there with snow, not a trace of stink: winter had seen to that.

Danielle burst around him, pushed him out like he was the turd, closed the door in his face, clicked the hook-eye latch in place, as if that were necessary. He slipped back under the hemlocks to get out of the wind. He'd just have to wait his turn, he thought grimly. She'd warm the seat, at least.

Seventeen

DANIELLE MADE COFFEE, a pointedly single cup for herself, stood at the butcher-block table drinking it ghostlike while Eric cleaned up the snow on the floor and rug, shuttled it out the entryway he'd made.

She called, "You should have fucked me while you had the chance."

A client on the way to federal prison had said something similar once, and meant it the same way, Turk DuFries: "You should have killed me while you had the chance." Eric clucked, that's all, irritably scraping at the accumulated ice and testing the door. He scraped more but still couldn't close it properly, a lot of work to go. He wasn't doing it for her, not really, but for his own peace of mind. The woman needed egress. It was as simple as a town ordinance. He joined her at the butcher's block, crossed his arms across his chest, cocked his head, an almost consciously intimidating pose. Someone had to take control.

"You don't eat Pop-Tarts?" she said.

"You didn't offer."

"They're on the house, dickhead. Don't wait for me." She

pulled her partly unraveled sweater over her head, knocking off the Rasta cap and getting stuck momentarily in the sleeves such that just her hair stuck through the head hole. Her hair, okay, wow. Danielle was not someone you smooched or got tangled with, no matter what drunken thoughts you might have had in the night. She was looking unhealthy again, some sort of missing light in her eyes and even her skin. "And then you have to go."

He said, "We both need to get out of here. But, Danielle, the snow's very deep. The snow's really deep and neither of us have the right clothing. And it's still coming down very hard. And if the road's not plowed there just won't be anywhere for us to go."

"It's a state road. This is Maine. It's plowed. You take those rain boots and whatever else you need and you start right now and you'll be home in a couple of hours safe and sound and smug as a cat."

"You're leaving someone out."

"Alison will be there to clean your litter box, don't worry."

He rubbed his shoulder. "I was talking about you."

"I take care of myself. Eric."

"Danielle. It has nothing to do with your taking care of yourself or not taking care. It's that no one should be down here in winter without a whole summer of preparation. Certainly not alone. You won't be fine. Things won't work out. You'd need fresh water daily. For a whole winter you'd need probably seven or eight cords of seasoned firewood, all cut and split. You might be stuck down here days at a time or even weeks. People die in these situations."

"That's for me to worry about."

"But think how I'll feel if they find you dead down here come spring."

"Well, how you feel is certainly the most important thing. Eric."

"You're deliberately misunderstanding me."

"Okay. Just have one. Have two. Like you ate all the Advil." She tore the subpackaging for him and handed over a Pop-Tart, like a small piece of painted plywood, not even sticky. He let it get very hot, almost smoking, picked it off the stove and passed it from hand to hand as it cooled.

Danielle watched with unhidden interest as he took his first bite.

The thing tasted pretty damn good, not what he'd thought, and damn it again if he wasn't hungry. He made a pleased face, took another bite, and another.

"Just don't think of all the chemicals," she said. "And that it'll be in your gut till you die. Or that you won't shit for a month. And, of course, that Alison the Good will never talk to you again, this level of sin."

"Thanks," he said. "Thanks for feeding me."

"I'm very nurturing," she said.

"I actually think so," he said.

She opened him another Pop-Tart and put it on the stove, stood over it, close to him, tended the thing, nothing more to say. When the Pop-Tart was warm she picked it off the stove and broke pieces from it and fed him solemnly, unreadably. Her fingers touched his lips every bite. But all of her attention was on the food, if that was what to call it, all of her attention on her hands breaking small bites from the Pop-Tart, her eyes watching every crumb.

"It's salty," he said. "That's the main taste underneath the sugar—salt."

"If you say so, mister." She dipped him a drink, bottom of the bucket.

"What's with the mister?"

"I suppose you think I'm mocking your paternalism."

"You're thinking of someone else."

"Mister, I'm thinking of you."

He was a pro, ignored her professionally: "We need to get you some water. How have you been getting water?"

She retrieved her Rasta cap from under her sweater on the floor, pulled it hard onto her head, made sure every chopped hair was tucked up there. She said, "I haven't, not really. It used to be easy, just walk down to the river. But it was so hard after the ice last week. Now probably impossible. I'm sorry, Eric. I'm sorry to be so mean. I am not a mean person. I used to be very nice. I went to church with my mother like every week when I was little, and Sunday school, too. I collected money for poor people in like a milk box. Even in high school I did stuff. I volunteered at the hospital. My father set it up. I don't know why I stopped. Maybe because I liked it. We could melt snow. Like you said. Eric."

"Melting snow is very slow. Very slow. Danielle."

"Okay, now you sound like Joan Baez. In a good way, I mean. My grandmother loved Joan Baez."

"I'm thinking, get down to the river."

"Still with the folk songs! Anyway. I tried that. Last week after the ice storm. And I even made it halfway back up. But the bucket was so fucking heavy, and I slid on the ice and fell all the way back down and went *in*. That's how I hurt my ankle. It's rocky under there—a lot of rocks. And it was awfully cold. But I never let go of the bucket."

"You were brave," Eric said.

"That's what my father always said. Like if I was just standing in the sun in the yard: 'You're so brave.'"

"I mean to hold onto that bucket."

"Instead of saying, like, 'I love you.'"

They considered that a minute, the constant mystery of human interaction.

"But, okay," she said, "let's get some water and then you *go*."

It wasn't the moment to argue. He'd keep working on her. He just said, "Mind if I make a cup of coffee for myself first and warm up?"

She pretended to ponder the request deeply, seemed about to deny it, seemed to think better of the negative impulse, said, "You were a perfect gentleman."

"Joan Baez is Cuban," he said.

"A perfect, perfect gentleman."

"Her heritage, I mean."

"Jim wouldn't be. A perfect gentleman. I kiss on him, that's it. Sometimes when I don't!"

"Well. I'm not Jim."

"I thought she was from California."

He touched the box of filters, examined them. "And you're married and even if you weren't I'd never take advantage."

"Take advantage of what?"

He felt a grin coming on, couldn't repress it. "You're vulnerable, Danielle. You're in a compromised position. That's what I'm talking about."

She wound up and slapped him hard—total surprise—slapped him again, the other cheek, a one-two sally, really forceful, and then she was laughing, a kind of startling chirp and burble. He

joined in, holding both cheeks, couldn't help it, the sudden re-
lease of tension, almost sexual.

As if it were funny she said, "You just tuck the filter in the
thing there and put a scoop in and rest it on your mug. Eric. The
water's hot. Don't pour too much in—it overflows everywhere."

Eric rubbed his face. "Talk about being in the moment," he
said.

"That was my joke," Danielle told him, no more laughter in
her.

Eighteen

THE HEMLOCKS ALONG the buried stairway down to the water were just overgrown enough that he could grasp branches on both sides of the way and let himself down and down toward the water's edge through the snowdrift, no footing at all in the cheap rain boots. The snow was still falling, blowing, dumping off branches, accumulating fast on his shoulders, his hatless head. He wished for rope, but there'd been none in the shed, all that junk and boating stuff and no rope, not even a ski rope, not even a clothesline, stuff you'd just expect to find in a place like that. But the depth of the drift kept him upright, the smelly old coat warm as a sleeping bag. He refused to pull the hood up.

He'd never seen so much snow on the ground, much less in one storm, and no let-up, the snow coming just as it had all night. The river below him was a black coursing, the only other life in all the stillness, the ice at its edges growing into architectural filigrees and ferns, ironwork wrought in glass, reaching hands of ice eventually to meet and cover the river. He thought of Danielle falling in, pictured her struggling back to the cabin, her ankle already swelling. Duty. That was the feeling that surged in his breast, that and no other.

His feet kept skating out from under him on the buried stairs, but the branches and the steadying depth of the snow made the trick seem possible. Danielle had provided her heavily spiked and grommeted belt, whipping it right off her bedizened skinny jeans, brief shot of her narrow hips in the process: underfed, but. But the clothes—once they'd been nice. Those pants hung. He'd looped the belt through the handle of one of her joint-compound buckets, five gallons. If he could scoop just two and a half gallons, that would weigh about twenty pounds, manage-able, maybe even a kind of ballast to help him keep his footing as he climbed back up. He wore his leather dress gloves—the fish-scaling gloves were just too soaked—thought about where he'd go to buy new ones when this was all over: trip down to Portland. Alison liked to shop. She'd know right where to go. And after maybe they could get a bite.

Incrementally, like an astronaut venturing away from his lu-nar lander, he made his way down, shoulder pulsing dully. The last hemlock branch was thick enough and long enough to get him to the river's edge, those soft hemlock needles in his face, fresh snow blowing down his neck. He'd never seen Alison's condo in Portland, much less stayed over. He kicked at the drift, opened a passage, took one last step, gingerly kicked out a plat-form he could stand on, never letting go of the branch. The river was actually shallow here and calm, a slack eddy, very clear, grasses under there showing the slight upriver flow, no rocks. So, Danielle had invented the rocks, lied about how her injury happened, weird chick. The current seemed a vestige of summer, the long river grasses like thick, luxuriant hair, bright green and lively, healthy, shining, tumbling, perilous. Alison never wore a belt, didn't need one.

He renewed his grip on the tree branch, his dress gloves giving surprisingly supple purchase, and leaned carefully, dangled the bucket by means of Danielle's belt, dipped it successfully, watched it fill, found he couldn't lift it: that shoulder. He shifted his footing, changed hands, gripped the hemlock branch, but the only position he could manage was just too awkward—he couldn't even collect half a bucket. And now the thing was sinking past his reach, and nothing he could do to stop it. He held on a while, but in the end he had to drop the tongue of Danielle's belt. The bucket sat squarely on the shallow bottom, flooded to just above its rim, belt trailing in the current, hopeless.

He said nothing on his return, just stood by the fire. Danielle was sewing at the kitchen table—mending her torn underpants, of all projects, not a word from her, either, chubby antique needle cushion at her elbow, more of the cabin's strange largesse. He could tell she'd just sat down, that she'd watched every move of his expedition through the shrinking lens of the front window. Good of her not to complain about the belt. She'd been down there in better conditions and knew how bad it was. If he couldn't solve the problem and deliver the big gallons they'd have to go back to melting snow, like maybe a quart of water or two an hour when what she needed for drinking and cooking and fire safety and cleanliness (and to get rid of him) was many gallons, plus a margin.

Once his hands were warm and his face had thawed, back to the shed. Under the simple workbench he'd seen a length of garden hose that conceivably could be tied around the hemlock trunk at one end and his waist at the other, give him two hands to work with. There was the garden hoe, too, which he might be able to hook through the handle of the bucket and in the process rescue Danielle's belt.

He warmed the hose by the stove to soften it, tied it around his waist over the big coat, carried the rest in a coil in front of him with one arm, the hoe with the other, like Don Quixote going to battle, or maybe like an ensign in an ROTC hazing. The path through the unbelievably deep snow had gotten pretty well traveled, so a little relief there, though new snow filled his footsteps even as he worked. He passed the whole coil of hose around the lowest hemlock trunk, rolled the coil down the slope and started after it, a garden-hose belay, the leather gloves perfectly grippy if not perfectly warm. The knot in his stomach loosened with each foot of progress: things were going better than he'd expected. He made the river's edge easily, sat back in the huge snowdrift, which was as soft and supportive as a lounge chair. From that position, using the hoe and all his strength, he was able to retrieve bucket and belt and maybe three gallons of water. After a rest, he plunked the bucket in the drift ahead, pulled himself hand by hand up the hose one step at a time, moving the bucket forward as he went. He stole quick glances at the big window, gratified to see Danielle up there watching him intently through the whale's eye.

In the cabin he ignored her unreadable gaze as best he could, moved the old copper slipper tub close to the stove, dumped his gallons in, like nothing in the huge vessel, a few inches at the bottom. But there by the stove the water would be convenient for her cooking and warmer for any bathing she might manage—straight out of the river it wasn't more than thirty-five degrees! And then another trip, plodding. And then another. And another.

By the time the copper slipper was two-thirds full (probably twenty gallons of water in there, two more solid hours of hard work), the operation had got pretty workaday, except for his hands, which were more and more painfully chapped and frozen, and his shoulder, miserable. One last trip and he filled up all the pots on the stove, including an old lobster kettle that held some three gallons. Twenty minutes boiling and she could drink it without worries. One last-last trip and he brought the five-gallon bucket back mostly full. He was done, water to last through whatever disasters awaited her.

"Mister," Danielle said.

Just the one word, but he knew by the tone of her voice that the subject of his leaving had been dropped. He'd been arguing his case in his head all the while: no one could make it up that hill through these drifts without snowshoes. Also, he'd exhausted himself on her behalf.

"Really," she said.

"I won't so much as touch the ladder tonight," he said.

"Perfect gentleman," she said again. She seemed to intensely dislike the concept: "Perfect, perfect. Gentleman, lovely gentleman."

"Now *you* sound like Joan Baez."

"She dated Bob Dylan. They weren't for each other, mister. My grandmother hated him for that."

Done-in, sweated, he pulled his chair away from the stove, out of her orbit, clear over to the table with his puzzle, sat heavily on the crunching cushions, sorted pieces of sky.

Not long and he felt himself nodding, caught himself with a jerk, sat up. Danielle was well into cooking something, or anyway chopping furiously at a pile of carrots on the butcher's block, one of the bigger pots he'd filled bubbling merrily all of a sudden. He nodded off again, woke shivering, his naked feet up on the coffee table amid his puzzle pieces and plain freezing wind, the interior drift growing, an elegant tentacle. Danielle was talking to someone. Stealthily, he turned to see: secret cell phone?

But no, she was holding a photograph, must have climbed the ladder to retrieve it, and yes, she was speaking to the thing, murmuring and muttering, like Hamlet speaking to Yorick's skull, if Yorick's skull had been an 8x10 print. Which made Eric into an 8x10 Horatio, alas, guy half frozen in a graveyard, barely a role at all, listening in on a private soliloquy, passionate tones. He didn't want to bother her, but he needed to get near the stove, needed to get there immediately. He stood, chair legs bugling on the floorboards, so much for subtlety.

She cried out as if caught at something, seemed to assume he'd been listening, rushed to explain: "I'd been about to break it off! That very night. Eric. I was going to say, 'Let's just pull back a little here, Jimmy LaRoque.'"

"Okay," Eric said gently. He tripped to the stove, all the pots of water he'd filled boiling, even the big kettle—he'd been asleep for quite a while, it seemed.

She gazed back upon the photo, kept up the monologue, but as if she'd been talking to Eric all along: "I mean, he was about to deploy, seemed like a good time, let me get back to school, let me get away from him, not to see anyone else, not like that, but to see no one, pull back, that's all, take the pillow off my face.

Then we had like six weeks and what we pulled back was the fucking trigger, all the way back, a wedding with his insane family and then a honeymoon, at least without them, at the Samoset in Rockland, constant lobsters, which I don't love. It's all at the airport now, the way they do it—'*Bye Honey, hope you don't die*—and he's off to advanced elite Ranger training, and then we get a weekend, which was severely off, like lobster sex instead of lobsters and sex. And then he's off to base in Afghanistan, two months of letters and e-mails and general slobber, phone calls every week. And then silence. Because his unit headed into Pakistan, as I'm not supposed to know."

Eric zipped his lips for her, wan gesture. His shoulder had all but seized. He wheeled his arm to stretch it. She joined him at the stove, one notch too close, briefly showed him the photo—a cheerful young man in shiny high health beaming at the photographer, full Ranger camo regalia, two long rifles crossed in front of him, ammo belts crossed on his chest, black service beret drooping spookily over one eye. He had a weak chin but strong cheekbones, deep-set eyes, a guy who hadn't slept and didn't care, definitely trouble.

Eric said, "He's incredibly handsome."

"Not really," said Danielle. She gazed at the photo a little longer, finally put it down on the butcher's block, retrieved Eric's socks, crisply dry, and then surprised him by bending to help him get them on. She even put his dried dress loafers on the floor side by side, where he could step into them like a school kid on the way out the door for the bus.

"Get your chair," she said. "Let's sit right here for lunch."

Her cheer made him suspicious, but not in a way he could say. He put a log in the fire, also a split of kindling to keep it hot, made the instant calculation that their wood wouldn't last, not even till nightfall, not at the rate they were burning it. But they had to burn it like that: the wind was beginning to pick up again, the snow coming harder again, whumps on the roof from all the burdened hemlocks and from the great twin pines high above.

He brought his chair to the stove, not too close to hers.

And shortly she placed a steaming bowl of ramen noodles in his hands, uneven chunks of carrot sunk in there unpeeled but healthily orange at least, spoon already in, its handle sliding along the edge of the bowl till it hit his thumb with a hot splash. "Thanks," he said.

"Three packets," she said.

"The carrots are pretty," he said.

"Oh!" she said, seeming to notice them for the first time. She served herself and sat.

Sodium. Was that the only food group anymore? The noodles were hard to capture with the spoon but they were hot and they were good enough. "Great idea with the carrots," he said.

And they ate, slurping and sighing.

Nineteen

WITH THE INDISPENSABLE hoe, Eric dug around the woodshed drift till he located the rest of the logs he'd cut, gradually levered them free using his feet and the hoe's long handle. After maybe half an hour of hard labor he had them all inside the cabin, small diameter logs from the top of the tree he'd brought down, enough wood to guarantee the night and the next morning, anyway, and that would have to be the end. No way Danielle was ever going to be able to stay the winter here, if that was her plan, no way she could spend another day. He rolled the carpet up and out of the way, and started in cutting with the bow saw, using the arm of the couch as a horse, his crumpled sports jacket as padding to protect the furniture. He rested after each cut, rubbed the kisses on his shoulder, gazed at the sky around Lichtenstein Castle, as far as he'd gotten, tried to find a piece to fit with just his eyes.

He pushed Lieutenant James LaRoque back down into his head as far as he could, all the way down into his toes, his toes inside the rain boots. Something about those crossed rifles, the winning smile, the weak chin, the exhausted, intelligent eyes. In the photo Jimmy looked like a good enough guy, someone you'd want on your team, manly and foursquare, someone you'd want taking care of business for you in Afghanistan or anywhere else, someone who deserved the best from everyone back home, someone who'd expect his wife to be cared for when necessary, and cared for honorably, in sickness and in health.

Danielle in her Rasta cap and huge sweater, Danielle in her filthy jeans, Danielle half catatonic, then tidying the kitchen area, Danielle frozen again, then looking at Jimmy's photo and muttering, then suddenly washing the lunch dishes with a rag. She seemed barely to register Eric. Her limp had increased, he noticed. She groaned audibly climbing the ladder to the sleeping loft. No doubt she was terribly hungover, too. He'd been the one to work it off. No doubt the morning's mercurial cheer had had to do with the wine still in her system. Of course.

Eric realized he'd been composing e-mails in his head all day, no whining and carrying on, just pleasant e-mails telling Alison what he was up to, this unexpected adventure he found himself on: helping the homeless squared. For the hundredth time he reached in his pocket for his phone—an urge to know the time, not to call anyone or check for messages, he told himself—but of course there was no phone, and no time either, not really, and no one: Danielle was right.

He sawed logs, and it got increasingly difficult as he went along, the muscles of his arms burning with the effort, fangs in his shoulder, exhaustion setting in. After their hookup in Beacon Hill, that first intimate sojourn, Alison holding all the cards, she came to Maine for a long weekend, one of the fall holidays. Not Labor Day. Later than that. She must have had Columbus Day off. You could look up the date in 2004, get it precisely right. If you had your phone. The seeds of their later disagreements were already in place. That, he could see clearly in hindsight: their first contiguous days together as a couple and constant small arguments over the minutest factual things, never personal, angry dissections, too, of very slight political divergences, these two people who deeply agreed on everything getting as hot over the details of their orthodoxy as the old protestant pastors, nuanced positions breaking the church of their romance into splinters and then splinters of splinters, sharp things to be deployed at any time.

He thought of the fact of churches for a while, and the way people must always form exclusionary claques, a long conversation with himself, aimed at a kind of vague jury, one of his habits of mind—constant, considered argument. A deflection, of course.

Back to Alison. The incremental sexual disengagement, one less sigh here, one less favor there. Her face came to him just briefly, her face very happy on vacation somewhere. Brazil. She had a warm, open, freckled face, brown bangs that aspired to blonde, a broad mouth and a ready smile that she'd deploy whether praising or eviscerating, very hard to know the difference till late in the middle of the night when you thought back over what she'd said. Her cleavage was freckled, too, structured by a variety of expensive bras.

She'd moved to Woodchurch after their wedding. They'd found a partner's desk at a high-end antiques dealer, and his parents had bought it for them. They'd rented a building with an option to buy—Alison refused to live where she worked—and the desk filled the conference room. They kept busy, then busier. She was a gadfly down at the capitol and brought in mountains

of state work. Across from one another at the enormous desk,
they put in long days, then longer. And the truth was, it was
fun. She had an ingenious way in court, which was to attribute
the weaknesses of their own client's case to the opponent's client. So if there weren't enough evidence that such and such a
big company was off-dumping chemicals into a scenic river (she
always called every river scenic), or evidence to tie the presence
of those chemicals in the scenic river to the company, she would
stand at the witness box and say, in so many words: You've got
no evidence, no paperwork, no taped conversations, no chain
of events that prove you *didn't* dump those chemicals in that
scenic river, that public treasure. No evidence of any kind. Who
did you expect to believe you? Not this court! The logic didn't
matter, and neither did the objections, always sustained: Alison
had a way of prevailing. And she brought in clients. Their two
years working at that desk were their two most successful. After
that, she took the job in Augusta.

Their sex life, which had never exactly sizzled (and Eric knew
sizzle: Iskra), fizzled, to use the language of a women's magazine
he'd seen at the dentist's office. A teaser had caught his interest,
and waiting for a filling he'd read the ten ways to put that sizzle
back. He knew flowers had no effect on Alison, and he knew
that lingerie wasn't going to work—she was a flannel girl. He
did offer a massage, item seven, which she accepted (the first
he'd seen her naked in weeks), accepted and napped through,
waking only to slap his hand when he reached too high inside
her leg. And he made her dinner, also breakfast, items nine and
ten respectively.

Talk of children didn't move her, not at all: she was not going to have a pack of stainers get in the way of a career. Stainers, that was her word! And since procreation was what sex was ultimately about, what was the point of pursuing it? Pleasure? Pleasure you could get from a meal! She'd been raised to expect the best in all things, and she studied the gap between her expectations and the reality of their lives with close attention. You have low libido, she said to him as they ate sometimes, you are bored by sex, you shut me out: but that was her jury-trial strategy. You never knew she was doing it till later, when it was too late to argue, too late to reverse the verdict.

Really, there wasn't enough wood. Eric cleared the way back outside—the snow falling so fast and dumping off the steep roof so continually that the doorway was already blocked again—bashed his way back beneath the underskirts of the hemlocks. In the near-dark and relative silence under there he collected dead-dry sticks and handfuls of fine twigs as high up into the trees as he could painfully reach, unwilling to venture back up the hill for anything more substantial. He made bundles of fuel, passed them out of the relative quiet and into the storm. The wind had definitely gathered force, seemed to come from a new direction. The hemlocks drooped and swayed. The two mighty white pine trees creaked and groaned overhead, flung twigs and bundles of needles. Another hour passed like nothing, or ten minutes, who could tell, except that the overcast got darker and then darker again, dusk coming, exercise endorphins coursing through him like whatever caused love, but darkened by adrenaline: something in him ready to fight.

The house was warm. He brought his bundles in two at a time.

Danielle was up, stood by the stove glowering, moody thing.

Eric patted his pockets, just a quick message he wanted to type into his phone, quick note to Alison, laughed at himself when he remembered.

"Merry fucking elf," Danielle said.

Twenty

IN THE SUDDEN dusk she went about making tea. He lit the kerosene lamp, placed it on the butcher's block beside Jim's photo, tried not to linger over that oddly kind face, pulled the chairs up to the stove, not too close together, sat and waited like a proper hired man, already chilled in his damp shirt and pants, blighted loafers, silk socks, the day gone by along with all hope of leaving. She spooned a blob of crystallized old honey into each mug. He resisted telling her how to recover the stuff—it would taste good whether recovered or not. The vintage tea came from a clever box and she simply spooned it into the smallest pot, let it sit in boiling water a precise while, finally poured it into the hot mugs unstrained. She handed him one and it was like a hardy little animal in his hands, quick and warm. He sipped at it in pecks, picked flecks of tea leaf off his tongue, felt the heat suffuse him.

"You're like the best girlfriend," he said.

"You wish I were your girlfriend," she said crossly. She coddled her tea and sat beside him, nothing more to say, none of his games. When they'd finished the first cup she poured them each a little more, pulled her big sweater off over her head. He liked her shoulders, nothing wrong with that. He liked her arm in the lamplight, the straps from her double camisole falling. She didn't sit with her tea but tidied some more, filled the little pot with cold water from the slipper tub, retrieved the lamp and set it closer with a quick look at Jim's photo. She padded over to the shed door, tested it, checked the front door, gave a long look at the emerging Lichtenstein Castle, straightened the little rug with her toe, collected Eric's jacket and shook it out.

"It's nice how you swept up," she said.

"We can burn the sawdust later," he told her.

She picked up *The Maine Woods,* stared at the cover a moment, brought it over and placed it on the arm of his chair.

"Let's read," she said.

She climbed the ladder and returned quickly with an old copy of *The New York Review of Books,* of all possible reading material, a large-format magazine printed on high-end newsprint, no doubt left in the cabin by Professor DeMarco. Settling beside Eric, she opened it right up and disappeared instantly and completely into the sentences she found there.

No choice, Eric started back with Thoreau, flipping to his place, not very far, gradually warming to the paragraphs. This was a different Thoreau from the one in *Walden,* who was two at once: cocky little bastard, delightful genius. In *The Maine Woods* he was much more the storyteller, older and wiser, less aphoristic, less moralizing, more seasoned, offered a story with characters, all of them marching through the woods. Starting with Polis, Thoreau's native guide, a man who, when the time came for them to paddle, walked into the forest for a single day and emerged with a birch-bark canoe he'd built from scratch, genius of another order. The Abenaki people, Eric reflected, had got through a thousand years of winter with fewer tools than this cabin offered. Outside the wind howled steadily, rocked the walls with frequent gusts. Maybe the cracks of the house had all been filled with snow and ice; anyway, the wind was nearly all outside now. Thoreau had been in love, loved the woman who had rejected him, loved her to the end of his days.

Danielle's arm was bent holding *The New York Review of Books,* her face buried in the pages (she read very close to the page—missing glasses?). Eric couldn't help it, examined a tidy biceps, the particular camber of her bones, not enough meat on them, but still. He read a page of his book, couldn't stay with it. The lamplight flattered Danielle. Even in the Rasta cap. She was older than he'd first thought, maybe closing in on thirty, and much smarter than he'd thought, so he'd seen. All the street talk, all the swearing and yo-ing—that was playing dumb, maybe for Jimmy, a wall she could put up around her, a wall that Eric wasn't going to be able to climb but that would have to be blasted away if he were to get her out of here and to safety. Quite a bit in her story wasn't coming together. She pushed on her soft nose as she read, flattened it, let go, flattened it again, a deep enough person for tangled undercurrents of thought to ripple in her face. That made her different from most of his indigent clients, who tended to have trouble concentrating on anything, ever. Back to the Thoreau, speaking of concentration. Her fingers were long. Polis stood in the canoe, used a pole, poled through the wildest rapids.

Eric and Danielle read as the night came down—seventy pages on Eric's part, so likely quite a bit more than an hour. He kept noticing the coat smell on himself, considered that he had sweated through his shirt and his boxers more than once in the course of this adventure. Gradually, he became aware of Danielle's scent, too, which was the coat to some degree, and the mildewy cabin to another, but more particularly that Ben-Gay smell (from a stash she was secretly rubbing on her ankle?), also something more personal, feral, not unpleasant, exactly. Surely she'd washed—he'd seen her wash—but there would have been no way for her to clean her clothes once the river became inaccessible, and after a while your own odor escapes you, as surely as no doubt his own odor was escaping him. The fire felt good and warm and the tea had heated his toes, but what he needed was a long, hot shower, and she needed one, too.

She turned a crackling page, studied a photograph.

Eric planned forward (always planning, as Alison liked to taunt): the storm would be done before long and he and Danielle could battle their way out and to the road and he could retrieve his car and he could get her to Patty Cardinal's house. Patty had taken in half a dozen lost souls in recent years and never been burned. She had a kind of halfway-house apartment over her garage with its own bath, plenty of hot water, no kitchen (because addicts start fires). But nothing would make Patty happier than to cook meals for Danielle, fatten her up. Patty was chair of the church clothing drive, as well, and would have decent pants and endless T-shirts and a few pretty nice things and very likely a good, warm coat all clean and ready. He'd have to be delicate bringing it up with Danielle. People in trouble didn't want to seem that way, he'd often noticed, and could be infuriated by the merest suggestion of help. Maybe if he said his poor, sad friend Patty was looking for a tenant. First couple of months free. Not charity, but that she needed help with shoveling snow, stuff like that. For Danielle there'd be the benefit that it would keep her alive through winter, and possibly help her get back to work or even school, keep her away from her in-laws in Presque Isle. She'd have her own door and stairway to the backyard at Patty's, and she'd be right in town, at least until Jimmy returned. And Eric would go after the guy who'd hijacked her vehicle, get her a little more money on the deal (threatened headline: LOCAL CAR DEALER TAKES ADVANTAGE OF AFGHAN WAR HERO'S WIFE). Her husband would thank him. Poor Jim, who had no way of knowing how bad things had gotten for his girl! Eric kept getting the picture in his head of this tough Army Ranger shaking his hand in gratitude.

"Yo," Danielle said suddenly. She crackled the magazine, lots of book ads on the back, didn't withdraw from its folds, read quickly and clearly, no stumbling, hint of the substitute teacher, an educated person, not who she pretended to be: "'In the American view, marriage remains the ideal state: only 10 percent of Americans endorse the idea that the institution is outdated, compared to, say, in France, where a third of people think it is.'"

She held the page so he could see it, but wouldn't hand it over, pulled it away when he tried to get hold. The article was called "The Marrying Kind" and was a review of four books about marriage, illustrated with a still photo from *The Graduate*: Dustin Hoffman making off with Katharine Ross in her wedding dress, Anne Bancroft holding on to her for dear life, playing Mrs. Robinson.

Eric said, "Did you know that Dustin Hoffman was already twenty-five when that movie was made, and Anne Bancroft just twenty-seven? They were only two years apart!"

She ignored him, went back to reading.

His response had been lawyerly, he realized, deflective. That's why she was irritated: she was saying something about him and Alison, and he wasn't hearing it.

She read to herself a while more and said, "Okay, mister, I'm getting to the good part here, listen up: 'Gottlieb thinks that she and other unmarried women in their thirties or older have gotten unrealistic notions of life and men, and are just too picky. Besides requiring that a guy be tall, have intelligence, education, kindness, a good income, and hair, he has to have an instant spark and avoid off-putting quirks like the wrong taste in TV programs or clothes. Her view that women have to learn to look for the good qualities of men who may not fit with their exigent dream lists, but with whom they know they get along, is exactly the advice mothers have always given daughters, but was somehow not transmitted to Gottlieb's generation.' Great, huh?" She studied him to find whatever effect she was having. "Discuss."

Intelligence is beauty, he thought, with all the force of a revelation. He said, "I like the way you read. You really are a teacher. I like how confidently you pronounce all those words—you've got precision."

"Eric. I'm sorry. You really are a giant squid. I like your clouds of ink. It's really thorough. The way you do it. Nothing to say about the article?"

"Ink," he said. In court, you repeated the question to gain time: "Okay. Something to say about the article. Women might need to look for the good qualities of men who aren't their dreamboat. But I guess I just don't see the point."

"The point is: doesn't that describe what happened with you and Alison? That after a while, she thought she could find a better model?"

"Why are you so interested in my wife?"

"Let go with your sucker arms."

"Tentacles, you mean. Squid have tentacles."

"The article."

"My dad used to say that there are two ways marriage can go: well or poorly."

"Squish-squish, mister. Clouds of ink like fucking fog. 'Well or poorly' my ass."

"Okay. I think you've got it a little wrong. I'd call it an essay. With a thesis. She's saying that some women never find a man to fit their ideal vision of a mate, that it's not possible to find such a man, that they have to learn to settle, and then learn to consider the man they've settled on the pinnacle."

"Just what I'm saying. With a thesis: Alison settled for *you*. And then, happily married, happily balanced on the pointed peak of *you*, she kept *looking*. Eric."

"She did find a better model. Definitely closer to her dream. I can admit that. He's got the height and he's got the high-visibility government thing going, and he's undoubtedly got the spark."

"As if you don't, mister. You're practically a TV host. In the store, I marked you for a grinner. You don't know what a grinner is? No? Aren't you supposed to know stuff? A grinner is, like, you can tell the checkout lady's mad so you grin at her. You grin at the people behind you in line. You grin at me, even when I'm, like, clearly fucking desolate. And when I'm . . . ? You grin. You're trying to look harmless but you're hiding this fat aggression. It's a little sick. You're grinning now, mister. It's like looking at a double exposure—you want to show how friendly and nonthreatening you are, but at the same time you look like you're about to bite me."

He composed himself, said, "You're the one that bites."

"You grin because you're afraid."

Eric said, "You don't smile at all."

"I'm sorry I slapped you."

"I wasn't afraid. Or if I was afraid, I was afraid you'd take offense. In line at the store, I mean."

"You were afraid. We're all afraid. Your greatest fear, what is it?"

"I don't know. Probably death."

"You grin."

"And car accidents involving death."

"Why does that make you smile? You're almost about to laugh."

"What's your greatest fear?"

"Being dumb. That's what I liked about college. Professor DeMarco was always giving us stuff to read. Stuff you would never have thought. A person is allowed to be interested in stuff. That's what I learned. And I just find this subject interesting. Male aggression. And by the way, your father was wrong. There are a million ways marriage can go, or anything else; well or poorly, those aren't even the extremes."

"You are funny," he said.

"Well, you are not." She made little squid hands, squirted ink.

Eric said, "I don't get the squid metaphor."

She said, "You are not too bright, clearly."

A silence grew. Eric got to his feet unsteadily and tunked a log into the stove, settled back into his chair, realized he was grinning very hard, couldn't make it stop. He picked up Thoreau, found nothing but strings of words, grinned more. He put his hand over his mouth, hid behind his book, but he was practically giggling.

After a few minutes, Danielle put her magazine down again, gave him a long, appraising look. She said, "He has studied Chinese. Mandarin, I mean—every Ranger in his unit has to have a fucking language. Some have several, like A-rab and Persian and I don't know, Russian. They all studied Pashto and the other one over there, which is Dari. For a month at LeJeune. I don't get how you learn anything in a month, but. One of them is fluent somehow, the language guy. And Jimmy, his legs are too short. In proportion, I mean. Very long in the body. Am I repeating myself? Like, a Michael Jordan body stuck on short legs. He's great at surfing and skateboard. And shredding. Because those short sticks give him low center of gravity. Put it this way: I would not have married him except he was on exit." She turned the big engagement ring on her delicate finger, clicked it against the tiny wedding ring that held it in place. "He paid, like, thousands."

Eric had thought it was fake. Finally his grin subsided. He said, "And you said yes."

"I said, Yo. And we fucked on the hood of his truck. Flinch."

"What kind of truck?" Eric said.

But she didn't get it, that Eric was refusing to rise to the bait, or maybe she did, went back to her reading, quickly absorbed.

Eric had always been in competition with guys like Jim. Stronger, faster, braver, often less intelligent, but handsome as oak trees. And as sensitive. Eric had that going, at least, sensitivity, though Alison was the one who claimed it, narcissist. He tried a little more Thoreau, the anti-Jim if ever there was one, found he could concentrate, began to enjoy Polis again, Thoreau and his Penobscot guide making their way into the forest:

> The Indian sat on the front seat, saying nothing to anybody, with a stolid expression of face, as if barely awake to what was going on. Again I was struck by the peculiar vagueness of his replies when addressed in the stage, or at the taverns. He really never said anything on such occasions. He was merely stirred up, like a wild beast, and passively muttered some insignificant response. His answer, in such cases, was never the consequence of a positive mental energy, but vague as a puff of smoke, suggesting no *responsibility*, and if you considered it, you would find that you had got nothing out of him. This was instead of the conventional palaver and smartness of the white man, and equally profitable.

Eric recognized his own style in Polis's, something Alison with her pop-psychological insights had called passive-aggressive, but which Eric had always merely thought cautious. It was also a great negotiating tool, his slowness at times, his silence after an adversary or interlocutor would say something like, "So, how's about ten K?" and Eric would sit at the other end of the phone stunned by the generous amount, thinking through all the possible replies, thinking how ten thousand dollars would help his client or how it would help himself or thinking about whatever issue was at hand, thinking and thinking in silence, dead phone till the other person would say: "Okay, twelve." And still he wouldn't get the effect of his silence—he'd only realize it maybe the next day—but think and think and feel the pleasure of the extra two thousand till the other person would say, "All right. Fifteen. But that's the best we can do. Final offer." And he'd hold a little longer silence, more aware of what he'd achieved, and finally say, "Well. All right. I think we can live with that."

Here, with Danielle, he'd been talking too much.

She in her quiet reading—still working on the marriage essay, in fact having turned back a page or two to start over, the thorough approach. She scratched at her cheek unconsciously in order to unconsciously signal that she knew he was looking. And he looked back down to his reading, sniffing a little to signal that he hadn't actually been looking, all this sub rosa communication between everyone always. Eric's affliction was being aware of it, but the awareness came from his experience interviewing liars and damaged souls and those in trouble, not from anything in his personal life. Or anyway, he had never been able to intuit anything about Alison, ever.

> Most get no more than this out of the Indian, and pronounce him stolid accordingly. I was surprised to see what a foolish and impertinent style a Maine man, a passenger, used in addressing him, as if he were a child, which only made his eyes glisten a little. A tipsy Canadian asked him at a tavern, in a drawling tone, if he smoked, to which he answered with an indefinite "yes." "Won't you lend me your pipe a little while?" asked the other. He replied, looking straight by the man's head, with a face singularly vacant to all neighboring interests, "Me got no pipe;" yet I had seen him put a new one, with a supply of tobacco, into his pocket that morning.

In other words, an intelligent and capable man quietly took the blows from inferior minds and made payback in his own way, in his own time. And on Eric read, more and more fully absorbed.

Until Danielle suddenly barked a laugh and raised her head. "Listen to this," she said. "This explains *everything*. Eric." And she read in her sure teacher's voice, not even stumbling over the biological words, but only on the second use of the word *sex:*

> Sex drive, for instance, is associated with the hormone testosterone in both men and women. Romantic love is associated with elevated activity of the neurotransmitter dopamine and probably also another one, norepinephrine. And attachment is associated with the hormones oxytocin and vasopressin. "It turns out," Fisher said, "that seminal fluid has all of these chemicals in it. So I tell my students, 'Don't have sex if you don't want to fall in love.'"

Something in the firebox of the stove popped then whistled long, ending in a sigh and a crackle.

"So it's all chemical," Eric said.

"Not exactly news, I guess," said Danielle.

They thought about that. Eric said, "I always thought it was something more."

"But what? What more? Exactly what?"

"I don't know. That it was the feelings that produced the chemicals, not the other way around."

"Okay. Or maybe we could just leave the chemicals out of it. Like let's say there was a kind of decaf jizz. Flinch. What would be left? For a couple in passion?"

Eric said, "Scientists are always trying to deny emotion. In psychology, as well. Like everything can be fixed with a pill. And everything you'd call human caused by an imbalance on one side or the other of a chemical reaction."

"But they allow for religion, right?"

"I don't really think so."

"But scientists go to church, right?" Danielle was onto something, or certainly thought she was. She leaned into him excitedly, said, "And people who don't go to church. What about them? They can have faith of all kinds anyway. Like faith in one another, or faith in a baseball team. Is that chemical? Does that come from sex? Answer is no. I think what love is, is that two people cross into a different world together because of a shared event or experience. Like, they cross together into one of the other worlds."

"I like it. And contemporary physics certainly leaves room for alternate universes. So, answer me this: Once the lovers cross over, do they ever come back?"

Danielle scratched her cheek, pushed at her nose, sat up straight, flushed from clavicles to throat, inspired, a kind of fresh beauty overtaking her, nothing to do with her features: "Like, you go through an act or an episode or a moment of transcendence together, not sex, I'm not saying that, though I bet it occasionally happens then—even sex where no one orgasms— but some big event of mutual transmogrification!"

"You did go to college."

"Something huge, something mutual, something as big as an earthquake or worlds colliding, something over the top, unmistakable, the sun exploding, though it could be too, like, *subtle* for others to see. And yes, they do come back to this world, because they never really leave. It could be as quiet as a blade of grass moving under the weight of an ant."

"So, it could be even something as simple as a conversation?"

"Doubtful, yo. Though I suppose maybe sometimes. Really, really big though, even if it's small, so that once you went through it, both people knew it. Something big, something majorly noticeable. It could be ecstatic, it could be tragic, it could be creamy, it could even really, really hurt."

"You and Jimmy?"

"It could be false. Even though you both felt it. Like an ecstasy brought on by drugs."

"Drugs like ecstasy?"

"Like crystal meth, I'm thinking."

"So you're saying yours with Jimmy was false?"

"I think it was. Though I felt it. And he felt it, too. Something exploding deep down under the world. But I never felt I loved him. No, I did, I felt I loved him, I feel I love him still, I was even in love with him, mister, but."

"There wasn't this transcendent event?"

"I think there was not. Or maybe there was. But maybe you only know after x number of years."

They thought about that.

Eric said, "To tell the truth, I'm really confused here. Can you give me an example of the kind of thing you're talking about? Another event of mutual transmogrification?"

"Birth."

"Wow, Danielle. Just wow. That's perfect."

She beamed. "But of course all that, all that care and love and duty between a mother and child, that could be seen as chemical, too. So actually, it's got to be more than that, too. A leap off a cliff, but you don't literally jump. Instead you are jumped. You become a jump."

Eric said, "You're a philosopher."

"More of an alchemist."

"And a ghost as well."

"I could eat," said Danielle.

Twenty-One

ERIC BOILED THE noodles from four boxes of her generic macaroni and cheese in as little water as possible, meanwhile dicing up some onion and jalapeno. Danielle read, one of those people who go through a magazine or book or instruction manual cover to cover and can't skip ahead, only go back, which she seemed to do frequently. There was a little spider pan behind the stove and he found a medium-hot spot on the wide stovetop and heated some of his fine Tuscan olive oil to sauté the vegetables. When the pasta was ready he used the back of a table knife as a dam and strained the water into the hole in the old-time drainboard. Probably it just fell onto the ground below.

"Isn't it time for wine yet?" Danielle called, as if he were far away, off in a proper kitchen in some other wing of some grand stone palace.

"I don't know," Eric said quietly. "I don't normally drink very much at all."

"Besides last night I haven't had a drink of alcohol for, like, weeks," she said. "And I was due. And my bag, that was gone a month ago."

Bag of pot, she must mean.

"For the best," Eric said.

Silence as she retrieved the second bottle of Alison's Côtes du Rhône, silence as he beat two of his eggs. She watched him a while, sidled up beside him, stood too close, then very suddenly slammed the wine on the butcher's block beside him. The pasta in its bowl jumped, the beaten eggs jumped, the other eggs in their carton jumped, the knife he'd been using jumped, and he himself—he jumped—practically onto her back. And then she did it again, slam! And everything jumped again, Eric, too. And once more, everything jumping. She bit the cork and pulled it out with a rude pop, held it in her teeth gazing at him, then spat it in his face, imitated his startled reaction.

Cheerfully she fetched their mugs and filled them both, then fell back into her chair by the stove. She clapped, she laughed, very pleased with herself. A kind of outsized joy seemed to have overtaken her. She slugged her wine.

Eric went soberly back to his project, beat the powdered cheddar cheese from several packets into the egg, beat in a little olive oil (butter would have been better), then grated a large amount of his Parmesan in. All of that he added to the pasta, dropped the sautéed onions and jalapenos in, mixed it all nicely, poured it into a bigger spider pan. Surreptitiously he opened her remaining bag of tortilla chips—he had the idea she'd protest—slid half of them out onto the butcher's block, crushed them up as quietly as he could.

She tugged at her Rasta cap, yanked it off, had a long look at it, tossed it on the floor behind her, took up the magazine again, read closely, spoke abruptly, more or less to him: "Totally."

"Totally," he repeated. "Totally what?"

"This article. About how women have gotten more and more independence because of education. And women know how to do things, and they have *confidence,* also money of their own. But that society hasn't caught up. Like that I haven't got confidence and I haven't got money, and like my husband's backward fucking family. And I didn't finish college." The wind outside added emphasis, a shocking hard blast that made the cabin whistle and shudder, no more comedy.

He covered the pasta and cheese with tortilla-chip crumbs, grated more Parmesan on top. He used a spatula to arrange the coals in the firebox, slid the spider pan in. "Dinner is in the oven," he said, no need to call her out: college, so what?

Twenty-Two

ERIC TRIED THOREAU again, lost interest quickly, distracted by the problem of Danielle and by the roaring, sustained gusts of wind outside. He kept looking to the window but the window was blank white, the eye of the whale completely packed in by all the blown and thrown and dumped snow, nothing there but the reflection of the room around him in kerosene light. So. Over the top edge of *The Maine Woods* he watched Danielle. She was one of those hypnotized readers—nothing could distract her from the sentences, her head moving in a complicated rhythm, the big stiff pages turning, every ad examined, every illustration. Eric tried to imagine her in some other setting, dressed and groomed for someone's wedding, maybe her own wedding to Jim, came up with positive results, a kind of auburn-y hair color—why not?—great waves of gleaming auburn hair. He sipped his wine and eyed the satisfyingly filled slipper tub at length, pondered thermodynamic calculations he was not fully equipped for: if you removed a few gallons of water from the twenty-five gallons in the tub and boiled it, then poured it back into the tub, and then removed a few more of the now somewhat heated gallons and boiled that, how long would it take (or would it even be possible?) to bring the water in the tub up to a nice, hot bath temperature?

He stood and stretched and yawned and had a look in the stove, used his stick to adjust the coals. Then, casually as he could, he tried the water in the tub with his fingers—very cold. He stirred it around with his hand, mixing the thermal layers— colder. With a shrug he pulled his sleeves down over his hands and lifted the lobster kettle off the stove, poured the couple of gallons already boiling in there into the tub, stirred again. Maybe one notch warmer?

He was always happiest when he had a project, Alison liked to say.

Danielle just kept reading.

The wind gusted again, an unceasing breath, a kind of burgeoning, louder and then louder yet. Even Danielle looked up. Something hit the roof with a thud. Then something else, and again, and then there was a roaring like unstopping surf and bigger, jostling thumps and then cracks like lightning straight above and something crashing toward them, rumbling louder and louder inside the howling, a tsunami approaching. Suddenly the cabin heaved on its moorings with a deep moan and squeal. Danielle shouted and leapt, slammed into Eric's chest such that he fell. The stove jerked, the butcher's block slid, the chairs followed, Danielle went down hard atop him and they tumbled together across the floor into the chairs and butcher's block in a heap—Eric over Danielle. Then it was over, a quaking, creaking stop, ramen packages still falling one by one from the kitchen cabinets.

"Okay," he said.

"What the fuck?" she said.

"I don't know," he said. "The snow must have let go. The snow on the hill. The ledge above us. All sitting so deep on that old ice."

"You mean like an *avalanche*?" Danielle said.

"Avalanche, yes."

"You're panting like a dog."

True. He held his breath a moment, lifted himself off her, got to his feet, helped her up. She'd been angular beneath him. One last packet of ramen fell. Then silence, then odd sighs from the woodwork, then a creaking that turned to a growling, like a creature in the yard, something that wanted to get in. The front door began to bulge, then humped into the room as they watched, thick wooden planks swelling like skin. Abruptly the latch popped and the door flew open and a loud, implacable tongue of snow high as the doorway and festooned with hemlock needles and bark and bits of branches pushed its way into the room a foot at a time, urged the couch sidewise, upset the table, spilled and overran Eric's puzzle, reached lazily all the way to the window, kept filling in behind itself till no more snow could enter.

The cabin shuddered, groaned, settled once again.

"Okay," Eric said. "It's over."

But a thunderclap sounded above, directly above. Then another —so loud that Eric bellowed in fright, grabbed for Danielle, who squealed. All but simultaneously a concussion, a blow to the gut, then the trailing sound, an explosion. The building lurched, and the far front corner, the permanent perpendicular meeting of two immovably heavy and well-made walls, *caved in,* a shocking snap of beams and boards and a shrieking of nails, the entire cabin heaving, bucking hard, grinding on its piers, then jerking dead, water splashing from the slipper tub.

Silence.

A few jagged breaths, Eric trying to settle his heart. He held Danielle without thinking, squeezed her to him—all bones. The little bookshelf upstairs teetered and fell over. The ladder slid along the edge of the loft, an afterthought, slid till it fell into the room with an anticlimactic crash. The wind whipped again, but this time into the new gape in the wall, blast of fresh snow, crisply frigid air, the storm reaching inside, a blast that kept coming, whitening the floor completely and all the furniture and Eric's very shirt, snowflakes sizzling on the stove. Danielle held on tight, keeping Eric between her and whatever had crashed into the house, her mouth still open in surprise. The cabin creaked ominously.

And here came the next gust and cloud of snow, a billow of wind like a hurricane come inside. Jim's photo levitated up past Danielle's face—the wind had found it on the butcher's block—made a couple of circuits of the room, blank white on one side, all Jimmy on the other. She reached for him, reached again, just out of grasp. The wind reversed, sucked the air out of the cabin loudly, sucked smoke and ashes from the stove into the air of the room, sucked Jimmy straight out into the night. The gale reversed *again,* clouds of snow and sticks and ice and pine needles pelting them, filling the house. Danielle pushed Eric to the floor, lay over him, protective. The wind roared doubly, then doubly again, and then another deafening crack, an explosion, the night itself breaking, a temblor rocking the very planet.

Inexorably then, two thick white-pine branches—tree-size branches—slid through the gape of fractured boards and tar-paper fragments and shattered shingles, a crazy slow inexplicable motion, a kind of reaching, the snapped branches like a giant's hands feeling for people to eat, bundles of pine needles on their thousand twigs, everything snapping and dragging and shockingly fragrant, huge ancient boughs pushing through the dense ridge of snow that had come through the door, pushing the mighty and immovable butcher's block easily, eerily, one inch, then two, then three, the great bole of the tree settling into all the snow out front, settling snugly against the cabin, which moved back in jerks, juddering on its piers.

Danielle's hands in his face, snow jammed in his eyes, jammed in his nostrils. She brushed at him, blew at him, patted his face. Another gust roared into the broken building, a sustained blast, the fire in the stove flaring, the kerosene lamp brightening, wavering, then going out, sudden dimness, just the hopping firelight, sudden silence. Danielle jumped up, found matches in the corner, lit the lamp again, her hands shaking violently.

Eric staggered to his feet, legs quaking, snow and twigs down his shirt, snow in his pants. There wasn't a tarp in the shed, nothing like that; he'd inventoried the place in his thorough way. In an emergency you acted. You did not just stand there. Navy training. Eric propped the loft ladder back up and Danielle climbed it, found the old wool blanket she'd let him use. In the shed he found a hammer and a coffee can full of roofing nails—big, flat heads, old-school.

At the broken wall Danielle held the blanket as best she could in the face of the wind, balancing like a surfer on the still inching and twitching pine branches, pressing a hem onto the boards, what remained of the cabin wall above the breach. Eric was able to get a nail in at that spot, then another further along, Danielle carefully smoothing the hem ahead of him, efficient team. The top of the blanket was securely in place as the wind picked up again, but the bottom was still loose, rippling. Danielle tried to get it under control with her feet, then all fours—he'd have to nail the bottom to the huge branches—but there was another strong blast, the ratty, dense wool billowing inward, flapping against them, knocking Danielle off her perch, nearly Eric, too. In the next calm she tried again and quickly he nailed the bottom hem in place, a roofing nail every foot or so, nailed it right to the encroaching tree, then nailed both sides to the broken boards that had been the walls, an imperfect and very permeable barrier. But snow would build up on and around it, he thought, seal the rift, become a wall. Or maybe not: the next gust came roaring. The blanket bellied inward, bellied out, bellied inward again, the cloth straining, both Eric and Danielle pushing at it ineffectually, then—*pop-pop-pop*—the nails let go. Then outward again, the blanket billowing into the darkness, held by four nails, then three, then two. With a shout, Danielle rescued it, holding shattered boards and leaning precariously out into the night, gathered the folds hand over hand, feeding the old wool cloth back to Eric. When the wind abated briefly they tried again, a nail every inch this time, nearly the whole can, nearly all of Eric's energy, too, the blanket doubled at the hem for strength—Danielle's idea, silently enacted—and at the next prolonged gust the blanket held, snapping out like a mainsail after a jibe, then filling with wind, sudden pop inward, equally sudden satisfaction: teamwork.

Twenty-Three

THE STOVE HAD shifted but hadn't parted with its chimney pipe, a good thing, plenty of disaster yet possible, plenty averted. The cold, however, had come inside. The fire had to be built back up, precious wood. Eric shoved the huge iron monstrosity back into place with his butt and the strength of his thighs. He remembered the spider pan in there with dinner only when he saw it, his creation blasted with ash and even coals but fragrant. He pulled it to cool on the butcher's block, blew what he could of the ash away. Not that after all the excitement they'd be able to eat. He built up the fire.

Then there was work to do, work to stay alive, and together they did it, not so much as a glance at one another, damned souls riding down the long slope on the other side of fright. Danielle swept, thousands of pine and hemlock needles and fine snow and bits of bark and plain dirt. Eric labored to finish securing the breach in the wall, but there wasn't much to work with, and in fact the blanket was holding reasonably well; already it had caught so much snow that the flapping in and flapping out had moderated to a heavy swinging—a relief—not so much like breathing as it had been, not so much the feeling of being inside one beast in mortal battle with another. He hoped the heat indoors would warm the blanket and melt the snow into it, moisture enough to build a gradual ice wall, real architectural strength. Meantime, he managed to pull two boards from the wreckage, used them to reinforce the weakened corner, nursing a rusty handful of assorted common nails, probably purchased down at Woodchurch Feed and Lumber in 1969 from Jack, free girlie calendar in the bag, Jack's wife still alive, his kids still babies, his house still a showplace, his quirks not yet evolved into madness.

This wing of the storm was following the same pattern as the first, the snow texture lightening, the temperature plummeting, the cabin losing its heat. Snow filled in around the huge branches of the pine and soon the many air leaks and snow siphons would be sealed. Sudden irritation came over Eric like a wave, like the avalanche itself.

Pure focus, Danielle swept and tidied and brushed snow off of everything and brought an increasing mound toward the damage, favoring her ankle again, he noticed, then piteously limping, no complaint, like a broken wind-up toy. The front of the house groaned—those two colossal trees pressing upon it. The long extrusion of snow and debris that had been forced through the bashed door had hardened and become structural, like a cantilever beam (Eric hoped), maybe the only thing keeping them from catastrophe, and the girl swept.

"Just stop!" he roared.

Danielle looked at him briefly, barely, and continued.

Twenty-Four

HE USED A spatula to carefully scrape off the ruined crust of his mac and cheese, added a little water, and put the dish back in the oven to crisp again. They had to eat, no matter what emergencies befell them. He'd kept the fire at the hottest temperature it could produce, so hot that the stovepipe glowed red. The food would be ready all but instantly. The kitchen area, at least, had warmed with the success of their labors, and Danielle had pulled off the huge cabin sweater once again, and then the top camisole (she wiped her brow with this), leaving only the pink camisole, a worn old thing. He could make out her steep nipples, briefest glimpse, then against his will looking again, against his will remembering the feel of her in the heat of the emergency, bony, protective. He'd feed her now all right. Alison was the big girl, lots of curves and cushions, lovely and feminine (if you didn't get too close), never protective, insulated, insular. Danielle more the stick, someone you could imagine staying up nights writing angry poems, making phone calls at all hours, opening little packets of cocaine or meth, filling her nose (and reaching for your cock, hard squeeze), but also the one to wipe the snow and hemlock needles from your eyes, your very nostrils.

The foot of the avalanche still pushed against the face of the cabin, unimaginable weight. The shove had already moved the structure appreciably on its piers, Eric was certain, and there were still creakings and groanings beneath—how far could the cabin move before it fell? And if it fell, what would become of the stove, for example, the stovepipe, all the hot coals, the burning logs, the smoke? And what would become of Danielle and of him, no way out? The shed with its girlie calendar might remain; perhaps they could retreat there. Or maybe they could smash out the front window. He stepped over the two trunk-thick pine branches, put the hammer on the sill, just in case. It'd be a soft landing in all that snow. Unless the house moved so far they ended up in the river, not more than ten feet away and twelve or fifteen feet down. Unlikely, he decided: the beams might fall off the piers, but then the piers would poke up through the floor between joists, and that would keep the place from going very much further.

But who built a house with only one exit!

"Yo, food," Danielle said.

"Okay, Miss Manners," Eric said.

"I regret the loss of your nice bottle of wine, mister."

"At least the wind's all outside again."

"Are we scared?"

"We're cautious," he said.

"I was like."

"We're going to have to find a way out, Danielle."

"Like, shaking."

He pulled his dish out of the oven.

She found her next box of wine.

The house seemed to be staying put. The groaning had definitely quit. Every flake of snow must have hurtled off the steep hillside, so no more slides. Unless a lot more snow came down, and in fact a lot more snow *was* coming down.

"We're okay," he said. He put a huge mound of mac and cheese on a plate for her, less for himself. Quickly, he scraped a carrot and cut it into sticks. Too much yellow and orange. He found the mango, peeled and pitted and cubed it (a little overly nicely, he thought, unaccountably worried about her reaction), still no green. They had nearly been crushed. He bent for pine needles, put a bundle of five on top of the pasta. This looked really nice. Talk about presentation telling a story! You had to take an interest in food if you were going to eat enough. The trees might have fallen more squarely on the house. Easily, that could have happened. And that would have meant death either directly or not. That's how serious everything had gotten, mortally so. And yet they were going to eat, and yet he was worried about making it pretty.

He patted his pocket, but the phone compulsion was growing fainter: he knew the thing wasn't there. He'd better write a note to Alison. A little note of farewell. Some kindly coroner's assistant (that silent Bruce kid with the pimples and glasses) would find it in Eric's pocket come spring, and finally Ally would know what had happened. Or was he just being dramatic? He knew what she would say. And she'd be right. If he seriously thought he were going to die he'd write a note to his parents as well, and in fact they had barely crossed his mind. His dad and mom, busy scientists still, poor correspondents, far off the grid as always, hard at work in the rain forest somewhere in Colombia now that the cartel was defunct, climate models, a lot of bad news, never great fans of Alison, not that they would admit it, Alison, who judged them flaky.

Very little wind was getting in anymore, amazing, all that snow out there, enough to plug a hole the size of a house, and their success in the face of disaster buoyed him, made him almost giddy. Unbidden, some sort of triumphal consonance, an image of Alison came to him, Alison crying at Portland Jetport, the two of them newly wed. He was headed for a Navy blue-ribbon environmental event, just a week's excursion. But Alison had cried, so unlike her, cried inconsolably. "I'm going to miss you," she'd said, over and over. They'd talked twice daily while he was away, and had phone sex, too. Hard to remember, hard to even believe. What words might she possibly have said? Perhaps it was he who'd done all the talking. But what it came down to was this: she loved him, she really loved him. And this: he'd needed that proof.

Danielle poured wine, sat in her seat, drank deeply. "Yo," she said when he put her mounded dish on the arm of her chair. "You think that's *enough*?"

"Probably not," he said. "Big person like you." He sat and began to eat. It was good beyond belief, smoky and like no mac and cheese he'd ever tasted, a dish of life.

She studied him, handing him a mug of wine.

He took it without a look, slugged at it, all appetite, blew out a breath, ate more.

"A pretty smooth operation," she said. "You and me."

"Please eat," said Eric.

And she did, working her plate over methodically, all of the mac and cheese, then the carrot sticks, then the mango, which made her sigh. She even picked up the pine needles and sucked on them.

"There's more," Eric told her.

"A houseful," she said.

Finally Eric let himself look at her. Tears ran down her cheeks. He was one of those who sneezed when others sneezed, and yawned when others yawned, and now tears came to his eyes, too, ran down his cheeks, tiny rivers of feeling.

"So," she said.

"So," he said.

"Do you really want sloppy seconds?"

He flinched.

"The bath," she said, wiping at her eyes, pleased with herself.

He wiped his eyes with his sleeve, and quickly. "So, you *were* paying attention."

"Jim's father put a camera in my bathroom but I found it."

"Jim's father belongs in jail."

"Oh, old dudes like him can't help it. Harmless."

"I hate that expression. 'Sloppy seconds.'"

"You are not big on expressions, mister."

"And stuff like that isn't ever harmless."

The eye contact went on a little too long. Eric broke it. She was the kind who won a staring game. He sipped his wine.

She kept studying him.

He said, "I'm just not sure we can heat it warm enough. That's a lot of cold water in there. We'd have to dip it out and boil it, keeping adding it back."

Finally she looked away, drank her wine, refilled it, drank

some more. She filled his glass, too, expertly manipulating the valve on the box, not a drop spilled. She mused: "How hot is a bath, anyhow?"

Something in the structure of the front of the house whimpered, but the jerking had stopped, the shifting. The food felt good in Eric's belly. The wine was actually very good. He sipped a little more. They had almost died—this was coming home to him. They were not out of danger, either. This came home, too. Who knew how badly the structure had been compromised? But the silence was comforting, reassuring: they'd had a close call, that was all. They could breath now, they could live. He said, "Like, a hundred degrees? I think a very hot hot-tub is around a hundred five?" The fire was going low. The lamplight was nice, lambent and serene, while outside all was mayhem. The wine was perfect, really. Who knew what bouquet in boxes?

She said, "How much water do you think's in the tub?"

"It's stamped 'thirty gallons.' And it's filled to maybe, well, about twenty-five."

"And how warm is the water in there now? Cold, right?"

"Right. It's cold. It's on the floor. It's maybe forty degrees. I mean, not much better than freezing. And that's after I already poured hot water in."

She sat up, smartest kid in class, no teacher's pet: "Okay, mister, we've got the lobster kettle and a couple of little pots, like four gallons we could dip out and boil, right? So that gives us twenty-one gallons at forty degrees, and four gallons at two hundred twelve degrees. Multiply twenty-one gallons times forty degrees, and four gallons times two hundred twelve degrees, eight-forty plus eight forty-eight. That's sixteen eighty-eight. Divide by twenty-five gallons, pretty easy, mm, mm, sixty-seven point five degrees. Do it again, four more gallons dipped out, same kind of same kind, and it's, mm, mm, like, mm, ninety-point-six. One more time and we're parboiled. Eric. So maybe just a couple of gallons to finish."

The front of the house shifted with a thump, and something underneath gave a great groan. Eric made a show of ignoring the noise: "You did that in your head? Ten gallons boiling? That's it?"

Rhetorically she said, "Okay. Truth. Is the house going to cave in?"

"It's just settling, I think."

"And yes, uh-huh, that's it. Ten gallons. There will be some minimal heat interchange with the environment, and with our bodies. But we'll have pots at the ready. Eric."

"I like when you call me Eric."

"Then I'll stop."

Twenty-Five

THE WOODCHURCH RIVER flowed from a series of eleven ponds that were in turn filled by a hundred small brooks and streams draining the mountains that pushed up against French Canada, forming the border in those parts: granite peaks, rolling spruce-fir expanses, hardwood valleys, endless hiking, the working forest, the other Maine. Eric and Alison found every feature, followed every old path and logging road, examined every wall and ridgeline, named every stranded boulder (*glacial erratics* they were called, enormous rocks carried by ice from what was now northern Vermont during the last ice age, hundreds of miles). Together they learned the plants, learned the mush-rooms, learned the topography, finding their way blind at times with a compass and map, or following waterways back down to the Woodchurch Ponds. These didn't have individual names but numbers: Woodchurch Seven with the best fishing; Woodchurch Four with the best campsite; Woodchurch Eleven the most remote, water clear as the sky, trees leaning in at the banks, not a sign of humanity. Woodchurch One was biggest, hosted several camps. It fell over an ancient beaver dam improved in recent centuries by loggers with cement, and that was the head of the Woodchurch River—nothing much but growing quickly as more streams joined in. It passed village and woodlot, farm and graveyard, bickering and boiling. It underflowed bridges, splashed over bedrock, outlived all human plans. It flooded yards in spring and fall, froze hard in winter, pooled sweetly in summer, always falling toward the sea. Through the town of Woodchurch, flowing deeply, it was crossed by five spans, two of them defunct railroad bridges, two of them major roads, one a covered bridge, condemned. Beneath town it entered a gorge, and down there it roared for an inaccessible mile or two, opening gradually into the deep vale where Eric had found himself. Funny you could live somewhere for years and still find new places, secret corners, lost history.

Eric dumped the boiling lobster kettle into the tub, refilled it from the tub, and put it on the glowing stove at the point of highest heat. He dumped and filled the three smaller pots, and fit them around it. "Minimal heat interchange." That's what had made him say it: *I like when you call me Eric.*

Danielle acted like someone who'd been handed all the power. She racketed around setting up her coffee system, two cups this time, one for her sidekick, her plucky trench-mate. She commandeered the littlest pot, poured boiling water over coffee she dumped in a filter freehand, a whiz at volume, too. There was still a wall of snow and hemlock pieces across the living room, a puddle growing, coolness emanating, the feel of a refrigerator door left open. She was married. She was married to Jim. Jim was a great guy. Jim was a hero. His face in that lost photo, warmth and depth. She handed Eric his cup of coffee. Wedding ring, engagement diamond, an antique pair, right there on the proper finger.

A medium pot was boiling. Eric dumped it in the tub, stirred it in, dipped out more, put it on the stovetop, added a log to the fire. It wasn't like they had endless firewood. The firewood might not last the night.

"The best coffee was in Mexico," Danielle said dreamily.

"Mexico," Eric said, surprised to think she'd been there.

"It wasn't that long ago. Jimmy and me on his brother's Harley. Rock's chopped Hog. Rock Knocker, they call him. He's got tats. He's got lots of tats. He's all ink. He has a bird on his dick, Eric, like a toucan!"

"Who doesn't, Danielle?"

She laughed, she actually laughed, something coarse about it, but pretty nevertheless: "You wish, mister. We were only in Mexico like a day, and stupid Jimmy got into a thing. This gnarly *hombre* looked at me wrong, and said some shit. But what José didn't know is that Jimmy *sabe* street Spanish. And he *sabe* street fucking violence, professional style. He's not supposed to use any of it outside the Rangers. Like ten guys in the end, trashing this *taverna*. He got his ear half bitten off and his nose busted. And he broke his own fucking wrist on someone's neck—everyone thrown all over the bar like a bad movie, and we have to escape on Rock's Hog across the desert in moonlight all the way back to Nogales, and Jimmy's going through customs all bloody and beat to shit. But those border guys?" She started to grin, loved this stuff inordinately: "They're all ex-military and they recognize a warrior and they love motorcycles and it's just like alcohol wipes and a rinse in the back room, splint on the wrist, and then we're free to ride all the way back to Tucson, no stopping, three in the morning." She thought about that a moment, her face falling, everything about her caving in. At length, she said, "This is a tough man, is what I'm trying to tell you."

"Probably Jimmy ravished you that night," Eric said, one of those things you wish you could retract: Too true, for one thing. Vastly inappropriate, for another. So small, so pinched, so mean. And when, plainly, Danielle was about to cry.

"Dick," she said. And then she did cry, pretending not to, even producing a fake sneeze to cover.

The coffee was very strong.

Danielle hadn't touched hers. After a long time she sighed and said, "He deployed to Afghanistan with his cast still on."

Eric couldn't help the cross-examination, thoughts that circled the cavern of his mind like blood-sucking bats he couldn't control, bad bats that flew from his mouth: "You left that out earlier. The cast."

She glanced at him miserably, no fight left in her: "I left a lot of stuff out. Eric." She gulped her coffee as if it were medicine, burped with no particular notice, seemed to think of something, hurried to the ladder without a word and climbed up to the loft, favoring the hurt ankle yet oddly athletic, a kind of physical confidence that no amount of hair chopping or self-starvation could hide.

Eric built up the fire, dropped one of the small pots boiling into the tub. The big pot was nearly ready, again, too. Danielle rummaged up there a long time, climbed back down with a stuffed FedEx mailer, sat with it in her seat, considered it. Eventually, she reached in, pulled out a precariously rubber-banded bundle of letters—very small paper and squares of card-board—the backings for all the notepads Jim was apparently using. She neatened all the edges at length, checked them for order on her lap, found various mislaid pages, got it all organized, all the time in the world, a familiar undertaking, it looked like, a child sorting her penny collection.

Her neck was long, without tension. Her face had changed yet again. Eric wanted just a single smile back. She was someone different when she had a project. She touched her nose, that soft addition, squashed it absently, pressed it sideways, pursed her lips the other direction, not very elastic, like she'd break something if she kept it up. He thought of her kisses. They had not been chaste, only a little passive, not like the bites: she'd been waiting for him, and he had done the right thing, exactly the right thing, which was nothing, and he was a good person, also lucky: Danielle would be nothing but trouble, and trouble you didn't fuck, because then you owned it.

"Here's one of the first letters," she said at last, having rejected the actual first and a couple more. She read with pride and ease and a little comedy and her mouth was free again: "'Dear Ass Attack: This ain't so bad as I said here. Errrr. In fact, it's pretty okay shit. Still in base. A-plus. Good as you could hope. Wendy's is here. Wendy's, aight? It's really like fucking home but zero foilage. I spent my whole pay stub on burgers. Beats a bag of nasty. Trojans in the PX for what? I thought it was Don't Ask Don't fucking Tell. Next what? Muslim Gerbils, right?'" She liked that joke, laughed with herself, but then dove noticeably inward, her mouth falling open. She read the rest of the letter to herself, her fingers tapping absently at those lips, which looked sore. And Eric had emphatically not kissed them, very good.

Several former clients came to mind unbidden: Pinky Daub, oh god, Pinky Daub, crazy as they come, but built like a muse, diaphanous dress to the courthouse and a reprimand from Judge Brackett: "This is a place of business," he'd said.

"Your honor, I *mean* business," she'd replied.

Another plea deal out the window.

No attraction.

He'd declined to represent Mary Alice Mayhew in her divorce because he'd dated her. She still claimed to respect him for that. He couldn't think why they'd broken up (way before Alison). Not a lot of heat there, generally speaking. You'd have trouble telling their fights from their conversations, deeply boring. She'd married the head of financial aid at the college, whose first name was Stratham, then cut Stratham loose.

When Danielle was done with the long first letter, she stacked the tiny pages fastidiously, placed them under her leg. She pulled out the next, and after a quick review, again read aloud: "'Dear Thing: Boredom galore. Bag of dicks. One-three-four mobilized and out yesterday . . .'" She held up the letter to show it had been scissors-redacted, continued cheerily: "'So there go half the balls here. Kirkpatrick made two LARGE on poker last week, all these fobbits from Nebraskaway. If not for Monday Night Football (first thing Tuesday mornings!) I would go shitbasket. TV comes in perfect, better than home. And we had the cleaning crew in to watch. They totally get it. Last night balls to eight hundred I could not sleep. Making movies of ya, babe. I will write my wet name on you.'" She read the rest to herself, her throat pinkening with whatever he had to say, her cheeks flushing next, and more and more violently, not that Eric was watching.

She skipped the rest of that packet, opened the next, read

lines randomly to herself, folded the letters quickly. Then she lingered, her voice different, channeling Jim: "'Errrr. As warned, you will stop getting any letters. Dreaming of that big house we saw down by Proctor's Store. Me pappy wrote and says it is still for sale. Me pappy says you are acting pretty dark shadows. What? You know you do not have to eat alone, baby. In that ass apartment. I got a whole pile of paper from you all at once, about sixteen letters from sixteen days running, nice. You don't complain enough! Ha. Ha. Ha. Ha. Ha. Tell dat fuckbasket Mr. Clancy I will have a word wit him and his fucking brat. He is chickenshit, believe me. Show him this here. Your kisses I misses, like at the Kidd's basement? Dat was some kiss. And about your little pants. Errrr.'" She read on silently, suddenly crushed the tiny letter into her lap.

Eric tried to imagine talking to Alison that way. Alison would mock him, at best. *Your little pants. Errrr.* He drafted his e-mails to her endlessly just to eke out steamy sentiments like "I miss you when I don't hear from you for two weeks, but of course I understand." Then he'd go yell at a client, some slip of a druggie girl caught passed out in a church basement with the alms box in her arms.

The fire was very high—their hot-water project in progress—and the outside was once again outside where it belonged, the wind howling wildly, their repair growing stronger by the minute, a wall of ice. Danielle read the next dozen letters to herself, put herself through a constricted but visible arc of emotion. Eric checked the water pots—two little ones boiling, so he dumped and refilled them in the increasingly warmer tub. He stayed at the stove, enjoying the heat, watched the three-gallon pot till it boiled, poured it into the tub, mixed the water, half of the big pot more. He built up the fire again, did some tidying in the kitchen, the buzz from the cheap wine moving into the head- ache range, fear returning: they were trapped, no egress, another night ahead, the hammer on the windowsill.

Danielle receded, flipping expertly through the thick packet of small pages, staring over them (here and there Jim had made a rough drawing), then carefully searching out the words she wanted, an album of greatest hits, inward smiles and small laughs, hard blushes, a lot more puffs of breath and sighs and a kind of private squirming. No matter what she said, she loved this guy, a love that Eric must help protect: Jimmy LaRoque was all she had.

With the fire so high and a cover it didn't take long to boil three more gallons in the big pot, the littler pots all boiling twice in that time. He found himself enjoying the rhythm of the work, each pot on its own quickening schedule. The water in the slip- per tub was plain hot: like compound interest, he thought, dip- ping out a little more.

"You about ready?" he said, unaccountable wave of anger.

Nothing from her, her brightened brown eyes skimming along whatever letter, from wherever, some bloody battle, more and more tender words no doubt as Jimmy marauded through the mountains of Pakistan, or wherever American military secrets had brought him.

He said it again, a little too sharply: "Hot bath."

"Yes. Yes, thanks." She read a little longer, then gathered her correspondence and climbed up to the loft where she rustled about the business of getting her clothes off, peed loudly into her pail. Eventually she descended in the big, filthy robe and equally filthy bare feet, difficult progress with that bruised ankle, stood by the tub. Eric poured new heat from one of the smaller pots, a couple of quarts hard boiling, stirred the tub, dipped the pot full again and back to the stove.

She touched the water, swished it around with her long hand, picking her feet off the cold floor alternately. "We got it, mister," she said. "Maybe a little too."

He could smell her, about half unpleasant. "You're good to go," he said. Really, he didn't mean to be so curt. "Be careful. Your feet are cold—it'll seem to burn."

She said, "No it will actually, really burn. Eric. Could you go on up? I'm feeling shy?"

"Of course," he said. "I mean, I was going." He hadn't heard her sound so modest, and it was appealing, chipped at his free-floating anger. He climbed the ladder and flopped on her bed and waited, privy to all the sounds of her getting into the tub: one foot at a time, a sloshing and sighing. He chanced a look and there she was with the robe pulled up around her slender thighs, warming her feet inch by inch, her legs very hairy, more like furred. He ducked back: of course he shouldn't be looking and wouldn't.

He heard the wind and he heard her drop the robe over her chair. He pictured the snow mounting, drifting. He pictured her placing her hands on both sides of the high part of the tub and sinking herself into the hot water, heard her huge double sigh, heaved for his benefit no doubt, a kind of thanks, and heard the wind. He thought of her desecrated hair, thought of her strong shoulders—she must have been at one time or another a swimmer—heard her finally let herself all the way in. Something clonked on the roof.

"Perfect gentleman," she called.

"Perfect," he said.

The FedEx envelope was at the side of the bed, one of the tiny letters on top. He didn't touch it but read what had been left for anyone to see, blockish handwriting: "Your skin in my teeth, baby. Slippery girl, ass girl, the Jim he kiss you endlessly. Like dat. You know. The way you push-push on my teeth." Well, it went on—it was what she'd just been reading—an act of lovemaking bluntly described, arousing in its privacy and not only in the pictures it evoked in his head, these starring Danielle and actually himself and not The Jim, just a long paragraph squeezed onto one of the little lined pages. He lay on his hand and read it again, dared after a third pass to flip the page over very quietly and read the backside. But the backside wasn't as compelling—the guy had started to promise her a good hard pounding and something about pulling her ponytail (a ponytail that had now gone missing, but not difficult to imagine) and the pictures in Eric's head turned to a lonely soldier stuffed with testosterone, wanking away desperate to come to orgasm before his fellows returned to quarters, or whatever they called it in the Army, using his pen to make his new wife complicit, nastier and nastier language, unpleasant. Well, all for the best: Eric shouldn't be reading her mail. And he shouldn't be getting himself all fired up, either. He flipped the letter back over, very precisely as he'd found it, flipped the FedEx package over, inadvertently uncovering the address:

> Ms. Inness O'Keefe LaRoque
> 146 Spruce Street
> Presque Isle, Maine

No doubt Danielle's mother-in-law.

"Need soap," Danielle herself called.

"Okay," he called back. He rearranged the whole FedEx tableau, gave himself a moment more of the compound-interest discussion in his head to derail his undoubtedly too-obvious arousal, climbed down to her in his own good time.

"Oh, thanks," she said. "It's in the cabinet over there, up over the flour bins. In a dish."

Lavender soap, pretty strong smelling, all but appealing, like the Walmart perfume aisle.

"What were you reading?" she said as he delivered it.

He blushed. "Love letters."

She didn't take him seriously, one of the great functions of the truth, as certain lawyers know. "Oh, Eric," she said suddenly fresh-voiced. "Sit here and talk with me."

She sank underwater, contorting herself in the slim tub to do so, and it was as if he himself had been dunked, that was how badly he wanted to get her hair underwater, that scalpy smell of hers. She stayed under, too. Her little breasts were plainly visible in the kerosene lamplight and it was very like the letters—you shouldn't be looking but how not, left out like that for a person to see? She emerged suddenly and sat up high out of the tub, rubbing her head with the soap, rubbing her neck. She dunked again, emerged, fingered the water out of her eyes, all business.

"I have nice tits," she said.

"Not that I noticed."

"They're lively, as my auntie used to say. Which she meant in a negative way."

"She was jealous."

"I need more hot," Danielle said.

Eric said, "Okay."

"That's about enough male gaze, mister," she said, looking at his shoulder, it seemed to him, looking at his chest.

He turned to the stove, two pots boiling. He selected the smaller of them. "You'll need to stand," he said. "If you don't want to get scalded. Use your robe, please. You learned something in college: 'Male gaze.' "

"Not just college. Eric. The eyeballs are everywhere." She retrieved the robe, contrived to stand up into it, wrapped herself loosely, one breast free to the air. He just couldn't help seeing it. Her shins were abominably hairy—dark sleek hair carried into rivulets by the water draining off them. He poured the new water in carefully, slowly.

"Tell me if it's getting too hot," he said.

"No, it's nice," she said, dancing.

He stirred the water with his hand, added more, stirred. The leg hair was primal and off-putting, not that he had anything against the body natural, just that there was the hint of neglect about this particular display, of depression, terrible isolation. He poured more. "Still good?" he said.

"I'm like Mrs. Bigfoot," she said. "I'm sorry. I've been alone."

"I'm not staring," he said: another thing certain lawyers knew, a corollary—state the opposite of the truth to own the truth. He poured carefully.

"Okay, whoa up," she cried. "That's getting pretty very all-the-way fucking hot." But she knelt, sank herself slowly back into the water, carefully managing the robe, covering her breast, suddenly shy again, always mercurial. She said, "My mom would sit and talk to me when I was in the bath."

He dipped the pot quickly just in front of her knees and put it on the fire, soap and dirt and all, took his chair, which was just slightly behind her.

"I can't tell you," she said. "It's been really months since I had an actual bath. Last time was, I don't know. This is a lot of water. It was the river all summer, like YMCA camp, and okay right up till the last time, in, like, October. I tried again a couple or a few weeks ago—Christmas Eve, I'm pretty sure. When it was cold as shit, yo. I got pretty good at the sponge bath. Though my hair paid for it. And. Um. I got kind of freaked out one night and tried to cut it all off with a filet knife, a fishing knife, extra sharp. It was in the drawer. Yes, that's what happened, Mr. Flinch. You've been pretty patient not to ask. It all ended in tears, as you can imagine. I cut myself and it bled and bled. I was just very fucking crazy from being alone. Also, hormonal."

"It's not so bad. You look fine. Your ear. And I didn't flinch."

"It's very bad. Eric. And I don't have a hairbrush. I don't even have a comb. And you flinched. I can see you, in case you thought not. Female gaze. Not something you learn in school."

Eric felt himself flush, got busy with a pot on the stove. He said, "Is there any shampoo?"

"Shampoo. I had a thing of Pantene. I was very proud of that. Pantene. First thing I bought with the car money. But I left it on the rocks down by the river that last time, conditioner, too, and towel and comb and brush and you name it. And the water came up after that week of rain? Like a mini flood. Carried it all away."

"We'll find it in the spring," Eric said, which as an offer of extended friendship was pretty oblique, but the joke made her smile. He searched all the cabinets in the kitchen area (Lux

dishwashing liquid, Murphy's Oil Soap for floors, Windex with
Ammonia D, all in ancient packaging, all potential havoc for her
already beleaguered hair), searched the various nooks of the big
room, boxes of this, shelves full of that, mountain of snow and
sawdust in the middle, crashed tree and the iced blanket holding up the corner, no luck. In the tool shed by kerosene lamplight inside a stack of four unequal rolls of duct tape he found
a bottle of dog shampoo, which in any other circumstances
would have made a pretty good joke, picture of a happy collie
on the label. But then in a line of another era's spray-paint cans
and wasp bombs and tubes of axle grease he spotted a (glass!)
bottle he recognized despite the missing label as Breck shampoo,
which his older sisters had used throughout their high school
years and which by default he had used as well. The conditioner
had been heartily electrical-taped to the shampoo, a length of
chain attached, a man's operation meant for the rustic bath in
the river. Eric opened the (frozen) shampoo component of the
clunky package, sniffed it luxuriously, and it was as if time itself had been trapped inside, how thoroughly his sisters leapt
back to him, the fraught hour before the school bus came, Ellen
and Tina, the steam in the family's one bathroom, the creams
and lotions and emollients and strange pads, the towels clutched
around them, the rare peek at private skin, their lingering scents.
He'd have to give them each a call when he finally got home.
They'd love the story of the taped and chained Breck, something
their dad might have done.

"Getting a little fucking cold," Danielle said when he returned.

He handed her the shampoo and she laughed, that chirp and
burble of hers.

"Dunk it under to thaw it," he said, and turned his attention to the stove. The smaller pots were boiling hard.

This time she just threw her two legs over the side of the slipper, lifted herself off the floor of the tub, left a spot for him to pour, things to see. Instead, however, he pictured the hot water mixing fast with the cooler and swirling up under her bum, didn't want to burn her.

"Woo, mister," she said.

"Too hot?"

"Very hot," she said. Then, "Jesus, look at my fucking legs." She turned them this way and that on the lip of the slipper.

"They're fine," Eric said.

"You mind if I wash my hair in your water?"

"Go ahead, yes, of course it's okay. There's enough fresh I think. And soap is soap. Damn."

"Damn, what?"

"I was just lamenting. I bought razors. Behind you in line at Hannaford? Cheese and wine and scallions and razors, of all things. But I left them in the car."

"No you didn't. They're here. I hosed you about them, remember? But I'm not going to shave in front of everybody, and not in your bathwater. Or maybe. But I'll do it after you're done. And what is it with you bringing all the shit I need? A little creepy, don't you think?"

"Well, it was all for Alison."

"Alison this and Alison that." She drew her legs back under the water, pointed at his chair. He was to keep her company, sit just behind, and watch the gaze, bub.

She washed her hair with the thawing Breck shampoo twice and plumped a good blob of the thickened conditioner on her head and waited. The fragrance was mild, floral, carried him back over mountain ranges to his Indiana home, to his sisters, his parents, his hours in the tub with model ships and wash-cloths, first experiments toward jerking off, which later like everyone else in the world he'd master. Danielle's hair looked better globbed with conditioner than it had looked at any time since he'd first seen her.

Danielle said, "Let's work on my hair." She dunked, rinsed the conditioner out.

"Work how?"

"The scissors, mister. Maybe a fork? Just make it all even if you can. Get the elflocks out? It's kind of gross. I'll get out of the tub first. You don't want to bathe in my hair."

"Elflocks?"

"That's what my mother called 'em. Like, knots. The elves make 'em while you sleep."

While she climbed out of the tub and got in the robe, Eric retrieved a fork and the pair of scissors he'd noticed in one of the drawers, old-fashioned black-handled things with overly long blades, slightly rusty. She sat in her chair by the stove and awkwardly he combed a little with the fork, used the scissors as a pick, decoded some of the easier tangles, got into it: elflocks, all right. Danielle was quiet, let him work, and so he made an-other pass, tugged at knots that weren't going to relax, the work of trolls. And she made no protest when he began to cut, an effort at a straight line or two, nothing fancy. When he was done—he worked fast, like a sailor trimming rope—she felt it all carefully.

"Mm," she said.

"Back in the tub," he told her, turning away pointedly.

And she complied, sank quickly under the water. When he looked again her knees loomed; she sank farther and her thighs rose, more downy than hairy, not like the shins, palest skin, not a blemish, not a mole. Her knees were scarred in the usual manner of the hoyden, which he was beginning to see was her history. She bobbed up again, ran her hands across her hair luxuriously, said, "Were you desperate to get married?"

He shrugged.

"I mean before you and Alison met? Was it all you thought about?"

"Hardly. What I thought about was law. About saving the world, to be honest. Delusions of grandeur."

"I had delusions of, like, worthless. Ness. I had no interest in marriage at all. Though I didn't not love Jim. He pushed and pushed. And look what he did to me! Total neglect. Sound familiar? At least you're a lawyer. I mean really a lawyer. And no doubt making money cock over cunt."

Eric flinched, thought it might be good to change the general tenor of the conversation: "Well, actually, there's a bit of a problem in that regard. I do far too much advocacy and pro bono stuff, and then, when I do work for money, I don't get paid half the time."

Her demeanor flipped once again. She said, "Counselor, that's fucked!"

He applied calmness purposefully. It starts with a breath. "Yes," he said. "Probably people owe me fifty grand or more. I mean, perfectly well-to-do people. You have to write it off after a while."

She just grew more aggressive: "No, you have to get some fucking *balls*. Eric. Do you need me to make some phone calls for you? Dooryard visits? And by the way, if people owe you money, you shouldn't be buying such expensive fucking *cheese*!"

She dunked herself again, came up patting at her hair, eyes tight closed.

Her little breasts, honestly. Eric felt himself a starving man, sudden insight. Alison had starved him, and purposefully, all while telling him that he wasn't hungry. Quickly he turned, this time all the way around, turned his chair, put his back emphatically to Danielle.

She said, "Would you ever date me?"

His answer came fast, too sharp: "I'd need a revival tent and a van."

"Probably true. But in a perfect world? Someone like me? Not a chance. Is what I'm saying."

"What do you mean, dooryard visits?"

"Well. It's like the Maine Mafia. You get a visit. They don't come in your house. You stand outside. You might not go back in. Ask Jimmy's dad."

An image came to mind, a man in a tank T-shirt, beer in one fat fist, Bible in the other. Eric said, "I would say yes—yes, of course I would date you. I would say yes very much, in my understanding of the word, if you weren't married and we could go out on a proper date. But only because your math is so good."

"Jim and me, that's over," she said. "So ax me on a date."

"If that were true, which it isn't, Jimmy and you, I would. And if I could be sure I wasn't taking advantage of you. Yes, surely. I would ask you for a date. And what would be your reply? In this perfect world we're talking about, of course."

Silence, some expressive sloshing. "You think you're so *fucking* superior."

Uh-oh. "No. I'm far from superior. Not to you, not to any-one." Not to Jimmy, surely. Jimmy the Army Ranger?

"And your accent changes when you're doing it. 'Surely' this, and 'what would be your reply' that?" Her anger bubbled like one of the pots on the stove; steam rose in her voice. "You couldn't say that—about taking advantage?—if you didn't think you were superior, very superior. Because you're saying there's a power relationship that you don't want to exploit, which is the same as saying you are superior. And that makes you a dick."

"No, not superior at all."

"Vulnerable! What about you? I think you're afraid I'm going to take advantage of *you*."

"All I meant by that was that you're not yourself."

"And all this high talk, but the only reason you're not slob-bering over me is that you think Jim will kick your ass. And you're right, he will." A big splash, and bathwater splashed in a fountain over his shoulder.

Eric said, "I'm not afraid of Jim."

"Everyone's afraid of Jim."

He turned so he could see her, said, "Jim and I will be friends."

"I've had a tough time. Eric. And you, you turn your back on me." She had a tiny mole on her shoulder blade, otherwise unblemished skin, brightly pink from the bath.

He said, "A tough time, I know. And I'm not going to take advantage of that."

A splash, and she was underwater again. For a long time. She came up gasping like a pearl diver, turned very naked to see him. Breathless, she said, "But I really, really feel like it."

Big flinch, he couldn't help it, knew she saw it, flushed, hit rewind, even as she held his eye, said, "What would we do on this date? I mean, what do you like to do on a date? A movie? I love a movie, good or bad, and then to talk about it after."

"I'd wear a skirt. I have a skirt. I had one, I mean. I had a few, actually. One was like this fucking short. I'll get a cute one. We'd have to be awfully quiet, mister."

"I always thought a hike was a good date."

"Always, like you went on more than two."

He turned away emphatically. "I went on plenty."

"I climbed Katahdin once. Jim is big on hiking. It was fucking brutal, more like a forced march. I did it in sandals. He sent me flowers you know, just last week. Flowers dot com and a guy drives down here all the way from Afghanistan."

"I would have thought you'd hate cut flowers."

"Eric. Come on. For a woman they're about equal to a blow job for a man."

Flinch.

Splish-splash. Danielle's breathing had calmed. She sighed. "Mm," she said. Then, "Do you know what I'm doing?"

"In fact, my first date was a hike. My dad dropped Callie DeMartino and me and a couple of other kids—her friends—at the Ribbon Rock trailhead down by Acadia."

Danielle moaned, but it was parody. She said, "No, really, do you know what I'm doing?"

"Tormenting me, that's what you're doing."

"Dirty mind."

"We brought a picnic. Just a nice baguette and a tomato, hunk of good cheese."

"You and your cheese."

"Ate on a rock high over the ocean, gorgeous."

"I have your knife. You keep it so sharp. If you don't turn

and see me I'm going to cut my wrists. First one, then the other, and not across but lengthwise, between the tendons. I've done it before."

"I didn't see any scars."

"And of course you looked."

"Your wrists are very pretty."

"You'd better stop me."

"That's enough."

The water sloshed. "You better." Her voice was breathy, then breathier. "You really, really better. Mmm."

"You don't fool me."

"God. Mmm. It hurts. That's a clean, yo that's a, that's a, shit, God, that's a clean. That's a clean cut." She groaned expressively.

"Very funny," he said, suddenly discomfited.

She must have seen him stiffen, breathed, breathed again, once more, not quite sighs, not quite moans, the real sound of pain.

"That's enough," he said.

"Now the other one," she said with a choked sob.

He almost turned.

She must have seen this, laid it on too thick: "Ouch. Ouch, fuck. Okay. Okay, mister, good-bye." The water sloshed.

The wind took over. The wind was everything, a roar all around, sucking at the stove, pulling air through the stove; it burned brighter, puffs of fragrant smoke, a whistling. Eric didn't look back, and he didn't look back. The kettle on the stove rattled once. He thought of his wrecked shoes. He thought of the veterinarian, a chain of causation starting yesterday morning with the tense weather reports. He wouldn't look. That kindly bagger at Hannaford's. The bitch of a checker. Not a sound from behind, not a telltale ripple, nothing. Five minutes, ten, plenty of time for a person so skinny to bleed out.

Finally a splash. "You are fucking useless," Danielle said.

He slumped, real relief, as he was unhappy to note. He said, "You had me for a minute."

"No, you had *me*. Eric. You had me and do you know what you said? You said no. You started talking about hiking."

"If you still mean it in a couple of months and if Jim and you have actually split—no way—and if Alison and I have split, unlikely, I'll say yes. Of course, yes. Anyone would date you, of course I would, and honored. In a perfect world. I would date a woman just like you, you yourself in fact."

"You'd want me to go back to school."

"That would be up to you."

"Maybe I could work for you."

"I could use the help, honestly."

Silence. Then, "Your turn."

"I'll bet you'd really enjoy being back in classes. How many credits do you need?"

"Like we're ever going to date. And like I'm ever going to go back to school. And like you'd ever let me work for you. Eric. Who can't even get clients to pay. Yo. I'm getting out of the tub. Your chance to see my fucking pretty wrists." The water sloshed. "Okay," she said after a minute. "I'm decent."

He turned as she was leaning, not decent at all, turned as she was reaching for the huge robe, the cabin's huge robe, a certain skinny elegance about her. He closed his eyes, pinched them closed, turned. But he'd seen plenty. The backs of her thighs had a distinct pattern of hair growth, a kind of staircase curve, symmetrical one leg to the next, not unattractive, fascinating in an animal way: on a horse this would be the color pattern, he thought—palomino, paint, piebald, skewbald, odd-colored, roan—thinking horseflesh so as not to think anything else. When he opened his eyes again Danielle was at the stove and covered.

"Water's all boiling for you," she said happily, and poured the big potful into the tub, dipped a new fill as he had done, put it back on the stove, poured the three little pots in, dipped again and back to the stove. "I smell so *good*," she said. And then, peering, "It doesn't look too dirty, sorry. Really you should've gone first."

She wasn't going anywhere so he just stood as if casually and pulled his T-shirt over his head, undid his belt, pulled his pants off, one hand on the chair to steady himself, hopped a little getting his socks off—that floor was deeply cold.

"Those boxers," she said, turning just as he pulled them off. He still had half a hard-on from all this overload, the letters, the scent of Breck, her pretty pink butt. She turned away quickly, only talked faster. "Jim wears these boxer *briefs*—you should get some. Sexy. You have a great body. Eric. Mr. Long and Lean. You should show it off more—everything you wear is so fucking baggy. As if I know what you wear. But I can guess: brown suits and pressed shirts. From that store in the mall down in Portland. What's it?"

"I wear casual to work," he said, mortified; she was right on the money: Brooks Brothers. "Maybe dress pants to court." L.L. Bean for pants, but that was a name he'd better not say.

"Just that you say 'casual,' and 'dress.'"

"You know, like jeans and stuff, versus suit and tie."

"Duh. And you say 'versus.' How did you and Alison meet? L.L. Bean adventure outing? Kayaking to the Isle of Conformity?"

He stepped into the not-too-cloudy water, hemlock and pine needles floating, found it hot, one leg then the next, very hot, nice though, waited a moment, too long for Danielle, who turned again to see him: "Oops," she said, but frankly assessing him.

The wind outside still howled. Amazing that violence like that could slip into the background of even such charged talk. Eric sat more quickly than he'd intended, leaned back against the slipper tub. He said, "We met on a blind date. My roommate at law school set us up."

"Before, you said you met at moot court in high school."

Busted. "We were acquainted, yes." When had he told her that? "But my friend didn't know it." And why on earth was he lying now? "And, um, we didn't realize it right away." Why was he still? Danielle's interest had surprised him, that's why. And something about the history between him and Alison seemed private.

"I'm not buying it, Counselor."

"Well, I'm not selling."

"You found her on that hike."

When had they talked about the hike?

"And then you met up in Boston."

"Okay. True enough."

"What happened at the moot court, through? That's what I want to know."

"Nothing. We were friendly."

"No, not nothing. You talked and talked. And realized you had soooo much in common. Even though you were rilly, rilly different. Like, I don't know, a dog and a cat. And after a week of this, you avoided each other rather than hook up, though it could have gone either way. Because you were a gentleman even then. And because she didn't want to go there. But then years later, you meet accidentally on a hike and it's like old friends, but still you don't kiss her."

"I went to see her in Boston."

"And you fucked in a parking garage."

"I don't remember telling you all this."

"Red wine."

"And then, just so you know, we kept going at her apartment."

"How's the water?"

"You know exactly how the water is. It's great."

"Hot and dirty?"

"No, it's fine. It's really nice. And Alison hates dogs and cats equally."

"Where's your dog?"

"How do you know I have a dog?"

"You said he went to the vet up there."

That miserable vet. "He's at Alison's."

"Alison who hates him?"

"No, she loves him, too."

"But demanded him because she wants all the chips?"

"I could get used to this."

"I'll shave while my skin is soft."

"We made out on the hike. Within an hour of seeing each other. Just so you know."

"Bold." She retrieved his five-pack of disposable razors from wherever she'd stashed them in the kitchen and collected the plywood cutting board. This, she placed across the low end of the tub over his knees and sat sideways to him but very close, also close to the fire, her foot up on the ash shelf of the stove, plenty warm. Carefully she bared a leg, examined it thoroughly, used the scissors to mow a while, harrowing patchy cuts and hair falling in little clumps on the floor around her, one leg then the next. She dipped a washcloth in their tub, wet her skin at length.

"This is the most intimate thing," she said.

He dunked himself awkwardly. "A little too," he said. And kept his eyes closed.

She said, "I mean the most intimate thing I can think of between people who aren't squishing. We're basically survivors down here. Right?"

"I think we're better off than most survivors."

"Refugees, then."

He swiped a hand across his eyes, bolt of panic, death *imminent,* found her looking at him very softly, anodyne.

" 'Modesty flies out the window,' " she said, quoting whom?

Hotly he said, "But the window down here doesn't open even when it's not packed solidly with snow."

She admired the razor in her hand: "Oh, *cunning.*" Easily, she drew it up the side of her calf, left a perfect, clean strip. *Cunning,* that was such a Maine word, something she'd learned from her in-laws, no doubt. She dipped the multiple blade in one of the small pots on the stove (she could just reach it, elegant once again, all gesture when she wanted), shaved another clean strip. "I have nice skin," she said.

"I'm not paying any attention at all," Eric said leaning back, sinking as best he could, his knees pressing up beneath her against the cutting board.

"Just no whacking off," she said as he went under.

Twenty-Six

HER THIGHS WERE next. She didn't seem in a hurry. She sat poised with the cunning razor in her hand. Her calves glistened in the lamplight. Eric felt he was losing his boundaries or, if not that, at least losing his moral compass. He felt himself falling for her, which he'd prefer not, altogether. He could already leap ahead to the pain: Jim would come back. Jim would come back soon. There'd be trouble, that was for sure, Danielle a woman for confessions, and Jim not one to hear such confessions calmly, at a guess. It was hard not to look at her.

She muttered, "But you still love her."

He said, "And you're still married."

She finished the one leg, turned just so away from him, drapery of the cruddy robe, finished leisurely, finally stood, removed the plywood seat and retrieved the three-gallon pot, which was boiling audibly. "You better move, yo."

He swung his legs as she had, but his were much longer than hers and it wasn't going to work, his privates very much in the line of fire.

"Just fucking stand up," she said.

"I'm embarrassed," he said.

"No doubt," she said.

He stood, turned away from her, made a little comedy of putting his hands over himself. Not that she could see, but surely she must know: he was rampant, rampant, and so close to her as she poured the water, and she poured it slowly, slowly.

"My god," he said. "That is very hot."

No mercy. No turning away. She said, "Jim was a fireplug in all respects. He was more like good engineering than anything beautiful. Eric. Can I say something? If you broke your dick off you'd be like a statue in ancient Greece." She dipped the saucepan behind him, hefted it to the stove. "In fact, a little chop-chop might be a good idea."

"That's very nineteen-fifties of you."

"No, more like three thousand B.C."

"I mean the castration-complex stuff."

"Nineteen-twenties then. Just sit."

Eric eased back in the water, displaced it nearly to the rim, unduly pleased by the compliment on his corpus, very hot water, bring it on.

Behind him, one leg shaved, she put a log in the fire, much bumping and clanging. She put on her big socks, corner of his eye. Then she was splashing their mugs full of box wine, sliding to him across the wooden floor. She handed him the mug that had been hers, her robe falling open, not that he saw.

Their blanket thumped rhythmically, beat of the wind.

"Thanks," he said. She'd switched those mugs on purpose, he thought, a kind of intertwining, a woman big on symbols. The wine was cold and tasted fine, better than the Côtes du Rhône, not so bloody thick, but he wasn't going to say that.

Danielle sipped, too, no comment, wine being wine, and no pretensions.

He'd have to get out of the tub soon: he felt almost queasy with the heat.

"This is a nice scene," Danielle said slowly, sitting back down on her board in front of him. "Intimate." She sipped at her wine. Then she repeated it, a whisper: "Intimate." And fell into a revery. Finally, she said, "The shrink used to ask what I thought that meant."

"What shrink was that?"

"Grief therapist. When I was, like, twelve. My father made me. The waiting room was always full of old men and magazines." She sipped some more wine. "But the lady was really quite chill. Dr. Dewanji. You'd wait and wait and then her inner office was like going into the sunshine. I didn't know why she asked. Intimacy. What the fuck did that mean? I wanted to tell her something smart, so she'd love me and would let me keep coming back, not that I knew that then. What I thought then was that she needed a definition for some other patient asking what the fuck she meant, that she'd just cop my answer and use it in the other room. I mean, we talked about it a lot, mister. What is intimacy? No, I'm asking you."

Eric had been thinking about the very thing, recent weeks. "Not proximity," he said. The wine stayed on your tongue. It stayed on your tongue a long time.

"Like you think I won't know what that means."

"Propinquity."

"Now you got me."

"Just a joke."

"Closeness? Is that all?"

Eric said, "A kind of shared privacy."

She said, "Loss of boundaries? That's another thing Dr. Dewanji liked to talk about, boundaries."

"No, no. I think that's something different, less healthy? Real intimacy, I think, you'd keep the boundaries, but press them together."

"Okay. Eric. I know what 'boundaries' means." The cabin made a miserable groan. "Do you think the front wall will cave in?"

Which made him realize he'd been staring past her at their makeshift corner. "I don't think so," he said. Now the water felt perfect. "There's a lot holding it up, when you think about it."

Danielle looked, too. They admired their repair a long time. It was still moving with the wind, but stiff with ice. That was something they'd done together, something that had happened to them. The huge tree trunks pressed against the front of the house had settled, Eric reasoned, would surely serve as buttresses. She stared at her wine then, drank it down, stood up pulling the robe tight around her. She shuffled to the kitchen in her big socks, found the open pack of razors—a lot of crinkling of plastic—brought them all back to the tub in a fist, offered him one, which he took. She retrieved the wine box then, poured them both more, sat on her board. Sumptuously, she arranged herself in the lamplight and let the robe fall open, turned sideways to him, put a foot up on her chair, dipped the washcloth in his water.

"*Hot,*" she said.

He looked past her to the broken wall, began to shave, starting where he always started, upper lip. Watching him closely, she put the dripping cloth on her raised thigh, turned slightly further away from him—he still couldn't look—stroked upwards neatly from her knee. "This is going to feel nice," she said. Sip of wine. "Nice and smooth, yo."

He felt his own razor's path over his face with his fingers, tightening his chin, pulling down his lip, tried to make it look effortless.

"Smooth on smooth," she said.

"I don't think so."

"I mean, on our date."

"Our date that won't happen."

"Don't you be so sure. Eric. Shit happens, including dates. I want to go to the beach. That's what I want. To the beach at Phippsburg. For our date. That very private beach with the huge rocks. Of course you know it. With a picnic. On a day no one's there—maybe say in June, or even May. The sun's high, then, and it's almost warm, we've got blankets. You have dared me to swim. Our skin is so salty. The sun is sparkling on the waves. That time of day—like late, but not sunset. A big pile of blankets, really nice blankets. Presents you bought for me. Like comforters and quilts and L.L. Bean blankets, those very thick wool ones. And I bet you made the bread. I bet you made the bread and brought some of your cheese and a thing of really nice, I don't know, olives. And those really nice kinds of salami you get at your fancy stores down in Portland, all those stores you know about. And tomato slices, and salt, one of those cardboard salt shakers, lots of salt and like leaves from special plants and that kind of really good cheese—it's salty, too. The theme of our date is salt, mister. And there's a fancy inn up the way and they have a room and we say what the hell and for us it's always these bathtubs and wine and all our blankets. And you'll be like a puzzle and I'll take off each little edge piece on one side of you and then all the edge pieces off one side of me, and we'll see if, if like, if the puzzles fit together. Smooth on smooth. Eric." Danielle swung herself back toward him, pulling the robe open, her thighs tight together and nicely shaven, pink from the scraping. She said, "I want to show you something.

"No," he said.

"Just look."

Her belly was too thin, actually concave, her ribs too prominent, her belly button tidy as he'd seen, stretched tight by the way she was turned, a vertical slit, that abandoned piercing visible. She pointed lower, a further contortion: "Here."

There.

As low as you could go and still call it belly. A tattoo—small lettering, plain black ink, very crisp, actually quite elegant, like a satin ribbon: *Jimmy Tremonton LaRoque.*

Twenty-Seven

DANIELLE QUICKLY PUSHED Jim's letters into the FedEx envelope and tucked it under the bookshelf, hidden nook. They got into her cold bed, which smelled of old smoke and Ben-Gay. But that only made the new scent of her hair sweeter: Breck. They kissed lying face-to-face in the lamplight, a kiss borrowed unspoken from their future date, which might never happen, and so. And then another, and then what you could only call a soul kiss, a long, sweet, stirring communication. "Hold my ass," she said into the midst of it.

"You said we'd just sleep." The house muttered and groaned. Outside, the wind was roaring harder than ever, puffs of sweet cold air and pricks of moisture through the boards of the gable wall behind them. He kept his hand on her back, just loose.

"You lying there in your pants," she said.

He said, "Is this really going to work?"

"It's already working."

In the loft, the wind could not be ignored, the thumps on the roof. How many hundreds of tons of snow pressed against the face of the building? They'd left clothes at the front window, boots, a Hannaford bag with the remains of their food, a roll of duct tape, the splitting maul. In a further emergency you'd smash the big window, dress fast, wrap up in the blankets, climb out and into the night, and hopefully not into the river. They listened a long time, their kiss having found its arc. How much more snow was coming down? After a long time, she turned away from him, pushed her butt into him. That was okay. It was all really going to be okay. He put his arm around her, held her breast. They'd invented a difference between sex and intimacy and it suited them both. Eric was glad he had his pants on, all philosophy regardless.

He put the lamp out, smell of kerosene after.

"Something I want to say," Danielle murmured at length in the dark.

"Okay," he said.

"Just. Okay. Just don't fuck me in the night. I've got no protection. Okay? Though it's not like I've been getting any monthlies. Too thin, way. But just don't."

He said, "Like I'd fuck anybody in the night."

"I'm not anybody," she said. "Remember?"

"Yes, yes you are."

"Actually, I trust you," she said, and pushed all the harder into him, both of them, he thought, full of the feeling that at any moment the cabin might collapse or slide off its piers.

Twenty-Eight

IN THE NIGHT he woke to her crying—no subtle tears or hidden sorrow but deep, desperate sobs and gasps and moans into their slack pillow, into the back of his neck, into the deep darkness of the cabin—they'd both turned over in sleep. He reached behind and put a hand on her side and she pulled herself very close to him, cried into his shoulders clutching him and wetting him thoroughly with her tears before she subsided under his awkward gentle backward patting and turned away from him. She fell again to sleep.

Now he was the one awake, staring and mulling, a good honest talk with himself—he'd embarked on the care of a delicate psyche, gotten involved with a woman who, no matter what she said, was vulnerable. He'd taken advantage, or nearly. And if he did take advantage it would be something akin to getting tangled with a client. He'd come this far in blindness, because of wine, because he missed Alison, and not a little because Danielle was manipulating him, he suddenly thought: toxic, expert, needy, a pathological liar. Or because she was very appealing, and smarter, funnier, wiser, sexier, more careful—also older—than he'd been willing in his various layers of prejudice to under-stand. Or far from it: insane. Flowers from Jimmy. What a load of shit. Like the FTD man had walked down here! How had he managed to believe that? He wanted his phone. He hated his phone. He wanted to text Alison, unreasonably wanted to text her, composed a text in his mind, then another and another, just about the danger he was in. Or maybe it was that a gap was opening in his dependence on her. He thought of the things she'd said in their last conversation, already more than a month past, sentences that were warm enough but unmistakably valedictory in tone, her phone call, in fact, made just to cancel another din-ner. No, Danielle, there hadn't been any discussion of Senator Spruce Boughs or any other boyfriend or lover and Eric did not want to believe it of Alison. He was the one breaking their pact and breaking it with someone who'd wet the bed with tears and chopped her hair off with a fishing knife. But whom he'd only kissed, and that kiss in *fondness,* he told himself, mere fondness. Glad he had his pants on. He heard and saw several versions of Alison's indictment in his head, offered his defense a dozen ways: text messages, e-mails, Facebook chats, on and on. He could see Alison's golden face as it fell into rage: she was ugly when she was angry, all her flaws accentuated, and terrifying, too, worse than any judge he'd ever faced—adultery was serious. Her adultery, which somehow she always managed to bring back to him, convincing him that he'd opened a gap in her life almost purposefully through his passivity, and all she'd done was fill it. He could do it, he thought suddenly. He could quit her. She had left Eric, after all, and pretty emphatically—though she made it sound like his choice, made him believe it at times, or anyway he'd hear himself apologizing. Danielle's heart thumped slowly at his back. The wind had died down. The cabin had ceased its complaining. Maybe the snow had stopped. He wondered if with your fingers you could feel a tattoo. He could hear the cookstove sucking air, that's all, the fire quietly popping and sighing, very close to the end of their wood supply. His body was clean and felt perfectly delicious and pure. Hers, the same, and separately, no doubt about that, delicious and pure, with just the ribbon of lettering to call it all into question.

Next waking there was light, muted and blue and arctic. Danielle was on her back beside him dreaming—he lay there a while and watched her eyes moving under opaque lids, her lips half-forming mysterious words, her shoulders square as architecture, a deep pool at the nexus of her clavicles, her jaw line strong as his own, her chin a little square, her skin shining. He was hard as the old marble hitching post outside the courthouse. But only, Your Honor, because he had to urinate. He'd have more to do to extricate himself from this situation than chop his way out of a remote cabin and forge a half-mile-long path up a steep hill through record snowfall. Gingerly, he disentangled himself from the warm but mangy blankets and sleeping bags atop him, slipped out of the spavined old bed, stood there tumid in his pants in the very cold loft. He thought of the weather maps he'd seen as the monstrous trio of weather systems had approached from their three directions, and the somber but clearly thrilled weatherman who'd pointed out the unusual convergences of warm and cool air masses, enough of a distraction from sexual thoughts that after a while he could use the thunder mug, as his grandpa would have called it. He unzipped and peed carefully against the metal so as to make as little noise as possible. His shirt and socks and actually underpants were downstairs with the hammer. The big window over the river was still completely blocked with snow, thickly covered, though that was where the light was coming from, a kind of glowing oval in the middle of the expanse of glass, the whale sleeping. It might be dawn, it might be noon, no way of telling. He'd avoided a terrible mistake, and was yet in the midst of it. He'd saved a life, however. That should stay clear: Danielle would not have survived without help, and that had been his only mission. He was Jimmy Tremonton LaRoque's ally, nothing worse than that.

"Okay, *mister*," Danielle croaked. She'd been watching him. "Planning your escape?"

"Planning yours, too," he said.

"No favors," she said. She was older than he'd thought and crabby again: "I'm already gone. I'm already escaped. You do what you got to do and leave me out of it."

"I have an idea," he said. "My friend Patty Cardinal has a room she rents."

"Fuck. No."

"No, it's nice. With its own entrance and stuff. Nice house, pretty nice. And she needs help with stuff. Like shoveling, that kind of thing. Her garden. I don't know. She'd let you stay there free till you got on your feet. Till Jim gets back, I mean."

"Jimmy gets back next week. Eric."

"Next *week*?"

"Think I tell you everything?"

"Well, next week. Then that's a different story."

"It's different, all right. It's really different." Quiet, a great muffled quiet. At length: "But I might stay with her a little. If he gets held back. They're always getting held back. When I talked to him he said he might be extended, actually."

"You talked to him? When did you talk to him?"

"Really. What's this Patty person like?"

"If he's out in Pak on patrol how did he call?"

"She's not a church lady, is she?"

"Older, and very kindly. And yes, I know her from church. She'll make you meals."

"As long as she doesn't make me pray."

"She won't make you pray. She won't make you do anything."

"Just so I don't have to stay with *you*."

Part Three

Twenty-Nine

In college, Alison had been a history/theater double major. These subjects, she felt, comported well with her dream of law. And she'd been the star in a number of musicals, which Eric could still sing, as Alison had so often in good humor sung around her Boston apartment, even acted them for him, the very best of her in the very best moods, often leading to lovemaking, not that that was all he thought about. In Woodchurch, she'd joined the Woodchurch Players and transformed the company, so everyone said, infectious energy and big-city talent, but probably primarily her sly ability to influence Crystal Crudhump, who was the founder, director, and chief benefactor of the Players, a quivering and imperious woman in her late seventies, now dead, famous for thick eye makeup and horrible taste in general and unfortunate casting, also shameless nepotism, the same handful of crotchety thespians in every production, year after year.

But Lady Crudhump, as she was called, had had to give over the role of Marion in *The Music Man,* because Alison could more or less sing and was actually the right age and was finally available, her promotion in Boston having collapsed. And as the theater pendulum swung, perennial leading man and big-hearted pragmatist (not to mention retired druggist) Chip Dennis had suggested in the very first rehearsal that Alison help them find a new Harold Hill, as it was time Carl took over the role of River City mayor Shinn from Bernard Lott, who'd fallen in the lobby of the Woodchurch Retirement Commons and broken his hip.

Eric was no singer, but he was used to standing up in front of people and talking. And so night after night for two months of rehearsals and in practice sessions at home and finally in six sold-out performances, he seduced Madame Librarian, and night after night she fell in love with him, even knowing better, singing everyone into tears.

Their kiss onstage grew steamier performance by performance, until the last night, when the audience actually cheered. "Goodnight, my someone," Alison would sing in the months after that, calling him up the half stair to their bedroom. "Seventy-six trombones," he'd sing, which was the counterpoint.

Their harmony often wavered, but they'd never been closer.

Thirty

THERE WAS THE matter of egress, which was heightened by the matter of his morning dump, and Danielle's, too, speaking of intimacy. The front wall of the place was bulging inward, straining, the sunshine on the snow apparently lubricating and quickening things. The snow that had come in the door was ice hard, nothing he could dig through, not with a garden hoe. He'd built up the fire with the last sticks of their wood. Nothing good to report. Just that he hadn't fucked anybody in the night, congratulations.

In the shed, yet another wave of anger, he examined the peak of the home-built roof, climbed up on the thick old workbench, knocked on the gable wall, tapped a screwdriver into the widest space available between the misshapen old sheathing boards, hammered it through tarpaper and then cedar shingles and made a small window to brilliant sunlight. He poked the point of the rusted keyhole saw into the opening he'd made and hacked away—difficult at first with only three or four inches of blade getting through, but gradually easier, cut a circle large enough for a person to crawl through, blessed sunlight as the first piece of board fell out, excellent bright sunlight glinting off an ocean of snow barely six inches below his vantage point, which was a good six or seven feet off the floor of the cabin, which was again three or four feet off the exposed bedrock. Ten or more feet of snow?

Impossible.

"I like the way you can do things," Danielle said behind him.

He jumped. But recovered with a scowl, gazed down upon her from his workbench aerie, said, "Well, sometimes you need to do things, I guess."

She was in the robe, and he could practically *see* the Jimmy tattoo, as if he were a kitchen match, and it was an unlit fuse: *Jimmy Tremonton LaRoque,* that elegant script, a first-class ink job. Her hair, all clean, stood up in a frizz, no great improvement but at least not a pestilence. She said, "Jimmy would have already, like, kicked his way out through the roof."

"Well, fuck Jimmy," Eric said quickly. He tapped the wall at breast height, well over her head. "The snow's up to right here."

The sun coming in his porthole lit the little room, lit her face as their predicament settled upon her. Just something about the way she set her jaw, freshly mad at him. How did the hormones work coming from the female to the male, if human interaction were purely chemical? Well, it was not purely chemical. Eric had never felt such an access of emotion, especially not for someone like her, someone so troubled. An access of irritation, too. Her irises looked black, no pupils, like bullet holes, but shining with intelligence and indignation. How could the unique soft shape of a nose cause such flummoxed rescission, bury his resolution?

Businesslike, he said, "I just thought we needed an exit. So

I'm going to try to make one. We need to get outside and see what's going on out there in front, and then we need to go."

"Actually. Eric. I'm pretty excited to be by myself again. I'm staying. And you can't stop me. It's my life. It's my decision."

"I'm sorry, but no. Not going to happen."

"Don't talk about Jim. Don't say, 'Fuck Jimmy.' Don't ever say anything bad about Jimmy LaRoque. Jimmy Tremonton LaRoque."

"You'd need cord after cord of firewood. You'd need water, too. I'll walk you out and you can go up to Presque Isle and stay with Jim's family, just as he wants. That's what's best."

"Oh, okay, mister. That's what's best? You maybe go where you wish, maybe up to Jimmy's family, *dickhead,* but don't tell me where to go, and don't tell me what Jimmy wants, all right? I'm not one of your fucking clients."

"But Jim is. Guys like Jim. Danielle. Dickhead, yourself. They often are my clients. Okay? I don't want to be hunted down and greased by some caveman."

"Greased? You want to get greased? You think Jimmy doesn't sign his work? Jimmy signs his work. And me, I see your plan."

"What plan? You never planned anything in your life."

She shrieked. Shrill, unexpected, very loud. She shrieked and turned and swept in her robe into the main cabin, jammed the simple door shut behind her, locked it emphatically—the old wood piece that served as a latch sliding into place. He laughed, not unaffected. Clearly she expected drama in return, the door kicked in, some big-time shouting and general knocking about, then ravishment. *Jimmy signs his work!* What a fucking bitch. Eric turned back to his task with new urgency. Stupid fucking girl. And now he had to go, he really had to shit. The problem

with climbing out the little porthole he had made would be climbing back in. You'd fall probably quite a few of the ten feet into the
soft snow, and then what? He patted his pockets for his phone,
Christ. What time was it? More quickly, and heart pounding as
in court before oral arguments—that fucking girl, who wasn't
even a girl—he cut his way down the joins of the two boards all
the way to his ruined loafers, not very difficult, then across the
grain just above the workbench top, exhausting with the little
saw and bent so low. Alison wasn't one to slam doors and throw
latches. She was merely one to quietly articulate a complaint (her
bad behavior reconceived as yours) and then step out for some
air. Often for days. He got down from the bench, kept sawing,
a better position. He'd already said too much about Alison to
Danielle. He'd already crossed every line. He shouldn't fool himself. Intimacy was intimacy. The old tears sprang to his eyes and the
old sinking in his breast overtook him, the Alison feeling ("There
were bells / on the hills / but I never heard them ringing . . ."").
He fought it, got to work, life or death, how about that, ungrate-
ful Danielle girl-woman bitch.

Cautiously he eased the boards down like an inward-falling
drawbridge, snow softly rushing through, no violence, just
powdered sugar sifting nicely over the workbench and to the
floor around his feet, cold and fresh-smelling. He wished for
snowshoes, then had a brainstorm, retrieved the wide old pair
of water skis with their rubber foot harnesses already adjusted
big. He broke the skegs off the bottom with a hammer, easy
enough, lined the skis up on the workbench, climbed up there
himself, found he could slip his loafers into the feet nicely, too
loose, so duct-tape the whole mess right to your ankles and
shins over your pants, several wraps (plenty of tape), then a few

extra to keep the snow out of your shoes. The sun out there was warm, but the breeze, *damn,* the breeze was sharp like broken glass.

Cautiously, using the hoe as an awkward ski pole, shoulder suddenly sore again, he glided off the workbench in the water skis and out through his makeshift door, patting and sliding as he went to harden a path out. First step into the drift and the day, and everything held. Next step and the next, and then he was moving, making a path he could just see out of, the top of the snow neck-high but very soft and light, classic powder, strata of other types of snow beneath, all those changing temperatures, all that wind. He moved through the drifts batting with his hands and slithering the heavy skis, made his way to the front of the cabin, which was unrecognizable, completely buried in snow and tree parts, the two great pines close against the house, one on top of the other, two or more of the huge hemlocks snapped off and crushed beneath, so much snow and so many broken branches that someone just arriving would not have been able to see a cabin at all, only a slight depression where the force of the snow had caved in the front door, pine branches bent hard against the façade of the building. The precipitous terrain above had been cleared of everything for hundreds of yards, stripped bare by the force of thousands of tons of unstable drifts falling. There'd be no getting to the outhouse! If the outhouse were even still there, doubtful. The pressure on the cabin had to be enormous, and as the snow on the other side heated in the afternoon sun, the pressures would keep changing: the building could easily be off its piers by nightfall. They'd been lucky to make it this far. No one could stay here, no matter how stubborn, not another hour. To leave was the only plan, to leave together, whether Danielle and her sweetly delicate *fuck-me* tattoo liked it or not.

He tramped in a widening, anxious circle, beginning to sweat with the effort, made a little yard in the snow maybe twenty feet in diameter, walls five or so feet high—feeling of an empty swimming pool, amazing—snow probably another five feet underneath, still packing down but likely to harden in the cold as compacted snow always did. He bashed out a side spur, made a deep hole with the hoe, backed out, turned, and backed in again, dropped his trousers, no real choice. Cryogenically preserved shit, great, nothing but snowballs to wipe with, then fill in the hole.

He patted out a lady's room in the same fashion, then patted his way to the river side of the house—cautiously, slowly, only a few feet between him and the rock face down to the water, that twelve- or fifteen-foot drop cleaned of snow by the sharp river wind. The current coursed black below, choked with snow and utterly inaccessible. He was a guy who prided himself on thinking his way forward through a problem. While meanwhile he was a guy who dealt almost daily with people who hadn't thought forward, who never thought forward, who were always crushed by the problems that not looking forward had caused.

Another stroke of alarm hit him, left him breathless. Once, crossing a long bridge in Florida, he'd panicked and stopped the car in four lanes of traffic, leapt out. Only Alison's calm voice had got him back in, cars skidding to stops behind them, horns blaring. She'd got him in and he'd lain on the backseat and calmly she took over the driving. It was a very high, very long bridge, the one into Tampa, and you couldn't see the supports and somehow that had triggered this thing, could have killed them both. "You're okay," Alison had kept saying.

"I'm okay," he said aloud, looking at snow, nothing but snow. Heart still pounding but thoughts reined in, he shuffled and stamped his way to where the big front window should be and cleared it off as best he could with the hoe, wary of the load of snow still on that side of the roof, which if it let go might crush him, which if it let go (more like *when* it let go) would lighten the cabin by thousands of pounds, make it even more vulnerable to the pressures of the snow and trees shoved into its face on the other side. He and Alison had been having an argument. Leading up to the bridge, the terrifying bridge.

His feet were half frozen but he stomped a new little yard in front of the window up to the precipice of the ledge so as to afford some kind of view out, stamped his way under the house a little, enough to see that he was right: the heavy, old-school wooden frame of the place had been pushed to the edges of the cement piers, a solid foot of movement, fewer than three inches to go, a bare toehold. He pulled back out. Looked up as if he knew: Danielle was at the window watching him, the evolution of her mood not discernable. He offered the same gaze, a couple of neutral faces.

The memory of the stab of panic was nearly as potent as the panic itself and echoed the panic on the bridge, and Eric felt suddenly that he had to be inside. He clobbered his way back to the exit he'd made in the shed, found her in there holding a mug of coffee for him.

"Wow," she said as if she hadn't just been shrieking at him. She climbed up on the bench and kissed his face and kissed his neck and put the coffee down on a paint shelf behind him and kissed his mouth hard. "You are soaking wet," she said passionately, "soaking wet and frozen, my god. Are you okay? You look freaked out. And your fucking pants are frozen."

"I'm sorry I said that about Jim," he said, tears coming to his eyes. "No more kisses, okay?"

"I'm sorry, too. Grease you. Where the fuck did that come from? Mister, I'm sorry."

"Just no more." He cried.

"Please feel better," Danielle said, patting him, not kissing. "I need you to feel better."

Thirty-One

To DRAIN THE slipper tub, handy Eric used the keyhole saw to enlarge a flaw in the floor enough to pass the length of the belay hose through, fifty feet of it. Danielle looked on with interest, a fresh understanding between them. He poured half a pot of the dirty water down the hose, which he capped with his hand very quickly then submerged into the bath, let go. Success: you could hear the water splashing under the house. He kinked the hose, bid Danielle hold the kink, and rushed back outside. The snow he'd packed had hardened per his expectation, and he was able to walk in rain boots around to the river side and duck under the house. He found the hose end and pulled the full length out, shouted for her to let it go, aimed gray water at the top of each of the piers he could reach—four on the river side, a quick five gallons of water each (smell of Breck), with the hope that the ice already forming would act as cement and not lube.

Back inside, Danielle crossed her arms in front of her chest. "How did you think of that?" She'd already wiped the slipper tub clean with her soiled robe. More reason to leave—their resources in every category were getting used up. He felt dangerously close to her, danger all around him. He'd never been a person who liked to bend the rules. Nor had he ever been bold in love. Nor had he ever much sought adventure. That explained Alison, at least till it didn't. And that's what had led him to the Navy instead of, say, the Army fucking Rangers. And that's why he hadn't traveled to Nepal in college when his friends had—a four-month trek—but had picked the London semester. And small-town law: your own office, your daily lunch in town, the same judge always, the same two prosecutors, the same kind of trouble, client after client.

"Danielle," he said too warmly, then explained the problem with the house.

She uncrossed her arms and reiterated what he himself had explained to her the night before: the place could only fall the width of the joists under there. The piers might pop through the floor, but the building would never go over the cliff, that was ridiculous.

"I'm worried about fire," Eric said. "I mean, I'm very worried about what might happen with the stove in that situation, if the house falls off its piers."

"I don't see how we can leave," she said. "I don't see how I could make it out, even if you can. How would we do it? I've got a situation with my ankle. And that's just one of our problems."

He went to the window, peered out at the landscape of snow. He said, "Maybe I could go for help."

She'd followed him, stood close behind him. "I don't think I'll do well left alone," she said. "And what about you? One slip and no one knows what became of him."

"We just have to keep thinking," he said.

"Some things, you can't think," she said.

"Maybe that's true," he said.

She turned him forcibly away from the window, made him hold her eye. She was a very deep person, if you looked, like looking into a well. She said, "You cannot leave me alone. Eric. You can't. I have been left alone before. It's not a good idea."

"It might not take very long."

"I'll walk with you."

"You can barely walk at all."

"Who can walk, over their head in snow?"

"So now you're with me."

"I was always with you. Eric."

"You little fucking bitch." Kidding.

She liked that, tit for tat, smiled inwardly.

And they stood twenty minutes side by side at the newly cleared window, Danielle's hand sneaking into his back pocket, a companionable fist, nothing grabby. The view was a revelation—just snow as far as you could see, all the trees across the river bowed deeply under it, so many knocked all the way down that it didn't even look like a forest anymore, more like a glade, all the underbrush buried, all the rocks, all the variegated terrain smoothed into a single, featureless plane, even the biggest trees adroop.

Thirty-Two

SHE MADE A breakfast of Pop-Tarts griddled on the stovetop as if they were pancakes, not terrible. And the oranges—she peeled three, broke them into sections, handed them to him singly, one for her, one for him, fair being fair: beautiful, juicy, sweet, cold, acid, perfect oranges. Implicit in each small grunt of pleasure was the thought that they needed to make their stock of food last longer than might really be possible. Implicit was the idea of leaving, too: the cabin was still making noises, shuddering on its piers, sudden small jerks that shook the furniture. Meanwhile, perfect gentleman, Eric climbed the ladder to the loft and retrieved their slops bucket—she'd made further use of it, a mess, so he threw her soiled old T-shirt over it, gingerly brought it down and then out through the hatch door he'd made in the shed and back to the lady's room he'd made, where he dumped it and swirled snow in it, buried the contents pristine, not a word between them about it after.

Then what? They pulled their two chairs up to the big window and simply watched the scenery—snow blowing in vortices, the river surging past with its load of snow and broken branches and once (like a plot development in a sluggish drama) a piece of someone's dock or maybe even part of a cabin, hard to tell, numerous boards and beams coming to a corner, anyway, the whole structure thumping along in the current. The thermometer in the shed said zero degrees, which if things stayed clear would mean a much colder night—twenty below, the weatherman had said, a dangerous aftermath to a dangerous storm, no doubt worse suffering than theirs at hand, and a fourth system on the way.

Eric felt already the sorrow he was bound to feel when this was all over in a day or two: Jim was coming back. No way around it. There weren't going to be any dates, no romantic dinners, no hikes along the beach, no days-long lovemaking, not for Eric and Danielle, and not for Eric and Alison, either. He had a faint glimmer of excitement, the idea that he might find himself single, dating, meeting a woman as yet unknown. But that familiar feeling never lasted and didn't last now, folded quickly back into sorrow. The river was thickening, snow blobs joining into one mass, probably backing up behind the Route 138 bridge a mile downstream. Soon, in a day or two, the whole conglomeration would freeze solid. One way or another, they had to get out. Danielle's kisses were firmer and faster and hungrier than Alison's, even just the small sample they'd allowed themselves serving as confirmation of something. Firmer and faster and more insecure: because who knew when you would get your next?

She kept looking at him, clearly expected a plan.

Eric said, "Thinking."

She merely stared.

He said, "You think, too."

"It hurts right now. Each thought, mister, it's like a needle in the brain. Whatever ghosts have for brains." She put a friendly hand on his neck, squeezed a little, kept squeezing.

At length he got his thoughts arranged, more like pitchforks than needles, cascades of hay, practical at least. He said, "We need to melt snow. Ten to one, snow to water. And work out some kind of canteen. Because if we walk out it's going to take a long, long time."

"How long is long?"

"All day, I think. All the available light. We'll have to leave at dawn."

"Oh, good." Another night, she meant, another night was good, more time to get ready, no need to motivate immediately, safety in waiting. "Awesome."

"Awesome," he repeated.

They watched the river.

At length, Danielle drew her hand from his neck, gave his shoulder a squeeze, patted the arm of her chair.

"How old are you really?" he said.

"How old did I say?"

"You didn't say."

"Well, you start," she said.

"I am thirty-four."

"Okay. I taught up in Presque Isle seven years, not one. And I was married five years, not just since September. I don't know why I changed it. I thought you'd think I was stupid. I'm twenty-nine in a few weeks. Which means I'm only twenty-eight, though, when you think about it." She put her hand back on his neck, a different kind of squeeze: emphatic. The river chugged past, seemed slower, higher, thicker, whiter.

Eric said, "And your name is Inness O'Keefe."

Danielle flushed to the roots of her hair, withdrew her hand once more, coughed, grinned defensively, then scowled, her face darkening, the fury visibly rising: "You were *stalking*."

"It's on your envelope," he said.

"You were on *recon*," she said. But she hated her own analogy, you could see that, anything military, hated it, and anything secret at all, and anybody's secrets, including her own. "Piece of shit," she said firmly. "I take it all back."

"Take what back?"

"All of it. Everything. Eric. You are dirt, you are crumbs, you are ashes in the fucking stove, and piss and shit in the bucket, and broken houses, and snot, and germs, and tears." And with that, she pushed back in her chair, hopped painfully to the ladder, climbed painfully to the loft.

He could hear her crying up there, then snoring.

Thirty-Three

AFTER A LUNCH of spaghetti with butter and small bits of vegetables and huge amounts of expensive raw-milk Parmesan (it was the fragrance of garlic cooking that had lured her down), all eaten silently, she apologized. "It's not like it's your fault," she said. "I just didn't want you to know my name."

"I can still call you Danielle."

"I don't know where I came up with that."

"But I like Inness, too. Inness O'Keefe. It's more like you."

"No, it's not. That's the thing. It's not like me at all. Not anymore."

"Okay," Eric said.

Enough talk. If they were going to leave at dawn, they had to get to work. Danielle or Inness cut a half-raveled old cabin scarf in two, sat him down and wrapped his feet, pretty nice wool, itchy and warm, stuffed him like sausages into the rain boots and duct-taped everything together. "I've had a lot of practice at snow suits and rubber boots," she said. "Duck tape, not so much."

"Duct," he said despite himself.

She didn't care, didn't even hear the distinction.

He ventured out in the noon sun for clean snow, back and forth to the door he'd made. Danielle met him there each trip and ferried snow to the tub, a nice wordless project together. She'd built the fire up and dragged the slipper tub to where it was all but touching the stove. They'd calculated that the snow would make water at the rate of less than one gallon an hour, easily speeded by packing pots with snow, too, and heating them on the stove, then pouring hot cups and pints of water back over the snow in the tub, a lot of work, which Danielle or Inness bent herself to. Eric outside, Inness in, they managed to melt maybe two gallons worth of the snow and heap the tub high with more, a precarious mound, maybe six more gallons of water to look forward to by evening—cooking, washing, drinking, a little extra in the event the stovepipe was compromised and they needed to put out the fire, plain prudence.

But imprudently they were using more firewood than Eric had anticipated. He made his way on the awkward skis under the window, forged a path downstream a hundred feet to a coppiced silver maple with a couple of dead trunks, the only dry wood he could see, difficult progress, ten full minutes. He broke off the few dead branches he could reach, dragged them back to the opening in the shed, where Danielle took them in. Around front, he was able to crack off some dead branches that the uppermost pine had shed in its fall, plucked and scavenged a good pile of sticks and twigs, maybe a half hour's worth in the stove.

A high bank of new clouds had begun to darken the sky. More snow wouldn't help their case, though the overcast might moderate the temperature. Really, Eric thought, they needed to walk out immediately. He tried to think his way through the problem, but the same loop had been playing for hours and didn't change, not a note: it wouldn't be impossible, getting out, only deathly exhausting, and at twenty below, if night caught you soaked in sweat, plain deadly. They had lingered too long this morning, had slept too late, had got too comfortable. They'd have to start at first light as planned—the plan was correct—make a steady march. They'd be well prepared, they'd be well rested, all the things they would not have been this morning. The trip up the hill was about a half mile, very steep, progress at probably half the speed he'd made to the silver maples, even less with Inness limping along behind. So, maybe three hundred feet an hour? Or make it five hundred: five hours to the road. Which might or might not be plowed. Well, they could smash a window at the veterinarian's if necessary: the old gal owed him. He rubbed his shoulder.

By way of a test he scooted as best he could on the ungainly skis around the front of the cabin, skirted the crests of the fallen trees (outhouse definitely crushed under there), battled up the slope blindly. Away from the river the drifts were so high he couldn't see out of his track and uphill progress was excruciatingly difficult. Ten minutes and he'd traveled at best thirty feet, with no sense of where the path might be and great banks of trees down in front of him and no doubt further trees down ahead: impossible.

He backed out through the personal canyon he'd made, faster progress than he'd achieved going forward, reached the juncture of his path to the silver maples. There he could see out over the snow, at least, a view down the valley of the great Woodchurch River. What if you walked out along the river, made your way to the Route 138 bridge? That way would be all downhill, and all fairly clear, flood-swept for millennia, the underbrush and everything underfoot completely buried in snow. If you could manage six hundred feet an hour, just ten feet a minute, worst case, the trip would take about nine hours, every bit of January daylight, plus some. And that was if it were really only a mile, and if Danielle could keep up.

He tried to calculate the strength it would take to push through this snow for nine hours or anywhere close: no way. But he made fairly easy progress back down to the silver maples, what with the path tramped both ways. At the maples, he headed downhill, kept tramping, put in what he hoped was a full hour in the fading daylight, six hundred feet, he hoped, maybe more (he was getting better with the skis): a head start for the next morning. If there weren't more snow.

He found himself full of the thought that he'd gone against his principles with Danielle or Inness and very much taken advantage of her distress, even just the kisses, the fist in his back pocket, the hand on his neck, and he hated himself. There'd be no more of that, said a stern voice in his mind, even while the picture of them in their endless blankets and quilts and comforters on an endless beach played again in his head. Puffing hard, suddenly starving (hadn't they just eaten lunch?), he saw that up ahead was a long inside bend of the river, another maybe thousand feet of progress blown almost clean by the wind, the long sandbar exposed. That would be easy going, and you'd be almost a third of the way to the bridge.

Suddenly there was a commotion, a mass fluttering, a small flock of common redpolls passing before his eyes like life to a drowning man. They landed in the snow-thick branches all around him, lively communication among themselves, bright crimson spots on their heads, streaked breasts, bright eyes, happiness with wings. Eric laughed, couldn't help it; and at the noise the tiny birds startled and leapt as one to the sky and flew in a kind of scattered precision down toward the bend, took up on the bare branches of a dead pine, lingered a moment, then, as though showing the way, leapt to the sky again, and onward!

Yes, he and Inness could do this. And if things got too terrible in the first stages, they could always turn back. He tramped a tight loop to turn himself around, rejoined his hard-won path, much easier to go where he'd been before. Almost cheerful, thick with hope, he made his way back to the cabin in his own tracks, picking up two dead tree branches along the way. And full of resolve: no inappropriate anything tonight, early to bed, out at first light, and everyone's life could resume.

Thirty-Four

DANIELLE OR INNESS was at the cookstove stirring a pot of ramen noodles and eating taco chips—the place smelled shockingly of salt and low-end spices. There wasn't a lot to add to improve the meal, just a few pieces of red pepper left on the drainboard, a little onion. Oh, but carrots. Silently in the face of her silence (moody again or just efficient?) he diced it all and simply tossed the mix in the pot with the noodles. He'd heated himself to a sweat—that would be dangerous if it happened on tomorrow's trek. Once again the loop played in his head, the various accidents they might have, the disasters. He'd got himself un-taped and barefoot, found that his pants were frozen, just office chinos. He skipped to the stove, hung the chinos on the peg behind, found his boxers soaked, too. His legs were pink as scrapes. He pulled off his shirt. Their robe was filthy, but it was going to have to do, dry at least, and warm behind the stove where Danielle had hung it. He wrestled with it, pulled his undershirt over his head, found her glowering at him.

"Okay," he said.

"*Asshole,*" she hissed.

"What now, Lady MacBeth?" He pulled the robe on—found it warm, tugged his freezing, dripping boxers down and off.

She said, "You go off for two hours out there? You don't say a word to me? I thought you fucking left! I was sure you'd left!"

Single-minded Eric, the constant complaint of Alison's: he'd forgotten to say what he was up to, how long it might take. "I'll try to do better," he said, just what he would have said to his wife, end of discussion.

But Danielle marched right up. He protected his face—she'd slapped him before—and so she kicked him smartly in the shin, those felt shoes. "You'll try to do better?" she said. And then she kicked him again.

"Hey!"

And burst into tears. He tried to think what to say, anger giving way to remorse, but she gripped his shoulders, sent the robe askew, tugged him to her, crushed him to her tight, a desperate embrace. "You are fucking *frozen,*" she cried, and pulled him tighter yet.

He spoke emotionally into the scent of Breck: "I was working on a path out there. I was working to get us out. It was very difficult."

"I can't leave," she said. "I can't leave this place. It's all decided. When I thought you had, like, *left.* That was a revelation. I can't leave. I remain. Like, oh, he listened to everything I said and he *left.* I was *glad.* Eric. I was *glad.*"

"I'm here," he said.

She was stronger than he would have thought, so skinny, held him tighter, pulled him in, the robe all but fully open. She said, "But you *left.*"

"Okay. Okay. Shh." And now Eric was crying, too. "I gave

us a head start. I guess I got scared and just wanted to give us a head start."

She hugged him harder, like trying to climb inside him between his ribs. "You were *scared*."

"Scared," he said.

She talked into his bare blue chest, full passion: "Most people don't say that, mister."

"Scared," he said again. "It's not something you feel every day." The cold had penetrated his feet. He shifted them. No socks to put on. No proper shoes.

"You better get the blanket," Inness said, releasing him abruptly and using a corner of the robe to wipe her eyes. As she stepped away, he realized his mistake: Inness was scared every day and had been scared every day long before any snowstorm.

Thirty-Five

WHILE SHE DRAINED her ramen, he opened a can of her Hannaford baked beans, dumped them in a pot, added a couple of chopped scallions, and after some brief but intense heating time and a hasty, hungry self-service, they ate with their chairs pulled up square against the stove.

"Ramen good," he said.

"You're learning, caveman," she told him.

"Baked beans good."

"We're going to fart," Inness said.

Eric smiled at that and at thinking of her as Inness and wrapped himself tighter in the smelly robe, his legs crossed under him, feet unwarmable. He'd have to saw up the branches he'd brought in through his hatch door, add the scant pieces to their wood supply. They'd be leaving a cold cabin in the morning, it looked like, the overcast having blown off, a clear, deep-freeze night coming fast, bright stars already visible out the window, thermometer in the shed reading ten below already, the temperature of the floor not far from that (anyway a pan of water he'd left there was frozen solid), a Côtes Du Rhône cork in the hole where he'd let the hose through. A dense island of snow still floated in the slipper tub, and seemed to be refreezing. Danielle pushed the island with her hand, set it spinning.

"But seriously," Eric said. He'd finished his share of the food fast. She was in her chair beside his, not too close, eating more slowly, enjoying each bite voluptuously. She wouldn't be hard to fatten up; she was someone who liked to eat. She kept complimenting him like he was a chef for adding scallions to the baked beans, for pairing baked beans with ramen.

"We're out of wine," she said. And kept saying.

But Eric was thinking forward, his proudest trait: "We can make wraps," he said, "just wrap your tortillas around whatever's left. We've got the grocery bags to put things in. We can bring a wine bottle full of water. Or probably maybe better to take two bottles, even if they're heavy."

"Haven't we said this, mister?"

"We've said this. I'm sorry. I'm anxious."

"Scared and anxious. Sad and lonely. I like the way you just put it out there."

"That took some time to learn." He didn't recall saying anything about being sad or lonely, tried to think about that.

But the woman was still talking: "And you cry whenever I do and you don't get mad when I'm mean to you. You're not at all who I thought. You're like the best girlfriend."

Girlfriend. He knew she was quoting him. He liked it. He said, "You haven't been mean to me. You've just been. Feeling your feelings." *Feeling your feelings*—that was a direct quote from a movie, something Alison had rented, disastrous evening, their last, and he'd been feeling his feelings quite a lot since.

"Yo, hello. I have been very mean to you. And you just listen and nod and wait for the, like, lava to cool. And you're taking your clothes off the whole time, you freakazoid."

"I was wet. Probably hypothermic, when you think about it. When we go, we'll have to dress in all the blankets, everything. I was disoriented. And you confuse me, too, gaping at me. I can't tell when you're kidding. That's one of the things about you."

"Seriously. Eric. To quote yourself. I've *seriously* got it: We dress warm. We prepare our food tonight. We pack up everything tonight. We get up at first light and we go, yo. Oh, and I eat like two Advil right now and four tonight before bed and like six tomorrow before we go, six more on the way."

"That ankle."

"Thank you, Doctor. And you, too, for your shoulder. See what you would have missed if you'd left me?"

"I wasn't leaving, Inness."

"Oh. Say that again."

"I wasn't leaving."

"The Inness part, I mean. I am Inness. I called you back to me with my heartstrings. My dad used to sing that. If I came home from somewhere, anywhere. It's a song, a sad Irish song. He was a very sad man. He is. Lonely. Kind of mean. I called you back with my heartstrings and you heard me, mister. Say 'disoriented.' Say that part again."

"I was disoriented," Eric said.

"And confused," she said.

"And confused."

"And scared."

"Very scared."

She nodded with apparent pleasure at the sound of that and scooped up the last of her beans, sucked the last noodles down, burped expressively.

After a while he said, "Your hair actually looks very nice tonight."

"Actually. My hair. Okay, before you start seducing everyone, please ask Inness some questions."

"I'm not trying to seduce everyone."

"And then I will ask *you* some questions, no singing."

"Like Truth or Dare?"

"No, just, like, truth. I've been trying so hard to grow. Because I know a person is supposed to grow. But I don't find I know what it means, to grow. Like you plant a seed, and somehow it gathers its life force with just the help of what? Like sun and rain and dirt? How the fuck does that work? It's magic. Super-fucking-natural. Where I'm just me. And anyway, what would the dare be? Eric. Go outside in two-hundred-dollar loafers and saw firewood? Or I'll shave my leggies in front of you drunk? I don't actually know you. Eric. I don't even know your last name."

"It's Neil."

"Eric Neil?" She made a complicated face. "What's your middle name?"

"DiGiacomo. It's Italian—my mother's mother. Lost heritage."

"Eric DiGiacomo Neil. At least you have *one* last name. The one in the middle. And honestly, the whole thing sounds a little familiar. Like, a lot familiar." She thought a moment. "Eric DiGiacomo Neil. Went down to the court for a deal. He tried something new and his client got screw-duh. And I can't think of the rest, la-la, la-da, da-da. And jail time for some poor slut. Now, ask me a question."

"So much for the public defender's zeal."

She just stared.

"The limerick, Danielle."

"Jimmy's father. Always with the limericks."

"You started it."

"Just ask me a question, yo."

"That's the first *yo* of the evening, if I may point it out. Or maybe not quite."

She gave him a long look. "No, it is certainly not," she said. "That's just a dream some of us had. Yo. And yo. What are you saying, yo? That I'm, yo, playing myself tonight in your production? Are you counting? Ms. Inness O'Keefe, no middle name? I'm sorry about the whole Jimmy routine yesterday. I see how it hurts you if I mention Jimmy."

He put everything into it: "*Yo.*"

She almost smiled. "See, you're getting it now." And then more thoughtfully: "I wear him like fucking body armor."

Eric didn't want to touch that, though it was impressive, real introspection. He said, "Why 'Danielle'? I mean how did you come up with 'Danielle'? It will be hard for me not to call you Danielle."

"I almost had a baby once."

"Almost?"

"Not with Jimmy. It was earlier. In high school. I didn't know who the father was. But before I had to deal, it went away on its own."

"You had a miscarriage."

"I was terribly sad. I had thought it was a girl. I had given it a name. She was going to be the best girl ever born. She was going to be my mom reborn. And I gave her my mom's name."

"Which was Danielle?"

"Oh, fuck you, no. It was Sarah. That's all. Pretty normal."

"Sarah. That's sweet."

"You can call me Danielle if you want. It's a good name. You don't like it? I just suddenly thought of it when you asked me. Because the Inness part? That's private. I knew someone in Presque Isle, Danielle Habegger. She was a student teacher, too, same building as Jimmy's. Fucking skank. We used to say. Which meant we were jealous of her. I mean, I was jealous of her, very beautiful and cheerful and tennis and these huge mountainous tits and big fine ass and cleavage everywhere, those coochie-cuttin' shorts, and blonde hair all long and very generous to me and dating everyone, and having fun and all the hard-ons following her around, and not married, like me, though Jimmy was always trying his coins on her slot. And Inness, my actual self, all chained to him and hard-wired inward and skinny. Really skinny, like kid's clothes at Junior Miss Parade in the shitty mall up there. It's only gotten worse. I don't actually know how I got down here the second time. I mean, after Professor DeMarco and her husband left. I just woke up one morning and I was back down here and it was cold and I didn't remember anything, not selling the car, not chopping my hair, not hurting my ankle, not anything."

The cabin had gone dark. The day had seemed very short. There was still work to be done. The night was perfectly still. Gently Eric said, "Maybe you mean something besides remember? Because, actually you do remember, because you've told me about these things."

"But I don't *remember*-remember, if you know what I mean."

Eric nodded seriously. No point in arguing: you either remembered or you didn't, he tended to think. Just ask any jury. He huddled under the blanket. Really, they should be making up their food for the escape.

He said, "I haven't thought of Alison all day." And wished he hadn't said it. He was steering things back to the date discussion, because he'd liked that discussion, steering things back all but purposefully, and of course he'd thought of Alison, seventy-six trombones, goodnight my someone, goodnight.

"Truth or dare," Inness said. "Who is the strangest person you've slept with?"

"You. By far."

"I mean, the most, like, inappropriate? And let's make it besides me. And you haven't slept with me, remember, only *slept,* you slut."

"I slept with one of my professors in college. Dr. Constable. She was youngish, not thirty. She had me to her house for a conference over tea but opened a bottle of gin and after about four glasses told me she'd fallen in love with me because of my midterm paper, which was called 'The Case for Atheism.' "

"She took *advantage* of you!"

"I don't know. She said she'd fallen in love with me, that's all. I tried to talk her out of it just the way you'd argue the existence of God. And next thing I knew she was bending me over the back of her couch."

"Redheads are always aggressive!"

"No, dark hair. Where did you get red hair from? Very dark hair. She was from Kowloon. Married to Dean Constable. She was a selfish lover."

"Like that matters to a twenty-year-old boy."

"I don't know. After a while. It mattered. I broke it off. You're the first person I've ever told. And she gave me a D! My only D. It kept me from getting honors. Nothing I could do about it."

"I'm the first person you ever told?"

"Yes."

"Not even Alison?"

"She didn't ask." He tugged the robe around him, stood wearily, checked his trousers on the peg (nearly dry), checked his boxers (crisp), put the boxers on, put his pants on, too, then went about dragging the branches he'd found into the room. It didn't take long to saw the load into maybe an armful of firewood.

Inness was waiting for him: "And who else?"

"Oh, okay. Jesus. You want a catalogue. It's not many. I've had long-term girlfriends, mostly. Iskra in high school. At tall ships camp. Broke my heart."

"She's sorry now."

"Ha. And after Dr. Constable, there was my college sweetheart, Emily Nadeau, very intellectual."

"And the best sex ever. I can see it in your face!"

"No, that was Iskra. But close. Anyway, Emily broke it off. Devastating. She was the redhead. I'd bought her a ring."

"Tall ship camp?"

"Long story."

"Then Alison in law school."

"No, then two short-term girlfriends. I had to break up with both of them, terrible."

"Not up to your high standards."

"Ha. No. Just. I don't know."

"They weren't very bright."

"They weren't very bright, you got it."

"Then Alison."

"Then Alison. But Alison you've heard about. How about you? Who was your first love?"

"We're not talking about *love*," she said. A movie seemed to play behind her eyes, and she seemed to watch it intently. She clacked her tongue privately, got suddenly to her feet, kept clacking her tongue, picked critically through his pile of wood, went about a scientific stuffing of the cookstove's small firebox, all the bigger logs they had left, and then smaller, dozens of sticks fit carefully then jammed into the small space, then twigs between those, scores of twigs into every little opening, and each seemed to represent a lover. The wood smoked on the coals, the smoke brightened, then the fire leapt, log to log, stick to stick, a show you never got sick of. She watched a while, and he watched her, the firelight on her face.

"Jimmy," she said at length. "That's all you gotta know."

Thirty-Six

ERIC SEARCHED THE house for items they might use on their trek out. There wasn't much, really nothing. A length of twine, a pair of pliers. Danielle or Inness sorted some food out, suddenly helpful. "I'll make wraps in the morning," she said. Eric tried not to seem too impressed. She was taking her Advil, too, and gave him his. And early she declared they needed extra sleep for the walk, climbed the ladder to the loft. Up there she undressed where he could see if he looked, her bare shoulders, anyway, a brief glimpse of her breasts, certainly not inadvertent on anyone's part, a lot of creaking as she got into bed. They'd said they would sleep in their clothes. For safety. In case something happened.

"Come warm me up," she called.

He brought all the duct tape close to the stove so it would be supple for the morning, fit a few more one-night stands into the firebox, banked the coals down, though the room wasn't even warm, the floor positively frozen. Forcibly, he put the next morning's project out of his mind. And then he climbed up the ladder, bearing their lamp. In its light her face looked fresh, as if she were someone he hadn't met, that soft nose and those full lips, the soft nose relaxing amid the generally harder features, her eyes dark and alert, always alert, wary and even scared, maybe that was it, at the very least closely observant, always ready to flee. Or maybe pounce: she gave him a long inspection. Gradually, then, she let her gaze go vacant, pretended to be asleep, a kind of invitation, he thought. Wrong guy. He blew out the lamp, stumbled around to his side of the bed, felt his way in under the covers, slid himself up behind her. She was naked, of course, save for the repaired panties, threadbare cloth that caught at his fingers. So make that all but naked. And what was he doing? Just an assessing stroke of the hand in the blackest dark, a friendly goodnight in the intimate space they'd carved out, the not-sex space. The skin of her back was taut and nice and really kind of cold and the smells of the cabin were theirs now. Her hair felt soft, and in the dark you couldn't see it, lingering scent of Breck. She'd asked him to warm her, he told himself, so he wasn't out of line.

Maybe she really was asleep. He listened to her breathing, felt her ribcage expand against his: very calm breaths, very quiet, very steady, but too shallow. So she was there, right there with him, feeling his hand on her back, on her butt. A wave of feeling rose in him and grew and finally crested, crashed on a rocky shore (maybe a sliver of beach in there somewhere, plenty of seaweed, one perfect shell amid the fragments), misery and ecstasy entwined into something new and for her alone; anyway, he hadn't felt anything just like it before, and never anything so strongly. He felt he had something to tell her. Fully dressed, boxers and trousers and shirt and socks, he pressed up behind her, let his hand drift down the side of her thigh, let it drift back up, warming her, smoothing a trail through goose pimples. Her butt was hard and thin and cold and her panties caught at his roughened fingers. He caressed the bony rise of her hip, gained the summit slowly, then even more slowly down into the next valley, tracing the shot waistband, lightly, lightly, two fingers only, his breath starting to rise even as hers grew steadier yet, his two fingers tracing the skin above the elastic, feeling for her tattoo—he could swear he felt her tattoo.

"Mister," she said suddenly and tugged his hand higher on her belly.

"Sorry," he said quickly.

"I feel you," she said accusingly.

"Yeah," he said.

She backed into him. "Something to look forward to."

"You're taking my part," he said.

"You can whack off when you're safely home," she said louder.

"And what about you?"

"More like twirling. But that's my business." She wriggled against him, and not subtly, comedy rather than passion, or so it seemed to Eric. Suddenly she turned to face him, a great, awkward thumping around, expressive squeaking of the old bedsprings, finally pushed her hands against his chest. Needing space? He backed off, but she followed, her breath in his face.

"What?" she said.

"I guess I want to kiss you," he said.

"You were smart before," she said. "You were very smart. When you were like three-quarters drunk. Smarter than me. Don't be stupid now."

"Just one small kiss," he said.

She seemed to think about that. She thought about it a long time. All the tension went out of her. She whispered, and soulfully, too, *"You are the best kisser,"* but pushed harder at his chest, pushed him away, turned up the volume: "But the answer is no. Not with all the trouble down south." Louder yet: "Police with nightsticks and dogs. Firemen with hoses. SWAT teams on call. Answer is *no*." Then angrily: "No way!" Of course she was right. But in the dark she slid her hands down his belly atop his shirt, bumped over his belt, massaged him through his pants. And whispered again, whispered to his mouth, working her way through two narratives: *"Just the way your fingers go? I can tell it would be really, really good."* He'd been that close, a torment, and now. She breathed, as if for him, almost silently: *"Just the way your kisses go."*

He puffed hard, and harder, trying not to be too loud, didn't want to seem too quick.

But she knew what she was doing, and quick was just what she wanted. To his mouth she said, "Baby," as if it were just a conversation. And then, all matter-of-fact: "Go ahead."

And he did, nothing for it, no way to command himself otherwise, trying to keep the motion to a minimum, the noise from his mouth. "Honey," he said. "Sweetie."

After a minute or two she took her hands off, found his shoulders, pulled him close. "That was legal," she said.

"Nothing's legal," he said.

"But mister. You don't get a kiss. No more of that. Dat be crime wave."

"Please don't talk like that." And despite the injunction he kissed her forehead, kissed her soft nose.

She ducked away when he found her mouth, she said, "Keep your fucking oxytocin to yourself."

He kept trying—really wanted that kiss.

"Behave," she said.

"I am," he said. "I will." He did.

She said, "Pretend you care about me. Ask about my family. Ask about my childhood."

"No," he said. "I can't ask about anything right now. And I do care about you. Obviously."

She commandeered his hand, slid it off her butt, kept it, brought it to her side, used it to strum her protruding ribs. And she whispered in his face: "Ask about my father. No one ever asks about my father. He's still in Jersey. He won't travel. He's never been to Maine. And it's not like I'm going down there. Haven't seen him in five years. Since Jim and I got *married*."

"Five years."

"Right? It's a long time. But he's a good dad, I guess. Quiet. A phone call is, like, excruciating. Three words: 'How's it going?' I have to drink four cups of coffee and just talk. He used to spank me for the smallest infractions. Till I was, like, sixteen. I hated him for years. Maybe I still do." Strum. Strum.

Eric found himself interested, also ready to sleep, very cozy with her, deep satisfaction and surfeit despite the thwarted kisses, a kind of inner glow, little guilt, none at all, no sign of Jim in his upper consciousness, her growing warmth, her compliments. There was the faintest flicker in the room from the stove downstairs, just the light that came through the vents in the firebox door, just those very small slits, and yet light enough for him to make out her eyes shining as she examined his face.

He murmured, "What does he do?"

"See?" Strum, strum. "You can do it. Ask me questions. I give you answers: He was a fireman when I was little. How cool is that? They brought the hook and ladder to my grade school and he let us climb all over it. You couldn't possibly be more popular in first grade after that. And later he was the fire chief in town, then the fire commissioner for the county, I think, then for the whole state, a pretty important job. Very Republican. Now he's head of Homeland Security for the state, which according to him means he does almost nothing at all for ten times more money than he got when he was doing everything. He's racist. His mother speaks Irish." Strum.

"Your mother was Sarah?"

"Sarah Elizabeth. She died when I was twelve. I thought of her when I was making ramen today. She'd cook me buckets of ramen. She wasn't well for the last couple of years and could be heinous. Now I can see it wasn't her fault but I wasn't very sad when she died. I got so much attention, for one thing."

"But the attention wore off?"

"Not really. I had some great teachers, and they took me under their armpits. I didn't fuck them like you did. Mrs. Kurtosh— we're still in touch. She's why I wanted to teach. She came to my wedding, which was nice except it caused a ruckus with Dad and his date, this Monica cow, who makes a big scene at my rehearsal dinner, *mine,* because there isn't a place for her, you know, but there's a place for my old teacher?"

"Under their wings, you mean."

"Don't be a dick."

Strum.

"Inness," he whispered. Then covered the emotion, spoke

louder: "Inness O'Keefe, no middle name. Went into the woods and was never the same."

"Heh."

He said, "Heh yourself. Where was this wedding?"

"In Providence, Rhode Island. Plain little Frenchy Catholic church. Jimmy's grandparents and like nine-tenths of the extended family live down there, a couple of hundred aunts and uncles and cousins and step-this and step-that. Really fucking nice people, *pffft*. And half as far for my family as travelling to northern Maine from Jersey would have been. Even though I only had, like, six people: my dad and his parents, who are bizarrely weird, and then my brother Kit and his boyfriend, the two most flamboyant Creamsicles on the planet, sweetie pies. And *Monica,* who matched them pretty well, accessory for accessory. We had our sort-of honeymoon at a rental house on the water down there, his uncle's property, but we had to pay for it, and not very nice, not compared to the Jersey Shore. Like, beaches made out of rocks."

"Before you said the Samoset out on the coast here in Maine. You said that your honeymoon was at the Samoset."

"Did I say that? I guess that was Danielle's honeymoon. Jimmy and I went to the Samoset before he deployed, though. It wasn't lovely. I lied. Your witness."

"You didn't say it was lovely." He tried dropping his hand to her belly, but she held it harder, strummed her ribs more emphatically with it. He said, "Jimmy's family is Catholic?"

"Catholic."

"So that revival tent? That was for real?"

"No. That was Danielle. Danielle makes things up, apparently."

"I'm getting it now. You were just protecting yourself."

"We can discuss that on our date. But I, Inness, had to turn Catholic for the wedding. To please Jim's mom. Because we're like Irish Protestant, that old business. Like I cared. I took a class for eleven weeks, half of it in like French Canadian. I didn't understand a thing. And it's all so bloody, why's it so bloody? All these Jesus dolls on crosses, dripping? Everyone in Presque was up in arms if I didn't go to church every fucking Sunday. And Jimmy, he was *into* it. Put the host on his tongue and he's got tears in his eyes, eating Jesus? What the fuck. He knew just how much to turn up at the cathedral, and he always did all the picnics and good deeds and everything. Somehow no one noticed that I was the one making the, like, Jell-O and fruit. He'd shout at me if I didn't dress up perfect. He punched the refrigerator and broke the toilet off the floor. I mean that was funny—the water was spraying up to the ceiling—and I laughed, big mistake. Really, it's too fucked up, what he would say to me. And what he'd do. I can never tell you. I never will tell you. It's very, very private."

Eric said, "You don't want to betray him."

"I just don't want you to judge him."

"Are *you* afraid of him?"

The front wall of the house gave a groan.

Thirty-Seven

WHEN HE WOKE it was only maybe five minutes later. Inness O'Keefe was still talking, something very involved about her sister. She still had charge of his hand. Her sister was not a lot of help. Her sister did not call. Her sister had disowned her, actually. Her sister lived in Maryland in a big house. Her sister was married to a finance guy. They had money. This was a moral deficit, it seemed.

When at last she paused, Eric said, "Say her name again?"

"You weren't listening?"

"I just missed her name, is all."

"It's Siobhan."

"Older? Younger?"

"You weren't listening at all."

"I fell asleep. Just for a minute. I heard about her kids. So she's older?"

"Much fucking older. She's like my spare mother. She's a Terrible and always was. And I didn't mention her kids. I never mention her kids. I'm not allowed to see her kids." Strum. "I was a pretty bad not-daughter to her. I admit it. I put her through hell."

His other arm ached, caught beneath him. So he rocked to free it and with one smooth motion pushed his hand underneath her, got his fingers on her warm back, his elbow under her, maybe not so comfortable for her, but she didn't protest. He said, "So, okay. What happened to your ankle? You wanted to tell me."

"It happened to Danielle."

"Or to that ghost."

"Let's say angel, instead. An angel sent here to tear you away from Alison. Also to test you. And by the way, you're failing."

"You will get your wings. You will get them."

"I hate that movie. The angel should have let him drown, I'm not kidding." Something was rustling in the eaves. A mouse that had stumbled on riches, shreds of raw-milk Reggiano.

Eric said, "What about your ankle?"

Strum. "What do you want to know?"

"Well, how long has it been hurt? A couple of weeks? That's kind of a long time for the kind of bruising you have. It might be broken. Seriously. Something's not healing in there. Maybe a bone chip? We'll get you an X-ray when we're out of here."

"Right, with my nonexistent health insurance."

"You've got insurance through the military, no? Tricare, right?"

Strum. "Do I?"

"I'd practically guarantee it. Spouse of an active-service Army Ranger? If not, we'll make it happen."

"Fine. Eric. Seriously." She pushed his hand off her, but didn't let go of it, in fact gathered it back in. "You're such a fucking lawyer. Am I under oath? Because I think I lied about my ankle. I can't remember what I told you. I'm sure I lied. But it was one of those first colder days, like two weeks ago, you're right. Only two weeks ago. Like a little after Christmas? I wasn't sure. I just guessed. I sang 'Ho-ho-ho, who wouldn't go.' But it was warm like summer. A few days after that."

"It was a long, warm fall," he said. "And Christmas was actually hot. People were out on the golf course."

"You play fucking *golf*?"

"Not any more. Very seldom."

"And you played on *Christmas*?"

"A couple of us who were alone, yeah."

"That is so *lame*."

Now his arm underneath her was falling asleep. He stretched it further, his fingers sliding down her back, found he could reach the band of her panties, then a little further.

She dropped his one hand, reached to control the other.

"You're a boy *after* all," she said, firmly placing both his hands back on her side, pinching his fingers together forcefully.

"My cage is open," he said. "Someone opened my cage."

She didn't seem to find that funny. She said, "You have to promise never to play golf again. Promise me. Golf? That's sick. Promise me right now."

"What's in it for me?"

She pinched his fingers together hard and said, "I already gave you a fucking hand job."

"Okay. No golf."

"Really, never."

"I promise."

"The guys in Jimmy's unit play golf. And Jimmy. He would kick your ass. He plays with one club, like a five-iron, even putting, and he still gets par, thinks he's all that."

"I've never gotten par."

She pinched his fingers harder.

He said, "Can we get back to your ankle?"

The mouse began its return trip to the kitchen corner, subtle passage in the silent eaves. They kept listening. No other sound. Maybe the river shushing by, full of snow. The heartbeat of Inness O'Keefe, or maybe Eric. After a long while, she began to whisper, a kid telling a secret that he had to strain to hear, words on the breath out, words on the breath in: "I walked down to the rocks like I always did, with both of the good towels and my Pantene and everything, the soap and everything, my brush, all that stuff normal people use, all my Inness stuff, and I'd been bathing down there all summer, you know, so I just stripped—my good pair of pants and my real sweater and Jimmy's thick, thick flannel shirt and my very good underwear, just piled it all on a rock, and then I stepped in and it was a lot colder than in the summer, of course, fucking freezing. And I dove."

"You *dove*?"

"I dove. I dove as far as I could. Past the rocks, missed everything. It gets deep. I hit my knee, but not too bad, and got out into the deep part out there, way over your head. It was really strong. And really fucking cold. I couldn't hardly breathe. And I'm shooting downstream. Professor DeMarco always said not to go out in high water, which it definitely was. She meant like don't go out in high water in *summer*. I'm a great swimmer. Eric. And it's a lucky thing, or anyway today it seems lucky, because I had to swim a long way. It was like my body took over."

"You did this intentionally?"

"I don't know. I'm not sure."

"But you swam."

She pinched his fingers together, controlling those hands, and a good thing. "My body kicked and swam. I was furious with my body. But now I'm glad. The river took me down a long way. Finally, I managed to pull up on a, like, beach—I'm nude and fucking freezing and there's nothing there but sand so I run up through the woods, but then with like a hundred yards to go I caught my ankle in the rocks and fell really hard, *really* hard, and that's when I hurt it, like crunch. And I hit my head, too. I barely got back up here, I mean crawling and shivering and bleeding and half knocked-out and panting and everything else. And all, like, 'Heaven Awaits,' which is what Jim's mother was always saying. It's all boulders down there. And I'm in the cabin and I'm like, you can't even fucking kill yourself right! I was so distraught. I didn't know what to do—I found that filet knife and couldn't do anything, I don't know, anything *real*. Instead I chopped my hair. I didn't light a fire after, nothing, just nude and naked and my hair cut off and my ear's bleeding like crazy and I'm fucking freezing and getting this feeling of floating off into the next world. But nothing like that, because I must have gotten in bed, anyway, I warmed up and was still here the next morning. I fell into total darkness after that. Like this total torpulent turtle under the mud with a twisted ankle. Barely alive, a couple of weeks maybe, no effort to live. Then one of those warm mornings came and I realized I needed groceries. I still didn't go out. Too afraid. But finally I did. And that's when I found you."

"And you hadn't eaten anything till that pizza I made?"

"I had a ramen left. And there was rice."

They lay quietly. Maybe they were going to sleep. Eric's post-orgasmic serenity had evaporated. His pants were plain wet. Inness O'Keefe's grip on his hands began to falter. What had he done now? Her breath caught, deepened. Her grip loosened on his hands. What had he done?

Inness snoring, Eric slipped out of bed, climbed downstairs, the only safe course.

Thirty-Eight

As for Alison and him, they hadn't fought, normally. They'd go through a kind of steaming détente, discuss whatever the issue was reasonably, no angry tones, though often carefully vicious phrases would go back and forth, stuff that would hurt only later and then echo and amplify, occupy whole afternoons and weeks of obsessive thought, phrases like "emotional impotence" from her mouth, and "coldhearted insecurity" from his. She might discuss his supposed low libido in clinical tones, but the very subject was meant to vanquish something in him, something that Inness O'Keefe had made rise again, and not his pecker. Alison was, in fact, nearly sexless, now that he considered the matter. Not an ounce of libido. Even in the height of their passion, those first few months of being in love, even then her hunger was muted, cautious, clipped and tidy. Anything more that arose was treated as a rebellion of her body. "Fingers aren't made for that," she'd said in the midst of passion early in their courting. Then how did she masturbate? He'd wanted to say. He hadn't asked, never asked, never had a glimmer of such a thing on her part in their years of marriage, had the impression, simply, that she never thought about her body or his, cared little for the whole panoply of human sexual feeling.

Then, of course, came that buffoon of a state senator to explode the myth.

Eric had forgotten to bring the lamp down the ladder with him, but preferred the dark warmth of the closed stove anyway, just glimmers of flame through the air intake on the firebox door, and more efficient. Then, suddenly, he was exhausted. He cleaned his teeth as best he could with the rag at the tub, scrubbed his face with hot water from one of the small pots, then stripped out of his clothes, washed under his arms almost violently, dropped his besmirched trousers and boxers and washed his privates, washed his butt, what they'd done in the Navy on maneuvers, peacetime, when their lives had been almost luxurious. The washing had a Navy name he couldn't recall, so what. He got dressed again fast and minus the underwear—realized that he still felt good back somewhere in him, some satisfied part of him, something slightly animal to pit against the guilty Apollonian: Dionysius, that's who it was, awakened within him, ardor and laughter and abandon, but caring, too, and warmth, and fellow feeling, compassion, the stuff Apollo couldn't muster.

Splash and dash, that was it, that's what they'd called it.

The floor was brutally cold, even more so through his absurdly thin dress socks. He retrieved the heavy couch cushions— dense old horsehair—and made a bed, lay on it under the old coat shivering in its stench, the dispassionate side of him trying to rationalize, rehearsing speeches, even a confession to Alison, then an apology to Inness O'Keefe, whom he'd taken advantage of. He got up twice and added sticks to the fire, but they were only sticks and burned quickly, hopeless. His boxers on the floor suddenly embarrassed him, and he stuffed them in the fire, too: might as well get some BTUs from his folly. After what was likely considerably less than an hour, all but literally freezing, he gave in, carried the dense cushions up the ladder one at a time—disaster if he fell—carefully lifted them past the bed in the cramped space and past Inness O'Keefe so as not to disturb her, went back for the miserable coat, climbed with it cautiously, slipped past Inness, made himself a little nest under the eaves in the insistent warmth up there, lay on it, pulled the coat over him. He'd proved he couldn't be trusted beside her, simple as that. The cushions were brutally cold. She'd had to fend him off. He had not even the excuse of wine, as she'd pointed out. He imagined Alison reacting when he told her. And he thought of all the men who'd used Inness O'Keefe before Jimmy grabbed hold, logs and sticks and twigs in the fire. He was no better than the rest of them. He'd trek her out in the morning, he'd follow up on all his promises, the help she needed, even the golf—he'd quit golf, show her what a man's word meant, not that golf was so important. And he'd leave her alone except for that help.

Then he remembered he'd left the firebox door open a crack in his quest for heat—that would only eat their last wood faster. The thing needed banking. He slithered back out of his make-shift bed, stole past Inness in hers, climbed back down the ladder quietly, poked at the ashes of his underpants (still pin-striped!), found a piece of bark in the woodbox, a stick on the floor, a bundle of pine needles, several cones, offered these to the coals, covered it all with ashes, shut the door firmly, stood in the faint, orangey light. Something popped sharply under the house, popped again. Then silence, or not silence but a kind of shushing, the river moving past. And the stove sucking air as the volatile pine needles caught. That mouse, somewhere close. I wish I may and I wish I might. Goodnight, my someone, goodnight.

He heard Inness stirring. Rustling and squeaking and then her pee hitting the side of her bucket. Their first night together seemed a month past, more than that, when he'd resisted her, when he'd still known who he was. How had the poles gotten reversed? He heard her fixing the bed covers, heard her sit back on the bed, heard her pat the blankets around her. "Jimmy?" she said. Very sleepy. "Jim?"

"It's me," he called. "It's Eric. I'm down here. Downstairs."

Her face appeared in the faint, faint light. Still confused: "Eric?"

"Yes. It's me. Eric. You were asleep. I think you've been asleep."

"You think I've been asleep."

"You've been asleep."

"But what are you doing down there?"

"I'm, I'm down here."

"I think I didn't finish talking to you."

"We had a very, very nice talk."

"We did. It was a good talk."

"I'm working on the fire."

"You're working on the fire."

"It's very cold."

"What were you doing coming up and down?"

"Up and down?"

"What were you doing? I heard you coming up and down."

"I don't know," Eric said. "I was. I just thought. I thought it wasn't right. I was trying to make a bed."

"You weren't thinking of Alison?"

"No, not Alison. If anyone, I was thinking of Jimmy. You and Jimmy. How important that is."

"And how you want to be back with Alison."

"Well. We have been trying to work it out."

"Work it out," Inness said. "I see. So why did you say Jimmy?"

"Because, it has not worked out."

"And you had to turn it on me? Like, you left me alone up here because of Jimmy? You don't even know Jimmy."

"You know what I meant."

"I know what you meant? You leave me alone up here. You want to kiss me then you leave me alone up here. Because you're thinking of Alison. Who isn't so much work as me."

"I didn't leave you. I'm right here. I'm fixing the fire."

"You got out of bed. You were thinking of Alison. How you've been with Alison so long. How she likes your fucking rock-hard Italian *cheese*."

"I was thinking of you. You and Jimmy."

"You were thinking of me and Jimmy."

"I was thinking of you and Jimmy, yes."

"You put your ring back on. Eric. Don't think I didn't notice."

Eric touched his hand. She was right. He'd put the ring back on, some absent moment, when? He had no idea. But that had been his right hand on her ribs. Oh, and his left on her back, the hand she'd had to collect.

She disappeared.

He shook his head, took the ring back off, buried it back in his pocket, sighed more loudly than he meant (that was his animal side trying to reach her, trying to tell her she was right), remembered the broken puzzle table, found one of its legs half buried in snow, put it in the fire. He stirred the coals with the table leg, got some light out of them, dropped the table leg back in, watched it catch. And that was it. Unless they burned the rest of the furniture, they'd be departing from a very cold cabin come morning.

"Eric," Inness said.

He looked up, couldn't see, something between them—a blur between them—Jesus! One of the couch cushions, flying down from above. It bounced hard off the floor and into one of their chairs, knocking it over with a slam. He laughed, couldn't help it. And then there she was again, and the next cushion came flying down, this one straight at him. He punched at it automatically, deflected it into the butcher's block, shouted: "Hey!"

"Fuckface!"

And here came the old coat, swirling down upon him. "Inness," he shouted.

But she shouted back: "You think you can just crawl off like that?" And disappeared into the shadows.

Give her a minute, Eric thought. She wasn't even awake. He couldn't see a thing up there. The stove was still warm. He stood close to it, the table leg crackling in there. "Light the lamp?" he ventured after a while. He could hear her shuffling up there. He said, "You have the matches. Light the lamp and let's talk." He patted his pocket. What time was it?

"Here's your fucking lamp," she said. And threw it emphatically, its fine glass chimney shattering on the floor, the steel base rolling clear to the far wall trailing kerosene.

"Inness!"

She appeared ghostly at the edge of the loft, flung her heavy mug straight at his head, water and all. He ducked and it hit the kitchen counter with a solid thud, unbroken.

A sudden brightness, an explosion of brightness—she'd lit one of the wooden matches, brief view of her face before she snapped it at him. It flickered out in the air and then the next explosion of light as she lit another and flipped it down, and then another.

"There's lamp oil on the floor," he said evenly. "Inness, there's kerosene."

Another match flew down as the first sputtered out. He ducked, jumped to step on the new one even as another landed on his shirt. She was getting faster at it, the sulfur still burning as the matches hit the floor. The smell of kerosene came to his nose. "Enough," he said. "Now, stop."

Her face lit up devilish; the matches came flying, little emissaries of her wrath, Eric like a dancer trying new leaps, stomping each one out. Finally the matchbox itself came flying down, a relief: she was out of ammunition. But here came the magazines from the little shelf up there, great velocity in the blue dark, like unkempt birds landing all around him, then the books, fluttering bombs, all aimed at his head. He ducked and dodged, tried not to grin, kept repeating her name: "Inness, Inness *O'Keefe,* Inness, *Danielle!*"

When the books were gone he stepped forward, arms out like Romeo's, or maybe Stanley Kowalski, anyway, beseeching: "Inness O'Keefe!"

But there was a smashing noise, then her face and shoulders, her scrawny arms, and here came the bookshelf itself, a heavy wooden thing that simply plummeted, landed at Stanley's or Romeo's feet, might have knocked him out if he'd been a step closer, might have killed him, ended the play right there. "Inness, goddamn it!"

Next her bucket of piss, unexpected, and it hit him square in the chest, a splash and a stench, real pain. And then the bed-clothes, next the mattress, major effort, then the bedstead, a lot of old springs in a flimsy metal frame, *sproing* on the floor, and now, nothing left, her discarded jeans, right in his face, then her shirt and her socks. Finally, she stepped out of the repaired underpants and threw them. Naked she came to the edge of the loft and kicked the ladder so hard that it swung out and fell, hit the slipper tub with a mighty, gonging boom. In solidarity the cabin lurched and shuddered, a series of loud, grinding crunches beneath.

"Inness," Eric said.

Her weapons were gone.

So, very softly, very gently, like singing a bedtime song, he sang her name: "Inness O'Keefe. Inness, Inness." Just her name, as soothingly as he could manage, given his emotion, given hers, something to fix her in time and space. "Inness," he said, "O'Keefe, Inness O'Keefe." He retrieved the tank from the lamp, set it right, wiped at the dripped oil—not a lot, thankfully—wiped at it with one of the paperback books she'd thrown, crossed the room singing her name, popped the book into the stove, a sudden explosion of light.

"Inness, Inness. Inness O'Keefe." He picked up a few more books, collected the bedding. He righted the bookshelf, but what-ever glue had held it together had let go and the poor thing fell into a sagging parallelogram. "Inness O'Keefe," he kept saying. "Inness, Inness."

Eerie silence up there, till finally there was a shuffling and she appeared at the edge once more, precarious and naked, the FedEx envelope in hand. She dug in, grabbed a handful of little pages and matching slips of cardboard and threw them, then the next handful and the next: Jim's letters, a thousand fluttering leaves, little helicopters in the dim light, finally the FedEx envelope itself, planing through the daintier flights and hitting the front of the stove with a slap.

Thirty-Nine

HE PUT A couple of more books in the fire—fat ones: Victor Hugo in French, and something gigantic called *And Ladies of the Club*. That gave him enough light to gather Jim's letters into a rough pile, stuff them back into the big envelope. He was not going to let her leave Jimmy Tremonton LaRoque's letters behind. He cleaned himself again, a laborious process, had to accept that his shirt was going to smell, used a few of the magazines to wipe up the piss that had hit the floor, already half frozen, put it all in the stove.

Upstairs, she cried very hard. He heard her blow her nose, but into what? There was nothing up there. She was naked without a blanket or scrap of cloth of any kind. And then, surprise, he heard her snoring, snicking, a kind of chopped and clicking and snotty breathiness, a woman who could fall asleep on a dime. He righted the heavy ladder quietly as he could manage, collected the worn sheets and the smelly blanket, climbed up there and covered her where she lay on the boards. Back downstairs he fed more books into the fire, dragged the mattress and couch cushions over near the warmth. He moved the slipper tub quietly as he could (the snow island now frozen in place, but free water under the fresh ice), made himself a new nest on the frigid floor, mattress then couch cushions, the remaining bed sheet, the coat. Inside his head he had nothing but Inness and her anger. And suddenly two negative Alison scenes: one, his attempt to stop her exit after their last dinner (several months before, maybe actually six months before, maybe more, if he admitted it), the arm of her sweater stretching in his grip, stretching, the calm hatred on her face; two, the last night that Alison had stayed over, all the way back in summer, when he thought of it, a swim in this very river but up near the college campus, her new very skimpy bathing suit, not bought for his eyes. Four small bruises—clearly the marks of a strong grip—high on her inner thigh. "Don't know," she'd said a couple of times when he asked. "Always banging into things."

A sudden roar and tremor and thudding brought him to sitting. He knew right away what it was: the snow on the river side of the roof had let go, tons of the stuff cascading and splashing past the window and into the river on the still, still night. When it was done, silence once again, but their only window was completely covered. Upstairs Inness snicked and snored, oblivious.

Forty

HE WOKE SHORTLY, shivering, no faint gradation of dawn light. There'd been some loud cracks in the air like shots, something in the structure of the cabin breaking. Their blanket-and-ice patch job seemed to be splitting down the middle, like a plaster wall breaking, though the snow wall that had formed behind it looked solid. And now there was a kind of rumbling, barely audible.

Which stopped.

He hadn't written his note to Alison. If he didn't make it. Their wills were unchanged. She'd get everything. Probably she'd sell the house. He stuffed more books into the stove to give some light, a little heat, dragged the metal bed-frame over quietly as he could manage, bent it more or less square, threw the mattress on. He collected more books, indiscriminately threw them in the fire, even *Madame Bovary,* even Balzac, finally *The Maine Woods,* and good-bye to Thoreau. He gathered up a pile of sawdust and fed that into the flames. Come morning, he and Inness could break up the bookshelf and burn it, make coffee before their

escape. He'd have to hide Jim's letters in his clothes somehow—
she might do something rash—he knew that in the end she
wouldn't want them destroyed. He found the thick FedEx envelope. The fire was bright for the moment. He pulled the first
page of a letter out at random, noted the salutation:

> My dear Inny: Nights here like nights in Maine but
> drier, and not many trees. I mean the pure silence. Errrr.
> Also the clear sky. The stars are about the same. The
> air is different. Smells spicy and burning. I don't know
> burning what. We on furlough three days. HYFR. After
> a clean-up near here. Something to say. I have some bad
> evil on me. It's very bad evil. Little shit turn out to be
> twelve. Twelve with Kalashnikov. We will have to live
> awful well, you and me, to make up for this badness.
> Kellogg is

And another, just a fragment on the light blue paper:

> gravel pit behind Clark's? And you be saying I could do
> it if I try, if I close my eyes. And you pull me in there. It
> was so humid, hot as shit. I never been afraid of the wa-
> ter at night again. And we slept on the slab of granite?
> I be saying the rest but I don't wanna give the censor
> a fucking chubby. Remember, yip? That was the other
> thang you led me through. I kept asking if

They were all like that, mysterious scraps of information, or
no information at all, the jaunty hip-hop language. Here and
there a firefight noted, or an old lady's corpse, an infant they'd
found in a tree after battle still breathing and the argument over
what to do with her, but she died. Eric put more books in the
stove for light: they didn't make much heat. No complaining

from Jim, no complaining of any kind, no introspection either. Just a soldier missing his girl and doing his job and counting the days, at least while the days were boring, which they were until they weren't—that kind of language. Jim was offering a report, not an analysis, mostly built on the clichés of his industry. Otherwise it was fairly moving declarations of love and memories of home, marred by efforts to turn her on, never an "I love you," though often promises of a better life when he returned:

> of names. William. Or Robert. Something simple. No, I ain't against it, baby. I know I said never, but I just see him at your boobs and then in a stroller, you know, and then we're throwing that football and he's swinging that bat and I'm coaching his team, you know. I coming around fer sure. I know it's the only reason you agreed to marry me! Errrr. My little wife. So if that be what you want, I think we know how to go about it. But let's get everything settled first. Our own place. Don't worry, I agreeing wit you.

In her handwriting along the scant margin a list of girl's names: Lolly, Holly, Merrily, Candy, Bliss, Margaret, Sue, Danielle—the last underlined, and underlined again. Upstairs, Inness mumbled in her sleep, turned in her covers, moaned something, sniffed and snorted a couple of times, fell back into her wracked breathing. He remembered the votive candles, climbed out of his nest, found two of them, placed them on the arm of her chair, lit them. Back to bed and back to the letters, a man to be found in the handwriting, Jim speaking directly to him the way he'd felt him speak indirectly through Inness's talk, and Inness's kisses, or anyway Danielle's, a page ripped in half:

People get a look at yo' booty, it's going to be like a line
following you down the street. But I know in Presque
won't anybody come after you, yo. Cuz they know what
we have and they know what they will get from me.
K-Bomb be teaching me skills! And I know you won't
go sniffing downtown

The next envelope was the thickest one, and had come from
the U.S. Government: Inness O'Keefe LaRoque, Presque Isle,
Maine. Eric weighed it a moment—he shouldn't be going
through her mail. But that thought was balanced by the sure
knowledge that she'd delivered this package to him on purpose.
He slipped the letter out, unfolded it, simple stuff, dated April
6, so nine months gone, and suddenly obvious, as if he'd always
known:

We regret to inform you that First Lieutenant James
Tremonton LaRoque has been killed in action near
Kandajar, Afghanistan.

Forty-One

THE LOW RUMBLING beneath the house resumed, accompanied by faint shuddering.

Eric dug through the FedEx envelope more urgently, trying not to crumple all Jim's little pieces of notepaper, found another official letter, this one on White House stationary, and not a form letter, either, but President Obama himself thanking Inness for her sacrifice, and praising Jim for his bravery, personally signed: dark, thick fountain-pen ink.

Folded inside that was a tightly handwritten letter from one Captain Frederick Kellogg, who must have been the Freddy that Jim so frequently mentioned in the tiny pages, also known as K-Bomb, apparently, as you put things together, the munitions man in Jim's Army Rangers unit. This had been crumpled and torn to bits, then meticulously taped back together, pieces missing:

> Dear Mrs. Laroque: Excuse this letter out of the blue and into your heartache I share it. I am home in Tennessee and finally I can hold a pencil again. I was close with your husband. He died as a hero. I expect you would want to know that he was a great leader and had

to do some very tough things. He had to keep the mission going when we were getting shot up. When Prince went down and DuValley got shot. That was the hardest thing and he did that. Kept going. We didn't know when we were training and before deployment or even in the first couple months in country that we were in actual danger not till the first man was shot. I mean really know. That changed us all. We became closer than already. And we became more real. And very angry with endless rage. But Jimmy was calm, always for the mission and made us a unit always. Never scared. That was us, and that was Jimmy. My heart is heavy for your loss. Which I hope you won't be offe

There was a gap, a triangular piece missing under all the tape.

six months. That is unofficial, of course, because extralegal. It was a quadrant we called Talibanistan. We had many contacts among the local people. They loved Jim and called him *Dratfhar*, that is a kind of river barge. It is very square and strong and hard to turn. *Dratfhari* just go where they are going to go. They are not afraid and that is courage, going where you have to go and doing what you

Same triangular hole, flip side, then:

n the morning I was out identifying fragments from the ordnance which was one of my jobs. The round was American made, both sides using ordnance from the exact same factory in Michigan. Jim said it was good for the U.S. economy. He was always humorous in that way.

You never saw the enemy they knew the geog so well and the towns. They'd find a hole in a wall just big enough for the barrel of their Kali and shoot ten rounds and move away. You just never saw them. But if you did you shot them, and that caused laughter and rejoicing. Jimmy thought he was getting a curse from laughing at these deaths.

That day we saw Taliban coming into the village across a little valley all in a line. Jim picked the lead man and we each called the number of our man and shot simultaneous. He was the only one who got his target. The others over there started jumping around and firing down the valley, where our shots must have echoed from we guessed. We saw which doorway they entered when they quit. We all shot after them and shot all the windows then their rounds starting come right at us. You couldn't see from where. And the bullets is flying. And they shoot through sheepskin to hide the muzzle flash. And it's getting dark, so no air support.

Mortar rounds came in all night, because we had compromise our position. Our translator was killed a nice man. Our medical officer was killed one of the team. Very bad. Four men down in two days. Not what you thought signing up. Just bad. Still bad. Very real. Not Sylvester Stallone. Actor gets up off the ground and wash off the blood and do the next movie and that's what I had pictured. Jim led a service after the choppers took them. That next afternoon which was April 5 Jim tapped me and we crossed the valley on our bellies, several hours by inches knowing we might be having our last day, not real. We caught them eating dinner and made them pay one at a time running after them up the stairs but on the roof

Another hole.

second I took him out face-to-face so at least you know
that and I stayed till the evac came in and got us both
out I did my part and my part was not plenty I agree.
None of it seemed real, or else nothing else was ever
real. Honestly I don't know which. This is hard to
explain.

And another.

hy of Jim's sacrifice. Every day I wish it had been me
and not him that day. He talked about you often especially your singing. When I'm released maybe I will
come to Maine and we can meet and talk about Jim and
I hope heal. And I will ask you to sing.

Eric found the letter from President Obama again, truly
signed in Obama's hand. Eric thought about that, how the
president's signing of a condolence letter was both personal and
impersonal. He tried to imagine Inness O'Keefe all alone at her
mailbox reading it, could not. Or maybe it was hand delivered
the way he knew the fatality letters were. Probably Eric had
heard about Jim's death on the news. Probably it was in the
news for days, Jim being a native Mainer. He tried to recall,
but there were too many kids killed, a disproportionate number
from Maine, it was often observed.

Eric put the president's letter on the butcher-block table,
weighed the paper down with the votive candles so that it
wouldn't go anywhere, and so that Inness would know that he'd
seen it, looked at it long, and blew the candles out.

Forty-Two

SHE CLIMBED INTO the makeshift bed with him at first light, her skin shockingly warm, like a fever. She put her face close to his. "Thanks for putting the ladder back," she said.

"I'm very sorry for your loss," he said.

She put her head on his chest. "Your heart pounds, mister. Like something down below on a ship."

"You'll be all right, Inness O'Keefe."

"I want to believe you," she said.

The front wall groaned, a sustained noise, almost funny, like something bodily, digestive. Then it stopped. They lay together in the blue and gradually pinkening predawn light, vague through the blocked front window.

Eric said, "I read the one from K-Bomb, too. That's a real friend. He said you sing."

"I do not sing. That was a joke of Jimmy's. He'd tell people I was a great musician and then out of the blue they'd ask me to play the piano or sing or whatever he'd told them. Very embarrassing. Please, no more about K-Bomb. K-Bomb is fucked. Right after that letter? I wanted to go see him? But he killed

himself. In the V.A. hospital down in Washington, or wherever
it is. Hung himself with a sheet."

Eric waited a moment, said, "Terrible."

She sniffed his cheek and said, "I thought I was going to
slaughter Jim's mother. After he was cremated. And we put his
ashes in the wind. She was all over me, like. Like I had done
something wrong. That's exactly it. The same little shit-squad
went to her door that came to mine, lieutenants with like stripes
on their pants, and swords. I thought it would be dramatic to
pull one of the swords and cut my own throat in front of them.
At Arnold Elementary they had an assembly without telling me
beforehand. Without telling me, Eric. Like, it was for his mom
and not for me. A memorial for Jim the beloved gym teacher.
And his celebrity mom in her black fucking gloves. Bitch with
her hands inside chickens all day. Or maybe I just missed the
announcement? Because I took two weeks off, which is the
maximum grief allowance. Or maybe they told me about the assembly and I misunderstood. I couldn't make sense of anything
no matter what people said. The way they look at you, mister.
Or the way they don't, is more like it. You turn invisible, like you
drank a potion. And the unbelievably moronic things almost
everyone says. You can't believe it." She put on a deep voice:
"'He was a great hero. He died for freedom.' And then they stuff
your arms with flowers. 'He would want you to know.' And all
this fantasy stuff about Heaven, how I'll see him in Heaven.
And I'm like, Jim is going to Hell, yo. He's killed people now.
He's killed a lot of people and some of them were innocent, and
like at least one was a twelve-year-old boy and probably some
were babies, too. He fucked me in the ass when I didn't want it
and pulled my hair and called me his ho. And everyone? He's

never been nice, not to any of you, and not to anyone. So don't talk about fucking Heaven and Jesus and God, not to me. Of course I didn't say any of that. I went, Thank you, Father. And, Thank you, Mrs. LaRoque. I went, He was good to me. True, when he was good to me, he was very good. He was a great gym teacher and all the kids loved him to pieces and I believe K-Bomb that James T. LaRoque was a great soldier and that James T. LaRoque loved me. His mother has the medal. He got a medal. At the assembly. The, like, whole fucking army was there in dress uniforms. And the governor of Maine, fat slob with Cheetos dust all over his suit jacket. Anyway. I shouted at the principal and at the officer guys for not telling me and for talking about Heaven too much and for talking about honor, like that meant anything, and the twelve-year-old boy, I said: What about him? And I said how the room was filled with twelve-year-old boys, how'd they like to see them all shot? And people tried to comfort me, then it became more like *restrain* me. And I got away and got in my car and I drove and I drove and I never went back. So I guess what I'm saying is that despite earlier communications, I am available, fully available, more or less, though who would want me?" She threw her leg over him, neither sauce nor supplication, something else in the gesture, something new to Eric, something he'd have to work to understand: plain affection.

That low rumbling under the house. A crackling in the front wall. A series of pops in the roof above them. A prolonged groan. They listened to the silence after.

"Damn," Eric said.

"Probably it's Jimmy," she said.

"Probably it's not," Eric said firmly.

She climbed up on him, rocked her pelvis on him. "Can we please, just please fuck?"

"Mm. No."

"I just think it would be a good idea to fuck before we go, I really mean it."

"Inness," he said. "Inness O'Keefe."

"Mister," she said.

"We can save it for our date."

"Are we still having a date?"

"If you want to have a date."

"It will be cold on the beach."

"Maybe we'll wait a few months. Maybe we'll wait a few months in any case."

"You are just you here, and that's what you say here, when you are just you, just Eric, but out there, you are a lawyer. You might not want a date. Or I might not. You represented my friend Carly, yo. You are Eric DiGiacomo Neil."

"You knew Carly Martin?"

"And Eric DiGiacomo Neil failed her."

Long silence. "I agree, I did."

She kissed him hard. Her mouth tasted like tears.

"Inness," he said.

Very fast and against his cheek she whispered, "There was this kid I met at a party in high school in Jersey and he was a stranger and I never knew his name and never saw him again. I just called him the Good Kisser. I thought if I ever found someone who could kiss like that, like the center of everything . . ."

"The center of everything . . ."

"Give me that ring," she said in the midst of another kiss.

"It's only an artifact," he said.

"I just want to see it."

"No."

"Give it."

He struggled to get his hand deep in his pants pocket, found the ring among useless change, drew it out, pinched it in his fingers where she could see it.

She grabbed it fast, plunked it in her mouth, swallowed it with a gulp.

Before he could react to that, there was a loud *boom* from the cabin, the whole building at once, it seemed, something crucial giving way. And suddenly, the whole place lurched and groaned and pitched toward the river, dove off its piers, the whole place wrenching and falling and thumping into the huge bank of snow that had dumped off the roof at river side, falling and settling and perching precariously right at the edge of the high bank, the front wall staying behind, the blanket patch ripping exactly in half, squeals and cries and a roaring, the shed detaching itself cleanly, nothing but tarpaper to hold it, the stove pulling free from the chimney pipe and sliding down the floor fast to the riverside wall just as the butcher-block table slid and just as Eric and Inness in their broken bed lurched and slid, right up against the kitchen drain board, Eric slamming into it, Inness into him with a yell, all of this a matter of seconds. The cookstove fell over beside them. The mostly frozen slipper tub came to a stop against it with a thonk. One of the kitchen cabinets tore from the wall, jars falling and exploding. The air in the cabin was all flying snow and bits of branches. Suddenly the loft was breaking free with loud snaps and screeches and itself falling with a percussive slam, finally the ladder landing with a clatter, just an afterthought, then silence. But no, it wasn't silent. The world went on—all the wind of the forest, all the music of the river, all the pink of dawn were around them, above them, and the penetrating cold.

Forty-Three

THEY LAY CRUSHED together in surprise. The cookstove smoked where its chimney had been torn away. "Here we go," Eric said firmly. They scrabbled up the inclined floor, collected Inness's clothing, collected every garment they had—the clothing would keep them alive—put it on piece by piece and very fast, Inness her underpants backward, her jeans, her shirt, the robe, Eric his sports jacket, Inness the smelly coat, Eric the wool blanket. Dressed, their sense of emergency began to abate: the cabin wasn't moving any further, though you didn't want to stay: the loose edge of the roof might easily fall; the floor was cocked at a crazy angle; the sky was up there where the loft had been.

"Let's keep moving," Eric said. "Food. And find your cap, your cap!"

She found it, also his gloves. She said, "Holy shit," and just kept repeating it.

Eric found the FedEx envelope under the stove and stuffed it up under the blanket and into back of his pants, loosened his belt to accommodate the bulk, tightened it back again. He found the jar he'd put water in unbroken.

She found the extra tortillas and the bag of carrots and the jar of peanut butter amid kitchen debris. "Holy shit. Holy shit." "Calories are heat," Eric said. "Let's take everything we can." They stuffed their food finds into a doubled plastic grocery bag, hurry, hurry, *holy shit* was right. Eric dumped out a loose jar of dry beans on the floor, scooped another quart of water from beneath the broken ice in the slipper tub, capped it. He stuffed that into another bag along with the nearly empty jar of peanut butter and one apple, grabbed the two oranges still left, upturned the slipper tub onto the ashes and coals that had spilled on the floor, the absolute end of their fire and water, one gesture. He remembered the duct tape—found a roll under the drainboard, jammed it in his jacket pocket. And then they scrabbled up to the high edge of the floor where the side wall had slid away, climbed down and right into Eric's snow yard, its surface nice and hard and dry, barely dawn, the first sun in the very tops of the highest trees across the river.

Inness said it one more time: "Holy fucking shit."

But they were safely outside, their heavy breaths coming in clouds of steam.

Heaped in his blanket, Eric kept running through an inventory in his head. Their shoes! His would be somewhere under the wood stove. Hers, no clue. The rain boots were in the shed covered in duct tape. They hurried to the makeshift door he'd cut: great danger of their socks getting wet as their feet heated the hardened snow. The shed was whole, only torn from its mother ship and a little twisted—it had never been a show building. A show building would have been dragged into the sky. Inside it, up high on the workbench, Inness helped him arrange the blanket into a cloak with a big pocket on the shoulders, duct-taped the whole generously so it would keep its shape, tucked their bag of food into the pocket, their jars of water. She packed his feet wrapped in pieces of scarf into the rubber boots, duct tape, duct tape, duct tape. They trimmed squares off the train of his blanket, no discussion, wrapped her feet over her warm wool socks, made shoes out of duct tape, ten layers, slipped her feet into the child-size pair of water skis, duct tape, duct tape.

She put her hands inside his blanket and then inside his shirt and he flinched at the cold and at the thought she'd find the FedEx mailer and the letters he'd salvaged, but she did not and soon her hands warmed. He gave her his fine leather gloves—like evidence in an O. J. Simpson trial at that point, but still functional—and she taped his feet to his skis generously. She had her Rasta cap, not warm, but the old coat had a hood, too loose: duct tape, duct tape. They could smell smoke from the stove; he thought of those hot coals on the floor in there, very doubtful he'd gotten them all put out.

"Gotta go," Inness said. "I mean, I've really gotta go."

"All right. And while you do I'll go back in, see what we've forgotten."

"You're not going back in there!"

"Matches, for one thing."

"I burned all the matches. I'm so sorry, Eric. I'm so sorry."

"Okay, but I'll make sure the fire's out."

"You're not going back in there."

"I need something for a hat."

"You're *not*, you're *not*, you're *not*. Do you hear me? You're not going back in there!"

She was right about that: he was already taped into his skis. She turned effortfully on the bench in her own skis and shuffled them out the door he'd made. Eric quick grabbed the calendar off the wall, folded it closed, the August girl safely inside, tucked the thing back behind him under the blanket and under his shirt with the letters from Jim, a lot of fuss for talismans. Finally he got himself aimed at the makeshift door and shuffled out. Inness had waited for him, but now she tested her water skis, slid them awkwardly step-by-step to the snow-carved lady's room. From the privacy of his own pretend outhouse he could see the cabin—the giant fallen pine trunks had shifted maybe three feet. The front wall had been pushed back, but was otherwise intact, the door swung open to nothing but snow. The entire rest of the cabin was tilted hard, almost forty-five degrees, the window side hanging over the river, nothing to stop it but the huge mountain of snow that had slid off that side of the roof in the night, more than precarious.

Danielle had eaten his ring. He laughed and kept laughing. Tomorrow, if they survived, maybe she could recover it.

"What's so funny?" she called.

"You ate my ring."

And then she was laughing, too.

Reunited, they stood side by side and ate more: tortillas with peanut butter. They sipped some of their water, broke into giggles, a function of spent adrenaline, he thought, not a word between them. After a while, the cabin groaning and creaking ominously, she pulled off her wedding ring—not the diamond ring below it, that she would keep—offered it to him. It was very small compared to his, hardly a Cheerio's worth. He ate it. And that ended anything funny about it. They gazed at one another, but briefly.

And grew anxious simultaneously. Her Advil! His Leatherman

knife! Both were in the cabin somewhere, necessary survival tools. He said so and she said, "No, no. Eric. No, no, no." Like she was talking to a grade-school kid.

The cabin lurched and lifted, the cement piers giving way and falling. Eric and Inness shuffled backward and away in their skis. The cabin lurched again. And then the heavy bank of snow holding it on the precipice over the river let go, a secondary avalanche straight into the river. All that snow formed an island that slowly became saturated and rolled and sank, moving downstream quickly.

Like a toboggan, very slowly at first, then gaining momentum, Professor DeMarco's family cabin slid off the high rock bank, the roof collapsing with a roar and clatter as it progressed, slid until the heavy beam of the front sill almost touched the coursing river, then slid a little more, notch by notch till the sill was dipping in. And then a little more, and more yet, enough finally that the deep current caught hold. The cabin jerked and turned, spun sideways, then fell the rest of the way off the bank with groans and sighs and the cracking of boards, spun in the river current, bumping and heaving, began to break into pieces.

"Holy shit," Inness said. "That was *us*, mister."

Forty-Four

HER SKIS WERE bright red, very wide. His were blue, narrower, might have been sporty back in the fifties or even the forties when they were bought, back when the flats dam was still in place and people boated down here. He had his hoe; she had two bamboo poles he'd broken mosquito torches off of, everything secured with duct tape, plenty of damn duct tape. His shoulder was already sore again. They crossed between the flattened cement piers of the missing house, and then they were on their way. He found the path he'd started. They looked back—you had to look back before you moved forward. The cabin had gotten stuck out in the middle of the river, three big pieces that would eventually be reduced.

Holy shit was right.

Those first thousand feet were heartening, smooth and fairly easy in the hardened track he'd made the day before. Inness immediately said that her ankle hurt, but only that once. He thought of her tossing everything out of the loft, grinned, couldn't help it: if they'd been up there when the cabin fell, they would most certainly be dead, or worse: hurt very badly and about to drown. Little stabs of regret: the Advil, various items of food, his Leatherman.

Well, fuck that. "My house by nightfall," he said. And he kept repeating positive thoughts: "We'll have hot showers when we arrive." And, "If the road isn't plowed, there's that big house by the bridge. If no one's home, we break in." And, "Steady progress."

Inness kept up a stream of curses, but she didn't make fun of him, didn't complain. A leader's a leader and Eric had assumed command. And she didn't say a word about Jimmy's letters, Obama's letter, K-Bomb's. You'd think she'd wonder where they were, or care.

The long curve in the river was as easy as it had looked—windswept sand, just a few inches of snow. But of course all that snow had been blown downstream, and so their progress slowed in the next leg, slowed further, one step at a time, long rests. The sun finally reached them, warmed their backs. Eric pressed his chest through the drifts ahead, moved a ski forward, moved the other forward, pressed his chest into the drift ahead, always keeping an eye on the river—at least they couldn't get lost—feeling with the hoe handle for holes and obstacles, skirting rocks, skirting the tops of tall shrubs that tangled him. Inness had it easier behind him, but that was only relative. He felt impressed with her uncomplaining courage.

She said, "Do I stay with Patty Cardinal tonight?"

"Later for Patty," he said after a few steps. "I have a guest room. You'll have your own bed."

A few more steps. "And a bathtub?"

"And a Jacuzzi, never used. All to yourself."

"And I'd like a massage."

"Well," Eric said, her tattoo coming unbidden to mind, that ribbon of ink. He pressed forward through the snow.

"That's a joke," Inness said at length. "No massage. You keep your fucking hands off me, mister."

"Yo," Eric said.

They made a few more yards of progress.

She said, "And you have, like, cognac."

"Scotch, I think it is. A client gave me a bottle of thirty-year-old something-something, supposed to be very *smooooooth*."

"We will drink in moderation, mister."

The banter was good; it kept up their spirits. They worked through a difficult stretch, came out of it, proceeded.

Inness said, "In your house. Are there a million photos of Alison?"

"Probably a few, yes."

She thought about that. "Well, you go in first. You go around and take down the photos. Easier than a tattoo. Just do it. All the wedding shots, all the shots of her family, all the cute kisses on the back of some motor scooter you rented on some honeymoon island, and put them away where I won't ever see them not ever."

"Roger."

"And don't use military lingo."

"Check."

And again they giggled, not for long. They came to another wind-cleared sandbar after several torturous hours of the deep stuff, scant progress. Eric was wary of resting, but they stopped long enough to sit down on exposed rocks and drink small amounts of water, tear up tortillas and eat them, open an orange, drink more water, eat snow.

Forty-Five

THEY GOT A workable rhythm going, and in fact the way was inexpressibly beautiful. Twice more they had to stop to laugh, snow caving in all around them, just something funny about swimming out of drifts with their arms. The sun grew warmer, and then warmer yet, and then the danger was sweating, and increasingly wet clothes. Heavy drifts then bare areas, slow progress then quick, no progress at all at the old dam site and so turn back, try a new route, success, the river roaring at their sides as the way downhill got steeper, more treacherous. But steeper took less energy, practically a glide. Eric's shoulder began to click, distinctly to click. Two o'clock, at a guess, only an hour more of the day, two hours more light, maybe two and a half if lucky, no sense of their progress. Gradually, Eric's thoughts grew black. Inness was slowing down, repeating that her ankle was fine, over and over, "My ankle is super fine," which meant it was not. Burst pipes to look forward to, if the power were down in town. If they made it to town. Inness close to tears: that ankle. Advil left in the cabin. *Click-click*. A long, costly rest. A creaky rising back to their feet. And onward resignedly, one heavy ski before the other, exhaustion looming, harder and harder to concentrate, sunset a terror. Ahead, suddenly, the oddest horizontal, a freaky illusion, like the sky had fallen sidewise, a great gray chunk of dusk, which resolved even more suddenly into a cement span: the 138 bridge! They'd practically forged their way under it!

"Bridge!" Eric cried.

To get up the embankment and to the highway was going to be the worst work of the day, a long, slow traverse. But gloriously, 138 had been plowed, it seemed. They'd made it! The resulting snowbank, however, was like a talus slope on a mountainside. Eric started the ascent, no more sliding along but instead a tough, lateral climb in soft, loose material—killer on Inness's ankle, no way around it, and impossible without the skis, so no relief. Leaning back to her awkwardly, he removed a glove and wiped her tears away with his bare hand, full of the feeling that they might topple and fall all the way back down and into the river.

"We're about there," he said.

"I'm crying," she said.

Where was his hoe? Her poles?

Long lost.

They made their slow way, incremental progress, long rests, the sky going dark, Jupiter appearing yellowy in the crystal sky, then the brightest stars one by one, then in the dozens, gradually the millions. And painfully they reached the top of the bank, no triumph. Because success unveiled the next trial, and then more. For one thing, Eric had been wrong about the house near the bridge. There was no house near the bridge. Which meant there were no houses at all until they reached Houk's Corners, a mile or more.

And maybe a couple hundred yards back up the road the other way, toward the veterinarian's, another discouraging sight: one of the enormous state plow-trucks, its lights flashing faintly under fresh-blown snow, stuck in a drift as high as its cab, higher in fact. The plow job the driver had abandoned was hopeless in any case, what the state called FRAO, First Responder Access Only, Eric knew from lawsuits, but a proven lifesaver and a lifesaver now: even in the dark of night he and Inness could walk to Houk's Corners and not lose their way: the banks were canyon high.

Inness said, "We'll have to think about names."

And maybe Eric was drifting, too, because somehow that made sense. A queer sensation came over him, the strongest feeling that the bridge they had to cross was unsafe, and further, that they had to think of names. The night upon them, the bridge's clear deficits making his heart pound, lists of names forming (Disraeli, DiGiacomo, Dirigo), he worked at unwinding duct tape—no Leatherman to cut it with, goddamn—gradually freed Inness from her skis as she said names, dreamy lists of names.

"You've got to stay awake," Eric told her. He lifted her chin. "Tell me another name," he said.

"Louise," she said. She sat on the crest of the bank.

Eric freed himself, then, stood in rain boots and duct tape, propped his skis in the snowbank, propped hers beside them neatly. "Maybe we'll come back for these," he said.

"Mementos," she said clearly.

The plow driver had escaped, and so would they. There'd be a radio in the truck! Eric said, "Let me check something."

Inness slumped.

Eric sat her up again. "More names," he said.

"Eleanor," Inness said.

"You've already said that one," Eric told her.

"Eleanor," she said again.

"Move your arms," Eric said. "Can you swim your arms? Can you roll your neck? Keep moving? I'll be right back."

"No. Eric."

"You'll see me the whole way. You can see in starlight. I just have to check that plow. Think of more names."

He slid himself down the bank, but a miniature avalanche started and grew and the bank caved and Danielle came down with it and on top of him on the road as he tried to stop her. He struggled from under her, and brushed himself off as he stood. She hardly seemed to know what had happened, still muttering names. He lifted her, sat her on a chunk of ice, and she fell off. He sat her in the road then and she slumped over.

"Right back," he said. And trotted all too blissfully unencumbered up the road and to the plow, climbed the huge bank of snow using the driver's footprints as toeholds, he realized, difficult going in rain boots, found the driver's door unlocked, the window opaquely netted in frost, dug barehanded to find the handle, yanked hard at it, got an inch, yanked again, bashed the snow with the door, yanked and bashed till he could squeeze himself bodily into the cab. Freezing in there. Why had he expected it to be warm? No keys, of course. And the radio was gone, just a steel rack and a couple of loose cables, electronics removed per Schedule Six DOT operator regulations, each driver assigned and responsible for a radio set. This cut down on thefts. Alison had helped write that boring bit of policy as part of a mitigation program she'd designed for this or that senate committee against the costs to the state of vandalism and petty theft, back when she was taking any work the state would offer. Upshot: DOT drivers took their radios with them. Likely the guy was picked up by his supervisor in a smaller state truck— looking at the road, Eric detected the tracks of a tortured triple k-turn beneath the fresh dusting.

He slid and shuffled back down to Alison, who lay in the road now—no, Inness, *Inness* lay in the road, in the middle of 138, which on a clear day you drove to town in ten minutes, give or take. He dreaded crossing the bridge to Houk's Corners, the surest feeling that the thousands of tons of cement and steel were about to fall, that he and Inness would be plunged into the river among smashed concrete and the crushing debris of the cabin, the cabin that even then was floating and bumping inexorably their direction, the jagged pieces of the cabin. Against panic he held his breath, he let it out, he held his breath, he let it out, he held it long and let it out. He reached Inness, said a few soft words about the snow plow, how it had saved them, urged her to her feet, got her under the arms and lifted her, made a soft joke about dancing, got a weak smile and a little effort from her. She stood on her own feet, swaying.

"Ready?" he said.

"Yo," she said.

He took her elbow and focused on her walking and they reached the bridge and began to cross over it (just a regular highway bridge, low steel railings, fairly new), and he tried not to think of the river and all the ice below but couldn't shake the image of the butcher's block knocking its way through the rocks down there, though of course it could never have made it this far, not through the jammed ice, the mess of tree trunks, docks, and all that must have come by in the night. Inness leaned heavily upon him and so all his focus was on her and she hobbled in her duct-taped socks and led him, whether she knew it or not, led him across the span, which held.

Forty-Six

ALREADY, ALPENGLOW HAD turned the sky lavender. Eric fished around in his makeshift hood for the water bottle and they drank the last of their supply. She'd begun to shiver and now he was shivering, too. They shouldn't stop moving. The walking brought them heat. He found the remaining tortilla and the apple he'd stowed, the last orange, and they took small bites, Inness trying to drop to the road and sit, Eric propping her up, keeping her on her feet.

"It's fuel," he said. He thought how much he'd like to take his blanket off, loosened the tape at his neck. "Ready?" he said.

She moved her feet, nothing to say, shuffled and leaned on him, and they slumped and hobbled a few hundred feet at best. From any distance, he thought, they'd look like a failed moose. Houk's Corners and the store were not more than a mile up the hill around a series of broad curves, twenty minutes' fine walk in summer, a two-minute drive. But the hill was like a mountain now, and the cold was deepening, flowing down the river valley in its own stream, a still, clear evening, his nose pinching with the cold, ice in his eyebrows. And they were sweated.

Eric's thoughts drifted. Ice skating when he was a kid. Mr. Gernitz would flood his yard, a dozen kids would skate back there, a kind of violent hockey with brooms and an empty tuna can, Mr. Gernitz's close interest in them unclear. He had to work to remember that Inness was beside him, that they were involved in an emergency.

"Honestly," Inness said, serene. And sagged, slipped out of his grip, thump on the road. She had icicles hanging from her nostrils.

He wiped them away with his bare hand. Where had he lost his glove?

"I'll sleep," she said.

Eric thought that sounded nice. They could sit a while, lie down a while. It was getting warmer anyway. But no, no, of course not. He swam his arms, he rolled his neck. He had to keep her moving. He thought to run ahead, get help, but if he left her she'd sleep and freeze.

"Come on," he said. "Time to stand. It's time. Not far to go."

She held up her arms for help and he pulled her to her feet, both of them wobbly. So in a motion, the only solution, he bent and hefted her to his shoulder, folded her over his shoulder at the hips, balanced her, began to march. She was lighter on his shoulder than she'd been on his arm; she was light altogether. He found he could really walk for the first time all day, walk like a human, head held up, right foot then left, right then left, Inness inert, the true night upon them, the true cold, the bite of it in his nose, enough starlight to make out the canyon that was the road ahead, rain boots and bits of scarf and duct tape bunching around his feet, blisters breaking, every bit of strength he had, no lights ahead, nothing. The road got steep and his step weakened. He needed a rest, just a quick rest, felt himself sweating under the big blanket. He should just take it off, get comfortable. He put Inness on the road and tried to figure it out, all that duct tape, sat beside her, got distracted by thoughts of a row of buildings he'd seen once in Europe, closed his eyes. Just a small rest.

Forty-Seven

MACHINERY BACKING UP, alarm beeping, a deep rumble, then an odd jangling like disconnected music: tire chains. Eric struggled up from sleep, struggled to sit. Far up the hill the forest was lit red with brake lights, and a white, glaring spotlight shone down the canyon of snow, backup lights and the beeping alarm, brake lights red and the sound of heavy chains clanging and the woods beyond lit up as if on fire, a truck coming toward them backward.

Galvin Roberts! In his big old industrial towing rig. Backing gradually toward them down the narrow canyon, expertise in the extreme. Galvin! Sent to recover the state plow! Eric managed to stand, shouted and shouted again, a muted human noise in the vast silence, waved his arms. Inness—oh no—Inness was face down on the road beside him. He lifted her to sitting, patted the snow off her cheeks and lips and forehead.

She murmured something, good.

The truck was backing slowly down the hill. Eric shouted louder but his voice was like nothing.

Galvin must have seen them there frozen in his spotlight, though, blew his air horn to say so—loudness itself—backed more slowly till he was nearly upon them, slowed perfectly to a stop, hissing of airbrakes, clank of clutch and creak of handbrake, squeal of door, idling rumble, diesel exhaust. He climbed down from the huge rig, hurried back to them, face set in amazement: Okay, here was Eric Neil, the lawyer fellow, Eric Neil whose car he'd towed just a few days back, Eric Neil the lawyer with a lady in duct tape sitting in the road nowhere near anything and twenty degrees below zero.

"Mr. Neil?" the driver said.

"Galvin Roberts," Eric said.

Galvin helped him get Inness to her feet and together they walked her to the truck, lifted her up into the cab. Eric hobbled around and got in on the passenger side, a ladder to climb, like Everest. Inside this truck, unlike the other, it was *warm*. Galvin took Inness's hand, tugged it unresisting out of the big coat sleeve, took her pulse against his huge black watch.

"I was worried about the bridge," Eric said.

"It's high," Galvin said. "Like a hundred forty, very high. She's hypothermic, Mr. Neil. That's my guess."

"I thought it would fall in. And the cabin."

"Okay, chief, you, too, I see. Let's get the heat turned up. And then I can get you home and you two get yourselfs into a warm bath. Mr. Neil? Focus up, Mr. Neil. A hot bath and blankets after, soup if you've got it. I'd take you to Woodchurch Memorial but they ain't plowed. Plus they got no power—generators is down, fuel gone. Trunk line didn't reach the hospital. You tell me why."

"They can't get fuel in?" Alison had been embroiled in the

trunk line dispute, that was what Galvin was saying, something about Alison.

Galvin said, "It's that bad, yup." He put the truck in gear and put the gas to it and they roared into motion, lumbered up the long hill inside the snow canyon so brightly lit, heater pumping gloriously, a couple of minutes to Houk's Corners, complete darkness in the buildings there, maybe a candle lit in the Clarks' house.

And onward.

Galvin took it as his job to keep talking: "Focus up, Mr. Neil. You got to stay focused. You both, you want to stay awake. State's got all four plows down. Town plows can't pass nowhere rural—just concentrating on the village. And 138 here? They just pulled Dick Wynot out of his rig an hour ago. I was coming down to collect it if I can. Believe I can. DOT garage is open. They're on the trunk line there, got power. Alvin LeGrande is there with parts. Just heard on the radio: drift heights fifteen feet and that's an average. I seen one thirty feet by the high school—I mean it's over the roof of the gym and that's three stories, wouldn't you say? May not make it. Hannaford roof collapsed early this morning! No one in there, of course. Oh, but imagine the mess. Got a crew shoveling atop Walmart right now, but there's going to be more to this disaster! Who builds a flat roof in Maine? They want to fix Dick's rig and get River Street plowed down over to Johnson's Feed and Fuel—proper shed roof there—get 'em plowed out so's Billy J. can get the tanker to the hospital. Ten thousand gallons number-two diesel, it holds. They burned some twenty-five hundred gallons running the generators at the hospital before they run out, tank on a quarter, is what I heard, budget cuts. Flat roof on the hospital,

too, come to think of it, but that's a fortress, there. Life Flight
has got every helicopter flying, now that the wind's finally down.
They took out some of the worst. But they ain't equipped to fly
in diesel, no suh. And the drifting, by god. Weight of the snow
broke the hydraulics on Dick's rig, froze the SDL direct wing,
and as you can imagine, with the wing seized up you can't back
out of nothing. And Mr. Neil—keep focused—the plow coming the other way was lost, too. He lost track of the road and
ended up in one of the potato fields up there north. So 138 is
blocked clear to Brighton, sixteen miles. Both them drivers near
to froze their ass. Roger was talking angels when we got to him.
It's a night to die." Talkative Galvin: "Hold her hands," he said,
meaning Inness's. "Pump her arms a little. And see if you can't
help him, honey. Pump your arms a little, kick your legs a little,
sweetheart. You hearing me?"

"Hannaford," Eric said.

"Yes, going to be a mess."

"Heater is fine," Inness said.

"Yes, it's good," Galvin said. "Just keep your focus, you two.
Mr. Neil, I'll run you home, and then I got to come back down
for the plow. I'm the only tow vehicle moving, maybe the only
vehicle at all at this point. Got to get some plows moving. We
got a single night here to clear some roads. Next storm coming.
For your part, Mr. Neil, keep talking to her. For your sake as
much as hers. You two are going to have to finish rescuing yourselfs. Warm layers, Mr. Neil, warm bath, plenty of liquids. Do
it gradual, don't just dive in. Are you reading me? I'm going to
drop you and you need to get warm gradual and I got to get that
plow in to the DOT garage."

"Hannaford just got that whole new organic section," Eric said.

Galvin shook his head, got on his radio, raised the DOT garage, explained what he was doing to the boys at DOT: Couple with hypothermia; Mr. Neil the lawyer talking nonsense, but they'll be okay; just a slight delay. It didn't seem to concern Galvin who the young woman might be or what Eric Neil might be doing with her.

Hypothermic? Doubtful. If you were hypothermic you got confused and Eric was not confused—he was clearer than he'd ever been. "Storm of the century," he said.

"Well, storm of the week, anyway," said Galvin. "Quite a bit of some more coming, from what they're saying."

Forty-Eight

TOWN WAS NOTHING but mountains of snow among other mountains of snow, every house and business buried to the second floor, all the streetlights on, eerie electric light, the first they'd seen in days. "You're on the trunk line," Galvin said, disapprovingly: the trunk line might be dependable, but it had been wicked expensive for the taxpayer, the workingman, a luxury meant for folks just like Eric. And hadn't Alison shoved it down the town's throat? Galvin knew right where Eric lived. Inness had begun again to shiver, shook helplessly. Eric wanted out of his clothes. He worried over the butcher's block. He worried over all of Galvin's endless monologue, the broken political logic. He worried about the mess at Hannaford. He rubbed Inness's cold hands, pumped her arms. She'd fallen asleep again in the heat of the cab, couldn't be roused, maybe best.

The mound that was Eric's house glowed. He'd left the mudroom light on, but the mudroom door was buried. The front door was worse, a drift covering the entire east side of the house to the roofline. Eric remembered tunneling through snowbanks as a kid. Towns advised against it now: kids got crushed. He shook Inness and she swam up as if from a deep dive, only slowly opening her eyes, smoothing her hair, wan hand.

"Jimmy," she said.

"You wait here. We're in Galvin's truck, where it's warm," Eric said.

"Don't leave me," she said.

Galvin said, "You'll get a warm bath. And warm clothes. And something warm to eat. Lotsa water. Lotsa extra water. Electric blanket, if you got 'em, but of course no one's got 'em anymore."

She nodded, blinking, shivering. "Don't leave me."

But Eric climbed down and stood in the street in front of his house, worrying about the weight of the snow and about the patients at the hospital out of power, the road there unplowed, acres of flat roofs all over town. Galvin got busy, retrieved a couple of steel shovels from a long tool locker built into his rig, handed one to Eric. It was heavy, hard to hold. Together, practically tunneling, they cleared enough snow to get to the mudroom door, which they found frozen shut. Eric warmed as he worked, found his thoughts coming in a straight line again: the butcher's block, caught up in ice floes and cabin pieces, his Leatherman knife. Galvin hurried back to his truck for a pry bar and used it to chop ice, got the door open.

"Let's get the girl in," he said. "I've gotta run back for that plow. The boys at the DOT are waiting, all the folks at the hospital."

"You are a hero," Eric said.

"Just doing what I do," said Galvin.

They pulled Inness down from the truck cab, sack of potatoes that Galvin put on Eric's shoulder. "You stay focused, now," he said to Eric. "And don't forget I got your car, not that you'll need it anytime soon."

Eric focused as best he could—Galvin had his car, right—carried Inness up the walk as the big rig clunked into gear, a great jangling of chains, blast of the air horn, and back out into the frozen night, life or death, that was Galvin.

Forty-Nine

ONE THING ABOUT the mudroom, it was warm. Eric lay Inness on the old wicker couch Alison had found along the roadside years before and painted blue, Eric lingering over the image of that project, almost smelling the paint.

Inness said, "Caroline. Catherine."

Focus. In the light she was a mess of duct tape and scraps of clothing more miserable than Eric had realized. She shivered and shook, seemingly more so as she warmed, which seemed to cue Eric, who shivered and shook, too. There was an awful lot of snow on the house and he didn't know how much snow a house could take, even a stone house like his own with steeply pitched roofs, and he pictured it all falling down around them.

Inness began to struggle with the huge old cabin coat. Good, she was coming back to life. Eric realized how stiff his hands were, realized again that one of his gloves was missing, the other rigid with ice. He bent to help Inness, couldn't negotiate the duct tape, so just peeled the coat over her head, like skinning a wild animal, the big cabin sweater coming off, too, just the girl down in there and not much of her, sweated camisoles and skinny jeans.

She said, "Bath."

And Eric's mind rushed all around the thought. He said, "It's a Jacuzzi. Never used. Also a fireplace. And of course the heat. Galvin said we're hypothermic, but I doubt that."

"Well, it's fucking hot in here."

"And later I can call Patty."

"Patty? Why?"

He wasn't sure. It had been an idea in his head, that's all, the idea that Patty was going to help. "I'm a little worried," he said.

"We're safe home," she said.

"You're shivering," he said.

"I'm fine," she said.

"You're cold," he said, shivering.

"You seem spacey," she said, her eyes closing. "You really do."

He pulled off the rain boots, unwound duct tape, got the blanket scraps off his ankles, peeled his office socks down and off his puckered toes, blisters bad.

"It's an intimate world we live in," Inness said.

"Probably we shouldn't drink," he said.

"Well or poorly," she said.

"You'll go back to school," he said. Not exactly what he meant to say. What he meant to say was. He didn't know what he meant to say. He said, "I'll go back to work."

Danielle said, "I ate your ring."

Eric considered that.

She said, "And you ate mine."

He said, "I suppose we can find them."

She said, "Shit into gold."

He peeled off her good socks, one by one, examined her swollen ankle, the skin damp and puckered, but no worse than it had been, he thought, not a blister on her.

"We'll take it slow," Eric said, realizing suddenly that they were safe. "We'll have our date. We'll go to the beach when the weather warms up."

"Seems a long time to wait."

"I've got a guest room," he said. He lifted her butt and stripped her out of her skinny jeans with great difficulty, those repaired underpants, so badly worn, pulled them off, too.

She put a hand over her tattoo, concerned only with covering the tattoo.

He said, "I don't mind," meaning the name there, the man who must be honored.

"You should mind," she said.

Under Alison's stone Buddha, Eric found the extra key. He wriggled it in the lock, pushed open the door, fresh wave of heat. He remembered turning the thermostat way up, had wanted to make the place a hothouse for Alison, who was an orchid.

Inness was the ice cube now.

Gradually, Galvin had said. Warm up gradually.

Eric ripped the tape off the breast of his blanket, wriggled and pulled and shed the thing awkwardly, tossed it in the far corner of the mudroom, spotted his insulated ski pants hanging on a hook above, grabbed for them, failed, grabbed again: success. "Put these on," he said. He had to help her, one leg, then the next, belly and tattoo and half-shaved fuzz, flannel-lined ski pants, heavy and stiff, but soft and warm, too, and she sighed feeling the fabric, finally lifting her butt and wriggling all the way into them, tugging the suspenders up and over her shoulders. "And this," Eric said. His big fleece shirt, just what he'd needed all these last days, his big blue fleece.

"I can't get used to you," she said, pulling off her sweated camisoles as one. She let him help her get the fleece over her head. She slumped and lay across the wicker couch, curled on herself. Her shivering had stopped, just a last involuntary spasm or two.

Those clothes were warm.

Inside, he pulled the packet of Jim's letters and the vintage girlie calendar from the back of his waistband, maybe a blister there, too, no idea what to do with them. So he just held on. Around the living room, every detail caught his eye. Galvin was right—he wasn't focusing. He had set a fire in the fireplace (built of stones from the Woodchurch River) leaving a little strip of birch bark licking out, a kind of magic trick for Alison, for his dinner with Alison. He put a match to the bark and in seconds the crumpled newspaper he'd hidden back in there had caught and the kindling, too, a fire now for Inness O'Keefe, plenty more logs where these came from, half a cord in the garage and three more buried under snow out back. He dropped his own pants, pulled his shirt off. Thoughts of the butcher's block kept arriving. He realized he was naked, suddenly, that his boxers were missing and he was naked and just standing there. Inside him, her wedding ring was becoming his, or theirs. He hobbled up the half flight to his bedroom, found his flannel pajamas, intimate world, slipped into them, warm.

He collected four Alison photos from the bedside (wedding, honeymoon, long-ago black-sand beach, a lost kiss in Prague) and then made rounds of the house, at least one image in every room, half a dozen in what had been Alison's meditation loft (cheerful shots with her parents, with his, the two of them in costume for *The Music Man*, she alone as the lead in *Hello, Dolly!*, a lot of happiness, really), several more in the argument bedroom, they called it (Ally as a kid with guitar as big as she, Ally and her three sisters in order of size, Ally holding her childhood cat, Arnold). The answering machine in the tiny den blinked threateningly. He hit ERASE without listening, unlike him, left a stack of photos in frames on the loveseat in there, added Alison's formal portrait from college (sweet, slightly unfocused-looking girl in combed hair and soft sweater, only two ways things could go). In the kitchen he pulled down a painting Alison had made in an early phase of their relationship, a lot of cheerful blues and greens, splash of red in the center, big thing in a heavy wooden frame, unbeloved no matter the compliments he'd given her, used it as a tray to load all the photos onto, all the years, well and poorly: down to the basement.

Down there, he inspected the plumbing—no leaks, nothing wrong, nothing at all: the power had never flickered, trunk line be praised. (Alison had fought for it on the behalf of the state. Her personal investment had been minimal. But it had made her enemies, even as essential as it had proved.) Damn—Jim's letters! The calendar! He found them on the hearth, brought the calendar to the kitchen, opened it to August, hung it where Alison's painting had been. That pulchritudinous sixties gal, pretending not to be innocent though innocent she was, coy finger in her mouth, those chubby legs tucked under her, breasts under tight-crossed arms, a kid with all her long life ahead. (Funding had been cut off before the trunk line reached the hospital, which had been the whole point, protecting the hospital, Alison filing suit, all pending.) He put the oven on. There must be something he could cook. He put a big pot of water on to boil. You always needed a pot of water. (Alison, who would never be coming back.) There was stuff in the freezer. Soup he'd made, big batches. There were all kinds of staples in the shelves. Rice might be nice. Plenty of not-too-old veggies in the fridge, too. He just had to think. That bottle of Scotch was on the counter. Thirty-year-old Macallan, so it said. He found a couple of small glasses, brought them out by the fire with the bottle, arranged two chairs, the ones Alison had never liked, would never sit in, big comfy things in leather, pushed Alison's stiff blue reading chair across the floor and into the dining room. He closed the double doors to hide it. Then to the linen closet and all around the house collecting blankets, at least a dozen, and that many pillows, too, and four sleeping bags and his grandmother's quilts and the two gigantic down comforters stored in his closet. He would let Inness pick the music, plenty to choose from. So much as he looked around seemed unnecessary—bowl of pinecones, clever little boxes, Mardi Gras masks. He put them away, empty closet shelves. On the mantel, a big glass vase full of seashells. These he scattered over the blankets, why not, put the vase away, too. In the closet he found Alison's full-spectrum therapy lamp, dragged it out, plugged it in, hit the switch: like sunshine, a heat of its own. Food, water, shelter, the light of day: these were the basics of human existence. You didn't need the rest.

The oil burner finished its cycle and the blower stopped and the house was very quiet—only the fire, those perfect ash logs beginning to crackle—and the strongly pitched roof above and the densely insulated walls and the stone structure all around and the mountains of snow atop it all and the new low-pressure system coming from the south with who knew how many more feet of snow and everyone around them suffering the same and the weeks it would take for the town to recover and the years it would take for the storm to be forgotten, the decades, the centuries, the eons: forgotten.

Inness, Jesus, what was he doing! He had to get the kid inside. Why had she joked about a massage? The not-kid, who couldn't get used to him. Eric hurried, but couldn't recall why. The bath! Of course. He hurried though hurrying seemed impossible, almost comical, his legs barely moving, hurried as best he could, hurried to the guest suite up the full stairs in back, checked the bed—nicely made, untouched since his brother's visit, his sister-in-law leaving everything hotel fresh, as she put it, Jeannie the suburban goddess. No photos to worry about in that room, which had once been Alison's closet, basically. Nothing on the walls, either, come to look, the dresser empty, the desk bare, unused TV on a low table, big comfy chair and reading light, lots of space: Inness could make it her own. They didn't need Patty Cardinal. In the unused guest bath he dampened a towel and wiped the dust from the enormous tub, started the water, felt it come hot, closed the stopper, crazy water jets, came with the house, never used, an absurd thing (Alison hated it for its representation of excess; Jeannie had made fun, found it decadent; he had found it irrelevant, but not anymore), an absurd thing that held about a million gallons of water (to go with the million-gallon hot-water heater in the basement, Alison liked to point out) and would warm Inness, save her yet again. His own teeth still chattered. He felt he'd never be warm, felt, in fact, as if he were losing heat rather than gaining. They'd best be

careful, he and Inness, find their temperature slowly, as Galvin
had warned. Eric could take a shower in his own bathroom. A
shower would feel damn nice. He watched the tub start filling, a
dramatic swirl, terribly worried about the snow weighing down
on everything, the image of that butcher's block sliding across
the cabin floor, the vision of it floating in the river, his heart
racing.

Likely he and Inness could find the butcher's block come
spring. Likely it would end up on the banks of the Woodchurch
somewhere above the 138 bridge, forced there by the ice, or
just below, all those snags and sandbars. It wouldn't make it
far, those stout legs to catch on something. They could go in
search of it in his canoe. He pictured it on a sandbar, a blocky,
stately thing, alone. Likely they'd recover it. They'd recover it
and float it downstream to a spot they could fish it out, and
they'd load it in the Explorer (with help if need be—Galvin?).
Home, they'd put it in his kitchen, and it would be the center
of all things. Funny to think the center of things right now was
floating among ice pans and chunks of cabin in the Woodchurch
River. More snow coming, Galvin had said.

My god, once again he'd forgotten Inness! He couldn't seem
to manage to hurry, made his way back downstairs, neatening
as he went. Jimmy's letters! On the hearth! Plain sight. He stumbled through the blankets he'd arrayed on the floor, grabbed
the letters, ran them upstairs, put them on the high shelf in the
closet there in her room for Inness to find or for him to tell her
about, just not right this minute.

Inness! He skipped to the mudroom, poor freezing thing. But
Inness was fine in his huge clothes, was asleep as in a cocoon,
curled tight, strips of duct tape arrayed around her, Rasta cap

pulled down over her face. He touched her and she woke instantly, tugged up the hat brim, gave him the patented long look. Which he returned. Eventually, he helped her to her feet, a laborious process, stiff muscles, of course. That had been one brutal hike. They'd been close to death, he suddenly realized. And realized that he was only just realizing it, that he hadn't known it, that they'd been spared grim knowledge by biology somehow, that they would not have made it to Houk's Corners, much less home, that they'd been *this close*. Galvin be praised, and luck, wherever luck came from, and the trunk line, too, and Alison!

Inness teetered, leaned heavily upon him, took a step toward the door, seemed about to fall asleep standing. He lifted her easily, she resisting, it seemed—don't pick me up—pushing him away but clinging, too, sudden arm flung about his neck. And suddenly again she turned her face to his and kissed his cheek, kissed his throat, bit his chin hard to leave a mark, tugged at his hair and kissed his mouth, not kidding, kissed him, kissed him. He kissed her face where he could, kissed her ear, got an arm all the way round her naked ribcage under his own fleece and pulled her to him hard, a crunch in the cold under the porch light.

He started into the house with her.

"No way," she said and abruptly let go, half fell out of his arms. She stood unsteadily a moment, then stumbled on her own through the doorway and into the lurid heat and sunlight, their beach.